A DARK ROMANCE NOVEL

INHERITANCE
Blood Legacy

TESS HOLLIS

First edition: March 2026

ISBN 979-8-9943451-1-5

Cover Design: GetCovers
Interior Formatting: RedFox Book Design
Editor: Kalynn Ligon, Page Turner Support
Published independently

For the ones that have stories to tell—
It's never too late.

AUTHOR NOTE

This is a dark romance with morally gray characters making choices that may be disturbing or uncomfortable. If any of these themes are triggering for you, please prioritize your well-being.

Your mental health matters.

This book contains dark and potentially triggering content, including:
- Graphic violence, including murder, torture, branding, and gun violence, with references to off-page mutilation
- References to human trafficking, sexual exploitation, and organized crime
- Kidnapping, drugging, non-consensual confinement, and surveillance
- Voyeurism and invasion of privacy
- Threats of sexual violence, including rape and forced pregnancy
- Childhood trauma, including a child witnessing extreme violence, murder of parental figures, and references to child abuse
- Extreme power imbalance, grooming dynamics, coercive and morally gray relationship dynamics, and dubious consent
- Explicit sexual content, including rough dominance, degradation, and BDSM-leaning elements
- Substance abuse, including heavy alcohol use, smoking, and being drugged without consent

If you or someone you know is struggling, please reach out:

National Sexual Assault Hotline: 1-800-656-4673 (RAINN)

National Domestic Violence Hotline: 1-800-799-7233

Crisis Text Line: Text HOME to 741741

National Human Trafficking Hotline: 1-888-373-7888

"Every saint has a past, and every sinner has a future."

—Oscar Wilde

PROLOGUE
Cal

I swirl the amber liquid in my crystal tumbler, the sounds of the crackling fire almost lulling me while I wait. Paging through the tattered manila folder lying on my lap, the last of my inheritance, I can almost hear my father laughing. It's the bastard's final curse.

A sharp rap on my office door snaps me out of my thoughts.

"Enter."

I hear the door open, and Raz steps into the room.

Without looking back at him, I have only one question. "Is everything in place?"

"The agency has secured her for the evening of the gala. If she shows, that is. As you know, Cal, she hasn't been the most reliable with her commitments. I don't know why you waste your time," he continues, annoyance evident in his tone. "She's proven she's not worth the time and energy you've already invested in her. With all due respect, she's a goddamned mess," he huffs.

His frustration makes me chuckle.

He's not wrong. She's reckless, yes, and definitely irresponsible. She lacks discipline, and her sense of self-preservation is almost non-existent.

"Well, it's not your decision now, is it?" I ask flatly.

I don't have to look at him to know he's running his hand over his closely cropped blond hair in frustration.

"Cal," he starts, "Your father is dead. You owe him nothing. His promises are not your responsibility to keep. When are you finally going to tell me who this girl is to you? Why is she so important?"

I throw the last of the bourbon back, feeling comfort in the predictable burn at the back of my throat, quelling the irritation of having this conversation yet again. This is the one story I haven't shared with my long-time friend. I close my eyes for a brief moment. We've shared death, destruction, and even women, but not this. I know eventually I'll need to tell him, but not yet. This secret is mine and hers, even if she doesn't know it yet.

I stand and face him, my expression set.

"You let me worry about her importance. You do what I fucking ask. If that's a problem, Raz, tell me, and I'll find someone else who can."

He lets out an impatient huff.

"You know that's not what I meant. Of course, I'll handle it. I keep handling it." With a sigh, he turns to leave.

"As I said, everything is set. For her, this is just another gig. She won't have any idea that this is another job she's getting paid three times more than what she should, or why. If she's smart, she shows. If she doesn't, I say be done with it."

He stops at the door and, without looking back at me, continues, "One more thing, someone else is looking into her. There was a ping on her juvenile record and the few college records she has. I've got the team trying to trace it, but they're good, Cal. Our team has done what we can to hide her, but whoever it is, they're getting closer."

I go still, the ramification of his words settling over me.

"Now, I'm going to check with the staff to ensure the rest of the details are set. You need this gala to be a success."

With that, he leaves, quietly shutting the door behind him.

I sit back in my leather chair and reopen the file. I tap my index finger over the latest image of her. If someone else has found her, then the time has come. I didn't want this for her. She was supposed to be safe. At the very least, I wanted to give her more time, but it can no longer be avoided.

Time to come out of the shadows, little hurricane.

ONE
Charity

Two days before the gala...

Answer the fucking phone. Answer the fucking phone.

I'm jolted awake with the sound of my cell phone screaming at me.

For fuck's sake, I need to change that annoying ringtone.

Rolling over, I grab it from the bedside table, my head pounding and every muscle in my body crying in protest. I squint my eyes, fighting to focus on the name flashing across the screen.

Winthrop Events and Catering.

Oh no. Please, God—don't offer me a job tonight. I press the accept button.

"Hello?" I croak.

"Charity Johnston?" a woman chirps on the other end.

"This is her. Can I help you?" Please don't offer me a gig, I silently pray again.

4

"Hi Charity, this is Ava at Winthrop Events and Catering. We've had an opportunity come up that we—and the client—feel you're perfect for. They requested you by name. It's Saturday evening, a gala at the International Museum of Art. Your uniform will be provided, of course. You'll be on the floor passing champagne, hors d'oeuvres—the usual. Be there by six for final inspection and instruction. Oh, and the best part,"—she pauses for dramatic effect—"the client is paying three times the hourly rate."

"Excuse me?" I stutter, trying to process the information she just gave me. "What is this for, and who requested me? Who the hell pays servers seventy-five dollars an hour to hand out champagne? Is this a joke?"

"Miss Johnston," her tone scolds, "I hope you won't be using that language while you're working."

I'm too hungover for this.

"I assure you, this is no joke. You were specifically requested. They mentioned that you did a remarkable job at the Heverfield engagement. They were quite impressed with your performance."

My mind claws through what little memory I have left at the moment. Heverfield? Engagement? Oh, right. What was his name? Ben? Chad? Some fuckboy name. I got fired after getting caught sucking him off in the restaurant bathroom. She's right, my performance was pretty spectacular that night. I smirk. This has got to be a mistake.

"Are you sure they asked for me?" I press. None of this makes any sense.

"Charity, if you don't want the job, I can find someone else." Annoyance seeps through her saccharine veneer.

As if on cue, my stomach rumbles, and my eyes flick to the stack of unpaid bills. I'm in no position to turn down a gig.

"No, no, I'm sorry. Of course, I want the job." I press my palm against my throbbing temple. "You just caught me off guard. I didn't realize I'd made such an impression with my, uh, service that night." I bite my lip to keep from snorting at the memory of exactly what services I'd provided in that bathroom stall.

"Wonderful!" she exclaims, the chirpiness snapping back into place. "I'll let their coordinator know. Your uniform will be delivered by courier on Saturday morning. Please be home to sign for it. Remember—six sharp. Guests begin arriving by eight. You'll stay until the event is cleared and clean. Charity, it should go without saying that this is a very exclusive opportunity. The agency and our client expect you to treat it as such. Understood?"

"Got it. Thank you, Ava. I really do appreciate it!" I try to assure her, even though I'm still confused as to how this came about.

Before I hang up, I remember Sam.

"Um, Ava?"

"Yes, Miss Johnston?" That edge is back in her voice.

"Can you tell me… is Samantha Kellogg on the list too? As a server, I mean. If the spots aren't filled, she'd be a perfect addition. Honestly, she has more experience in these types of assignments than I do. She should already be in your database."

Sam has become my only friend since moving to the city six months ago. We hit it off after working a pretentious wedding where we spent most of the night mocking the guests and sneaking drinks from the bar. Despite her busy schedule, we've become best friends. We try to refer each other for these side hustles when we can. Well, side hustle for her, at least.

I hear a sigh.

"It would be highly inappropriate to discuss the other staff members. But I'll look into it."

She hangs up without even a goodbye. Rude.

TWO
Charity

The day of the gala…

The morning sun filters in through the side of my tattered Venetian blinds. I grab my phone to check the time, eight a.m.

Ugh, no. It's Saturday. I shouldn't be up this early.

I catch a whiff of myself and wrinkle my nose.

"Jesus, Charity, you stink," I mutter to myself.

I smell of stale beer, peanuts, and strangers' regrets. I should've showered when I got home, but exhaustion overtook me, and I fell into bed instead.

At least I changed into a clean t-shirt, and I'm not hungover.

I call that progress.

The Downtowner, a dive bar a few blocks over, allows me to pick up shifts when I need cash, and I always need cash. Greg, the owner, never asks questions. He hands me an apron and puts me to work. We're doing each other a favor. He pays me cash under the table so both of us can avoid the taxman. It's a symbiotic relationship.

Peanuts in the shell are always kept in the warmer for the customers, compliments of the house. The clientele, mostly locals, come in, get drunk, and crack peanuts, all the while being encouraged to throw the shells on the floor. It's gross and a health hazard, but no one seems to care. I get paid to pour and deliver drinks. At the end of the night, I sweep up the mess and forget who I saw or what I heard.

I hoist myself out of bed and make my way to the tiny bathroom, kicking the dirty clothes I've left scattered out of the way. A shower, toilet, and a small sink with a vanity fill the space. It's all there's room for, but I don't really need anything else.

Turning on my portable speaker, I hit play on my phone, and the sounds of Bohemian Rhapsody fill the room. I turn on the shower and wait while the water heats up, scrutinizing the image in the mirror staring back at me.

There's no denying it. I look tired. My hazel eyes have dark circles, and it's not only the smeared mascara from last night. My complexion is dull and sallow. These bar shifts are killing me, but they pay the bills.

I need to find a sugar daddy who'll send me to the spa and treat me like the princess I aim to be. I chuckle to myself.

"Keep dreamin'," I tell the woman looking back at me. "Girls like us don't get guys like that." I stick my tongue out at my image and jump in the shower.

My cheap bottle of cucumber body wash is almost empty, so I fill it with water to make sure I use up every last bit. I'm out of shampoo, so this will have to do. I've just lathered up my dark hair when I hear it.

Bam. Bam. Bam.

What the fuck?!

Bam. Bam. Bam.

"Just a fucking minute!" I yell over the music.

Who the hell is knocking on my door so early? I fight to get the soap rinsed out of my eyes, jump out of the shower, and grab one of my beat-up towels.

Bam. Bam. Bam.

Racing toward the door, I yell, "Goddammit, I said just a fucking minute."

I throw open the door and freeze. Standing in the hall is a man, well over six feet tall, dressed in a black tailored suit. His blond hair is cut in an almost military fashion, and he's got the most striking green eyes I think I've ever seen. My eyes roam over his face, the right side covered with veiny white scars.

"C-c-can I help you?" I stutter.

The man cocks an eyebrow and looks me up and down with a smirk. I unconsciously clutch my towel tighter.

"Miss Johnston?" he queries.

"Yes, that's me," I respond hesitantly.

It's only then that I notice he's holding a garment bag.

"Your uniform for tonight's event." He holds the gray bag out to me and smiles.

It's then that I notice how beautiful he is. Terrifying, but beautiful.

"Oh, right. They said you'd be coming." I take the package from him, and before my mind can stop it, my mouth spews, "Aren't you a little old to be a delivery boy?" I slap my hand over my mouth, my face reddening.

"I'm so sorry. I didn't mean that. I promise I'm not always a rude bitch."

To my shock, the beautiful, scarred man laughs.

"Ohhh, Miss Johnston," he drawls. "Something tells me that's not quite the truth."

His eyes scan the apartment behind me and then lock back on to mine. His expression hardens, and I feel the air shift. I shiver under his gaze, suddenly feeling too exposed.

"This is a very important event. To avoid any mishaps, my employer insists that these types of deliveries are handled personally." He narrows his eyes, and his voice drops to a rumble. "Six p.m., Miss Johnston. Don't be late."

With that, he turns around and silently disappears down the stairs.

I blink at the empty hallway for a moment, my wet hair dripping cold water down my spine, then slam the door, twisting the deadbolt.

I can't help but wonder what kind of event has "six-foot scarred and scary" personally delivering uniforms at eight a.m.

Still clutching my towel, I carry the garment bag the few feet into the living room and throw it on my ratty couch. Looking around the room, I imagine it from that stranger's eyes. No wonder he looked at me that way. My living arrangements don't exactly scream "Trust me with your high-end events." The couch is lopsided, the coffee table is littered with magazines and old take-out bags, and the plant on the end table is half-dead. For the first time in a long time, I feel self-conscious before I shake it off.

Fuck him and his judgmental ass. This place isn't much, but it's mine.

I eye the bag again. There's no label. No tag. Just sleek gray fabric with a black zipper running down the middle.

Fancy.

Maybe I should've asked his name? No, fuck that. That man gave off leash and leather energy, and the last thing I need right now is that kind of trouble.

I pad off to my bedroom and finish toweling off, pulling on my usual t-shirt and leggings. I throw my hair up in a messy knot before heading to the kitchen to make coffee. It still seems odd that a client would ask for me by name, but I try to shake it off. I think back to the Heverfield engagement party. How in the hell did that gig get me a reference? They didn't even pay me for the night. Instead, I was unceremoniously fired for giving a groomsman a blowjob. It was not a great scene. In my defense, I didn't know that he was married. If a man's not going to wear a ring, how am I supposed to know? He was cute, and I was horny. We had a few shots, and one thing led to another. What can I say—I let the tequila do the talking.

I take a deep breath and unzip the garment bag to inspect its contents.

The agencies that I've registered with have my measurements—that's standard. What's not standard is the dress I'm looking at.

Usually, the uniforms are nondescript, polyester-blend pants and white stain-resistant shirts. This is not that.

I lift the dress out of the bag, and my eyebrows rise in appreciation. The soft, buttery black fabric is unlike any uniform I've been assigned before. When I hold it against myself, I notice the slit climbing up the right side, practically to my hip. It's cut to hug every inch of me, with sleeves that stop just below my elbows and a neckline that plunges dangerously low. At the bottom of the bag, I find a pair of pristine kitten heels to complete the look.

This is something that would hang in a boutique window with no price tag. If you have to ask, you can't afford it.

Well, this explains the pay scale. I guess the museum's art isn't the only thing meant to be on display.

"Eyes on the paycheck," I say to myself. "You've done more for free."

I eye the dress one more time before zipping it back into the garment bag.

This is either a setup or a miracle, and I have a way of fucking up miracles.

THREE
Charity

I try not to make eye contact with the Uber driver or the hula dancer bobbing on his dashboard as we make our way to my destination. Instead, I concentrate on the city blurring past us. I know from the follow-up email that the museum is around thirty minutes outside of the city. It's not a cheap ride, but since it's reimbursable, I can justify the expense.

Staring out the window, I try to focus on anything but the knot in my stomach. Anxiety skitters along my skin. I feel too exposed in this dress. I'm also wearing more makeup than normal, and I'm fighting the urge to wipe it off my face. I'm used to working weddings and the occasional corporate affair, but this is way out of my comfort zone. I squeeze my eyes shut, willing my speeding heart to slow down.

My nerves are just starting to calm when we turn down a dimly lit road. Trees hang over the path forward in a perfectly straight line. As we approach the museum, my breath hitches. Breaking out of the trees, the building comes into view. The lights reflect off the steel frame covered in windows, looking both out of place and perfectly situated at the same time.

The car stops, and I mumble thanks to the driver before stepping out. My legs wobble slightly as I follow the path around the imposing structure, searching for the staff entrance sign that will lead me where I need to go.

As I enter the building, a woman with a headset and a clipboard approaches, tapping her pen against the edge of her mouth. She gives me a quick once-over and then jerks her chin at the dress.

"It fits. Good. You're in zone two, champagne rotation. You'll move clockwise around the perimeter. Stick to the marked path and do not cross into guest seating. No refills. If they want more, you give them a fresh flute. Every. Single. Time. If you spill, you swap trays. You will have at least two glasses on your tray at any time. No standing still. Keep moving, keep smiling, and keep your mouth shut unless spoken to. Yes?"

"Yes, ma'am," I respond. Nothing in her speech surprises me.

She nods, accepting my agreement, and looks at the rest of the group gathered around her.

"Eyes up, shoulders back," she continues, "You're expected to be visible but neutral. No flirting. No names. No commentary. If a guest touches you, smile, redirect, and move on. I'm talking to you, too, gentlemen. This event's guest list is filled with both notables and the notorious. If anyone crosses the line, you find security first, and me immediately after. Let me be clear: that line is very broad. Is this understood?" We all nod in agreement. Her eyes sweep the group like she's searching for the weakest link.

"Now go. Guests will be arriving in the next thirty minutes. I expect to see each of you standing immaculately and invisibly, ready to serve," she waves us away with a stroke of her hand.

"Well, that was... something?" I turn my head to see a pretty, tall, blonde, freckled girl to my right. "Way to tell your employees that sexual assault is not only excused but expected." She rolls her eyes.

"Sam!" I squeal as she gives me a tiny hip bump.

"Looks like we're both in zone two. Nice uniform, right? Do you think they'll notice if we keep them? I mean, seriously, I could wear this at a club, and no one would bat an eye. My girls have never looked so good!" She giggles as she gives her breasts a little shake, completely amused with herself.

I can't help but grin back at her. Sam has this way about her—unshakeable confidence that's impossible to ignore. Six months ago, we were strangers working the same shitty catering gig. Now she's the one person who can make me laugh when everything else is going to hell. I don't usually click with people this fast, but Sam's different. She's the person who makes even these ridiculous gigs bearable. When she walks into a room, her presence fills it without trying. There's no performance, just pure Sam. I've spent years trying to perfect, and failing, at my customer service mask, but Sam's never worn one a day in her life. Even now, standing in this pretentious museum in our ridiculous dresses, her laugh cuts through my anxiety like sunlight.

"Yeah," I reply, "this is a bit more over the top than I'm used to working. Honestly, I didn't even know this place existed until I got offered the job. It's amazing."

"My cousin got married here a few years back. It's impossible to reserve unless you're somebody. He married a trust fund princess, and her Daddy made sure to give her the day of her dreams. You should've seen the looks on that family's faces when my middle-class, low-brow family arrived," she laughs again, eyes dancing. "Oomph, that bride was pissed when she found my cousin, her groom, drinking beers in the parking lot with the rest of the guys. Granted, not cool, but she made a whole scene of it." She shrugs. "They're divorced now."

We chat easily as we walk to the exhibit hall. Like me, Sam is also a transplant. While I moved here six months ago and am barely getting my feet under me, she's been here since graduating from college. Unlike me, she didn't blow her college experience. She earned a degree in finance. While I'm working these server jobs to survive, she sees them as an opportunity to network as well as supplement her income.

Sam swings open the gallery doors, and I stop short in awe of what I'm seeing.

"I know. It's beautiful, isn't it?" She sighs, and we both take in the scene before us.

One side of the room is a floor-to-ceiling glass wall overlooking a wide expanse of green. Fairy lights dancing through the swaying trees remind me of the fireflies I used to catch and hold captive in old mason jars. I was convinced I could keep their light for myself.

I take in the rest of the gallery. Low lights from above illuminate the long rectangular room. Flickering sconces line the walls, meant to mimic fire-tipped torches, casting shadows up the sand-colored marble. In the center of the room, surrounded by a small flowing river meant to keep out intruders, stands the large temple. Blocks of weathered stone etched with Egyptian symbols tell stories no one remembers. Music drifts through the hall from the string quartet stationed at the far end of the room. I don't recognize what they're playing, but the melody weaves into the sound of the bubbling water, creating a new symphony.

I glance at Sam. "That's one hell of a replica," I say, bewildered.

She snorts. "Oh, that's not a replica, baby. That's the real thing. Straight from Egypt. They shipped it stone by stone and rebuilt it right here."

"You're kidding," I say with disbelief.

"Nope. They're still studying the hieroglyphics, trying to piece together whatever ancient drama's been carved there." She grins. "Probably some long-dead king bragging about his dick. Times change, men don't."

Both of us snicker in hushed tones.

"Okay, girl, show time. Hey, quick, give me your phone. I lost my phone last night along with all my stupid contacts. Forgot to back it up."

"Again?" I laugh. "Well, that explains not calling me back. Didn't you just get a new number like a month ago? You do know you can get a new phone and keep your old number, right?" I ask.

"Yeah, yeah, I know. I'm hopeless! I like change. Besides, it's an easy way to shed the douche bags I seem to attract. New number—new dating pool," she smiles at me and shrugs her shoulders.

I unlock my phone and hand it to her. She enters her number, taps her phone to mine, then hands it back to me. We hear a ping, and she holds hers up, showing that my contact information successfully transferred.

"You're a mess," I laugh.

"Yeah, but I'm your mess." She throws me an air kiss.

"Ladies, phones on silent and away please," a deep voice rumbles.

Startled, I turn and see the scar-faced man who delivered my uniform.

"Oh, sorry," I say. I double-check that I've turned off my phone, then stuff it back into the short apron they've supplied.

"Miss Johnston, good to see you were able to get here on time," he smirks. "Almost impressive."

I narrow my eyes at him when I notice the twinkle in his eyes.

He gives Sam a once-over and walks away.

"Oh my God. Who is that, and how do you know him?" Sam is practically drooling at the retreating beast.

"I don't know him," I shrug. "He's the guy who delivered my uniform. Fucking terrifying if you ask me."

"He delivered your uniform?" she asks, raising an eyebrow. "How the hell did you arrange that? And you think he's terrifying? Shit." Sam huffs. "The only thing I'd be terrified of is him breaking my pussy. Oh, to be so lucky," she sighs wistfully.

Before I can respond, we're both handed trays full of champagne.

"Okay, everyone," the woman with the headset is back. "To your stations. Doors open in exactly sixty seconds."

FOUR
Cal

I watch from the atrium overlooking the temple's gallery below. It doesn't take me long to locate my little project, chatting it up with a curly blonde with freckles. I see the blonde grab Charity's phone, enter something, and flash the screen at her before handing it back. *Curious.*

Right on cue, I see Raz approach the two women. He says something, and both hurriedly tuck their phones away. I catch Raz wink at the pretty blonde. Raz, you cagey son of a bitch, I chuckle to myself. Good luck with that one, my friend.

My attention turns back to my little hurricane. Her dark brown and auburn locks are done in a neat updo. The body-hugging dress, with its plunging neckline, accentuates every curve of her frame.

The door to the secluded atrium opens, and Raz steps in.

"Cal," he starts, "we may have a problem."

I turn to him and raise an eyebrow.

"No, we are not doing fucking problems tonight, Raz," I argue. "There are millions of potential dollars drinking my champagne and eating my canapés. What do you mean we have a problem?"

"Nikos Vardis just arrived," he replies.

"Goddamn it, Raz," I swear, "how in the fuck did he get through the door? What am I paying security for if they can't manage to keep that motherfucker out?"

Vardis is the last thing I need tonight. The fat fuck. The last vestige of the filthy legacy my father left me. I've worked my ass off to separate my business from that world. It's cost me a fortune. In the process, countless unsavable souls were wiped from their worthless existence, but no price was too high to eradicate those ties. Like the cockroach he is, Vardis survived. I may have spent millions getting out, but my independence also cost him one of his most lucrative supply pipelines, not to mention the only son he was able to sire. My only regret is that I didn't put a bullet in his head myself.

"Well, he's here now, Cal. He has an invitation somehow, and unless you want to cause a scene with those million-dollar ass lickers drinking that champagne and eating those canapés, you need to prepare yourself. Get your mind off the brat and Vardis. You need to focus on the room."

Raz is the only person on this planet who has the audacity to speak to me like that. As my business partner, he's as invested in tonight's success as I am.

I give him a nod and take one more glance at the crowd below, then straighten myself.

"Okay, let's go. You keep your eyes on that motherfucker, and if he blinks wrong, you blow his head off. No hesitation, understand me, Raz?"

"You've got it, brother," Raz affirms, both of us knowing he won't. He'll be much more discreet. It's what he's paid for.

FIVE
Charity

I weave through a sea of elegantly dressed people, carefully balancing the tray of liquid gold. Eyes down. Respectful nods. Polite smiles. No empty glasses in sight. I play the part, but I've never felt more out of place. The room is packed with the who's who of the upper echelon. Some faces I recognize from headlines, the rest are a blur.

The clink of flutes, hushed conversation, and the soft bubbling of the reflecting river blend with the quartet's melody. Like me, the musicians are invisible. No one notices them until silence hangs too heavy in the room.

A guffaw of boisterous laughter jolts me from my rhythm, and I steady myself and the tray I'm holding. "Shit," I murmur. There's always one in every crowd. I look over and see a barrel-chested man in an ill-fitting tuxedo that should have been retired twenty pounds ago. He's standing with his arm around a petite redhead's waist, obviously too old for her, but rich enough to excuse it. Typical.

I hand off my last two glasses of champagne, place their empties on my tray, and work my way over to the bar for refills.

I see Sam and immediately smile.

"Hey girl," she beams. "How's your section?"

"Jesus, Sam," I respond, "if one more old man sniffs me, I think I might lose my shit. What is with the sniffing?"

She gives a little laugh.

"Have you run into any gropers yet? I've had two so far. Clumsy me," she sighs, then continues in a mocking falsetto, "So sorry for stepping on your foot!" She dramatically bats her eyes at me, and I can't stop myself from laughing a little too loudly.

The woman with the headset, whom I've learned through the night is named Janet, gives us both a death glare and a sharp "Shhh!"

Sam gives her a warm smile and a "Sorry, Janet!" before turning back to me.

"Okay, so they're about to start the speeches. 'Give us your money' blah blah blah. It's for a good cause, the best cause, blah blah blah. Once they start, we can sneak out for a quick break. We'll snag some of this overpriced chill juice and go out back for a smoke. Meet back here in ten?"

"Oh God, yes!" I confirm. "This past hour feels like it's been a full damned shift. See you then!"

We both grab our trays and head back into the crowd. *Clink, Click, Clink.*

An overhead announcement breaks the hum of the room.

"Distinguished guests, please make your way to your tables. Opening remarks will begin shortly," a faceless male voice announces.

Guests begin dispersing to their assigned seats.

I make one final round to ensure everyone is adequately supplied with drink and drift back over by the bar to stand by Sam and the rest of the serving staff.

"Great job, everyone," Janet whispers to us. "Once they're settled, and the speeches start, the food service will begin. Each of you can take a fifteen-minute break. No more than two at a time, please. Cover each other's tables while we're getting breaks in, and," she adds, her eyes narrowing at Sam, "for the love of God, don't come back in smelling like cigarettes!" Sam flashes her a guilty grin, which causes me to snort.

A hush settles over the crowd as the spotlight hits the temple's stone façade. A woman in a floor-length sage green gown steps out from the entryway and onto the pylon with smooth, practiced grace. She lifts the microphone with both hands, smiling.

"Good evening, and welcome to the 10th Annual Phoenix Gala," she announces, her voice warm and welcoming. "Tonight, we gather not only to raise awareness about the horrors of human trafficking but to fund tangible change. Your generous donations provide counseling for survivors, transitional housing, and education opportunities that not only give back their futures but help ensure that they are afforded every chance to thrive."

Polite applause ripples through the crowd.

Sam, standing next to me, gives me a gentle elbow nudge and tilts her head, pulling my attention to the right of the temple where the scarred deliveryman stands. I look at her, and she waggles her eyebrows with a mischievous smirk.

"Look," she whispers, "my beast awaits." I roll my eyes at her, but I can't help laughing just a little.

"Sam, No!" I whisper back, "That man looks like he grinds human bones for his protein shakes!" We laugh again and turn our attention back to the pylon where the woman is still talking.

"It is now my great pleasure to introduce the man whose generosity and vision brought tonight to life. Honored guests, I present our host and benefactor, Mr. Calahan Mitchell."

A second spotlight flares to life as Calahan Mitchell emerges from the shadows of the temple behind her. Dressed in a crisp black tuxedo, he takes the stage with a calm, commanding stride. I feel my pulse jump.

"Wow," I mutter under my breath.

"Ohhh, of course that's your type," teases Sam. "My beast may look scary, but Cal Mitchell *is* scary. Stay away from him, Charity," she warns. "That man's got a history that you do not want to get involved with."

"*Your* beast?" I ask with a grin. "Don't worry, that man up there is so far out of my league. I can still appreciate a gorgeous man when I see one." I give her a wink.

We watch as Cal, as Sam calls him, reaches for the woman beside him and offers a polite kiss to her cheek.

She tries to linger, but he doesn't allow it. With barely a shift in posture, Cal steps back, avoiding her. It's impossible to read unless you're looking for it. The smile never leaves his chiseled face, but the message is clear: Not tonight.

Hmmm, well, that was interesting.

Sam leans over to me, "Ready to hit our break?" she whispers.

"Um, do you mind if we let the other set go first?" I answer, not taking my eyes off the stage. "I'd kind of like to hear what he has to say." I try to hide my blush, not wanting her to see how much this man has piqued my interest.

"Fine, but only if you promise to introduce me to your delivery boy before the night ends."

"Deal," I confirm. She steps over to a few of the servers to let them know they can break first.

I watch as Cal takes the microphone from the woman's hand, his fingers brushing hers for the briefest moment.

"Thank you, Helena. Beautiful as always."

He tips his chin, dismissing her without a word, then turns his attention to the crowd, leaving her to drift offstage.

He scans the crowd, as if he's taking the measure of every soul in the room.

"I'm honored to welcome you all tonight. I won't waste your time with platitudes. You're not here for a tax write-off or a photo opportunity. You're here because somewhere in this city, a human being is being sold while we sip champagne. Your donations matter, yes, but your presence here tonight tells me you understand what's truly at stake. You've chosen a side in a war most people pretend isn't happening."

His ice-blue gaze sweeps across the room, landing on me. The intensity makes goosebumps rise on my skin. His eyes hold mine a beat longer than they should before continuing. It's only then that I realize I've been holding my breath.

"In a world where evil hides in plain sight, tonight is our chance to shine a light on its darkness."

He lets the silence hang a beat, holding the room captive.

"So eat. Drink. Enjoy!"

A slow smile curls at the edges of his mouth.

"And when the time comes, don't be shy with your generosity." He gives the crowd a wink and then walks off the stage to the sound of applause.

SIX
Charity

As the first overpriced course makes its way to the tables, Sam and I head out for our break, a half-full bottle of champagne hidden from view.

Outside the employee entrance, she takes a swig from the bottle and hands it to me.

"So," she starts, "want to tell me why Cal Mitchell of all people looked at you like he knows what you look like naked?" She lights a cigarette and offers her pack to me.

I tip the bottle back, taking a drink, the bubbles tickling my nose, and hand it back to her. I shake my head at the pack of smokes. "No thanks." I desperately want one, but having quit a few months back, I can't afford to pick that habit back up again. "And no," I continue, "he did not look at me that way. I didn't even know who he was until you told me his name. What's with the ominous warning anyhow?"

She widens her eyes at me.

"Are you being serious right now? You really don't know? Cal Mitchell has a reputation, girl. The only reason he's the so-called 'benefactor' for this charity is that his father was one of the biggest sex traffickers in the northern hemisphere. I mean, some of it's probably gossip, but his father was supposedly ruthless." She takes another swig off the bottle, and we continue to pass the stolen champagne back and forth.

"So, if that's true, why this cause? I mean, it's a bit on the nose, not to mention bad for business, wouldn't you say?" I ask.

"Well, rumor has it, his dear old dad died mysteriously when he was around our age, and Cal wanted out of the skin trade. From the sounds of it, Cal wasn't afraid to spill blood to get out. I only know the details from hearsay, but what a great story, right?" She inhales a drag of her cigarette, and she catches me looking longingly at it.

"Are you sure you don't want one?" she asks. I shake my head.

"I know, it's a filthy habit. Someday I'll quit, but today is not that day." She takes another drag and snuffs it out against the building, throwing the butt into a nearby trash bin.

"So now," she exhales, "Mr. Mitchell is known in all the circles as the great antiquities dealer. His father collected women—he collects rare treasures of a different sort. I hear that he's even returned pieces that he's found on the black market to their original countries. A real Boy Scout," she huffs, "if you buy that."

I tilt my head at her, "You don't?"

She shrugs.

"All I know is that the man has more money and power than my rinky-ass job will ever see. Maybe he's not selling people, but he's still got his hands in some dark shit."

Before I'm able to probe further, the scarred deliveryman comes around the corner.

My stomach drops, and I quickly hide the champagne bottle behind my back.

He narrows his eyes at me.

"Ladies, shouldn't you be getting back? The guests should be finishing up dinner and will be expecting fresh beverages." He raises an eyebrow at both of us.

"Miss Johnston, the champagne bottle, if you please." He holds his hand out.

I blush again and hand it to him.

Sam starts to explain, "Hey, I'm the one—"

"Miss Kellogg, I'm fully aware that you are the one who walked off with the half-finished bottle. What I don't recall is alcohol consumption being part of tonight's compensation." He looks at her sternly. "Am I mistaken?"

"Well, no, but it was just going to get thrown out, and that seemed wasteful, Mr... ahhh...?" She raises an eyebrow right back at him.

"Verrick," he responds. "Raz Verrick. Now, if you would both please return to your stations before I have to do something we'll all regret, I would be much obliged." He cocks his head at her. "And you, Sprite, watch yourself!"

She gives him a wink and laughs.

"No problem, Beast." With that, she grabs my hand and drags me back into the building.

SEVEN
Cal

As dinner is cleared and guests begin to mingle, I check the time. Raz notices my restlessness and leans in. "Just a bit longer, boss. It's almost over. Once they start filing into the auction, you can slip out without anyone being the wiser." He's been with me long enough to know I hate this part of my position. I started the Phoenix organization to atone for my father's sins. Sins that I've spent years trying to wash away but still stain the Mitchell name.

I look around at the fake smiles, the plastic conversations. Some are here because they actually give a damn. Most are here for the press they'll get for the donation they make. As long as those donations are large enough and the funds clear, I don't care what their reason is. The money spends the same.

"So, I found your brat outside drinking a half bottle of Dom with the blonde," he chuckles. "She's fiery that one. Those two are trouble with a capital T."

"She's not *my* brat, Raz." I narrow my eyes at him. "Regardless, who is she? The blonde, that is."

"Samantha Kellogg. Junior Analyst at a small financial firm on the east side. MBA. Good at her job, from what I gather. According to the paperwork, she's been taking these server jobs for a while. Only the higher-paying, higher-visibility gigs. I'm guessing she's networking, maybe paying off some student loans."

"Hmm…smart," I reply. My attention drifts and lands on Charity. Not taking my eyes off her, I continue, "Seems you've learned a lot about this Samantha." I turn to him and give him a knowing smirk.

"Hey, I'm just keeping an eye on your interests as you've asked. Besides, it's my job to know who is working in your periphery."

"Tell me, Raz," I gesture toward one of the male servers, "what's that guy's name and where does he work?"

"Fuck off, Cal. You've made your point." He shakes his head, grinning. "Now, go mingle. Make these assholes believe you're the reformed man you claim to be." With that, he walks away.

I snap the mask I've spent years honing into place and step back into the crowd.

EIGHT
Cal

I migrate around the room, greeting as many guests as I'm able, counting the minutes before I can slip out. Without meaning to, my eyes track Charity's movements. I've watched her through paper reports and photos for almost seven years, but being in her presence is different. I can *feel* her.

I catch Raz circling the perimeter of the room, always watchful. His training as a special forces soldier and medic has been an asset to our business. After his discharge from the service due to injuries from an IED, he had trouble finding work. Admittedly, he's a scary sight with the scars that twist up the side of his face. In our line of work, being scary is an advantage. My father found him, a drunk, scarred-up twenty-two-year-old kid in one of our clubs, and offered him a job. We became friends as he rose through the ranks. The only good thing my father ever did was hire Raz. His friendship is priceless to me.

When I took over the business, I gave him a choice. Stay with me, help me clean it up and rebuild, or take a check and keep quiet. Fortunately for me, he chose to stay. Thirteen years later, and there is no one on earth I trust more.

I watch Charity out of the corner of my eye as she politely takes orders and returns cocktails for my donors. I know her work history, and I'm not surprised she's able to handle the room with ease. It's her temper that gives me pause. All the reports point to the same end. Her seemingly easy-going nature hides her hair-trigger temper, filthy mouth, and a mean right hook when provoked. She's been dismissed from the last handful of jobs I've arranged, for insubordination.

It's then that I spot him. Fucking Nikos Vardis. His eyes lock with mine, drift over to Charity, and back to mine. His lips curl into a half-smile, half-snarl.

Fuck!

I watch as he casually makes his way toward Charity, and I know I need to stop this. Excusing myself from the couple I've been making insufferable small talk with, I make my way toward him, but I'm too late.

Charity's eyes go wide as I approach, and my cock swells, oblivious to the terrible timing. *Well, fuck me.*

"Calahan," Vardis oozes, his Greek accent thick and out of place. "Great party. I was just about to request another drink from…sweetheart, what's your name?" He places his hand on the small of Charity's back, and fury roils in my gut.

Charity jolts at his touch, but to her credit, she holds her composure.

"Charity, Sir," she replies. "What may I bring you from the bar?" She tries to step away. Her voice is measured, but her eyes fire disgust at him.

Good Girl, but you're still too close.

I need to get her away from him.

I snap my fingers at her, and her gaze shifts to me.

Forgive me, I silently breathe at her.

"Are you here to work or find your next rich fuck?" I snarl at her. "Two Dalmore 25s, neat. GO!" I order dismissively.

Her eyes flash with a moment of surprise, then darken.

"Very good, Sir," she bites back at me, her fury evident.

Oh, little hurricane. You are not equipped for this game.

She doesn't deserve my harsh words, but at this moment, I can't care.

I turn to the man to my right as she stalks away.

"What the fuck are you doing here, Vardis. You're not welcome." I keep my voice even, my face betraying none of the vitriol I feel for this man.

"Now, Cal, my boy," he smirks. "Is that any way to treat an old friend? Isn't my money as good as," he waves his hand across the room, "these pompous fucks?"

"Your blood money is no good here. Get. The. Fuck. Out." I scan the room until I locate Charity, the need to ensure she's safe overpowering my usual control.

"Well, well. Charity. Interesting girl that one," he smirks. He's also tracking her.

It takes every ounce of control to stop myself from plucking the motherfucker's eyes from his skull.

"She looks so much like," he turns to me, "*her mother.*"

My pulse spikes and my blood turns cold.

He knows? How in the fuck did I miss this?

"Oh yes, Mitchell," his smile is cold and calculating. "I know exactly who she is."

I grind my teeth. "Enough, Vardis."

He grins. "Enough? Oh, you idiot boy. I haven't even gotten started."

NINE
Charity

That asshole!

My hands are shaking so badly that I nearly drop my tray. I try to take deep breaths to calm myself. It doesn't work.

How fucking dare he talk to me that way! He might be paying me to serve his overpriced champagne, but how dare he think he can treat me like that.

I slam my tray on the bar, drawing the attention of everyone at the bar.

Sam appears at my elbow, her eyebrows pinched together.

"Whoa, Charity. What happened?" she searches my face with concern.

"Oh, I just had the fucking pleasure of meeting tonight's benefactor," I huff. "No worries about any illusions I had, that man is a total bastard!"

"Okay," she says, still scanning my face. "Tell me what happened?"

"He called me a whore!" I blurt louder than I meant to.

"He WHAT?" I see the rage fall over her face. "Oh, hell no!" she exclaims. "Absolutely not! Give me the word, and I'm on it." Her pale face turns completely red.

Something in my chest loosens a fraction as I watch her ready to battle for me.

"Sam, I don't know what happened. I was serving drinks like I'm paid to do. The bastard walked up and accused me of trying to 'find my next rich fuck.' Who does that?" I rage.

"Charity, let me take the drinks. You don't need to put up with that shit. No one deserves that."

Her anger steels my resolve. I know what I need to do.

"No, I'll be fine. I've got this. No one treats me like that." I straighten and square my shoulders.

Jeff, the bartender, finally wanders over.

"Two Dalmore 25s, neat, please," I tell him.

He blanches. "Oh, you got him? I'm sorry."

I look at him with surprise. "Sorry for what?" I ask.

"The Dalmore 25 is about two grand a bottle. Mr. Mitchell has it brought in exclusively for his personal use. I know from other events that most of the staff tries to avoid him," he continues, "He's been known to be a bit, um, prickly."

"If by prickly, you mean a raging fucking asshole, then yeah—on fucking point," I sass back.

Poor Jeff winces.

"Sorry, Jeff. I just want to get this dickhead his drinks and get the hell out of there."

Jeff gives me an understanding look and places two glasses of amber liquid on my tray.

"Good luck."

As I turn to make my way back over to 'Mr. Mitchell,' I carefully balance the crystal lowball glasses, my rage simmering into a full boil.

Who the hell does he think he is?

I march toward him, feeling the room go quiet around us, conversations dropping to whispers as I approach.

"Dalmore 25, Sir." I offer a strained smile to the man Cal Mitchell is still speaking with and hand him one of the lowball glasses.

"And for you, Mr. Mitchell." With the slightest grin, I reach the glass out to him, but then impulsively, never dropping my gaze, pull back. I spit in his drink and push it forward to him again. "Choke on it!" My voice drips with malice.

I hear gasps and a distinct chuckle from Cal Mitchell's current companion, but I don't react.

Calahan Mitchell narrows his eyes at me, the animosity in the air palpable. Without hesitation, he grabs the tumbler, swallows the contents, and places it back on my tray. "Miss Johnston, I believe this concludes your service for the evening," he sneers. "Raz, if you would be so kind as to show her to the door. Oh, and do ensure that she receives proper payment for her services this evening."

Before I have a chance to offer a rebuttal, a firm grasp clamps on my arm, pulling me away from the night's host and his companion.

"Let's go," I hear his henchman say. But my attention stays locked on Cal, unable to look away from his cold, dispassionate eyes.

It's then that the slightest twinge of panic hits me.

Oh, Charity, what have you done?

As Raz starts dragging me toward the exit, I twist, trying to break out of his vice-like grip.

"Knock it off, right now!" he snarls. "You couldn't handle it, could you. All you had to do was show up, do the work, and go home with another one of his padded checks. Oh no, you had to make a goddamned scene. I warned him that you weren't reliable."

"What the hell are you talking about?" I ask, trying to make sense of his statement. "What do you mean, another one of his checks?"

"Get your hands off her!"

I turn my head and see Sam trying to catch up to us.

She meets up with us as we reach the corridor leading to the employee exit, grabbing at Raz's arm, trying to loosen his grip.

"I said, get your fucking hands off her, asshole!"

Raz looks down at Sam like she's an annoying gnat that he wants to slap away.

"Unless you are planning on joining her, Sprite… Get. Back. To. Work. NOW!" he hisses, each word slicing through the air.

"Sam, go," I plead. "Don't get yourself into trouble on my account. I knew what I was doing," I glare up at Raz, "and I'm not fucking sorry!"

Exasperated with both of us, Raz growls again.

"I don't get paid enough to deal with this bullshit!"

"Sam, go! I'm fine." I assure her. "I'll call you tomorrow."

Sam's eyes dart between us, her fists clenching and unclenching at her sides before she finally takes a half-step back.

"Fine. I'll go. I swear to God," she says, pointing her finger at Raz, "if there is one mark on her, I will hunt you down and make you sorry!" she promises him.

He lets go of me, pushes a wad of cash into my hand, and points at the door.

"You, OUT! And you," he points at Sam, "Back to work or join her. I don't give a fuck!" He crosses his arms and waits while I slip out the door.

TEN

Cal

I watch Raz pull the hell cat out of the event. The crowd begins whispering warily, not knowing what to expect next.

"People, please," I say, trying to diffuse the situation, "Let's not let one mannerless guttersnipe ruin our evening. The auction will begin shortly." I smile reassuringly. "Freshen your drinks and prepare to go home with some amazing treasures."

When I turn back to Nikos, I see the dark smirk on his face.

"Interesting development, Calahan. So, are you fucking her already, or was that your version of foreplay?" he taunts.

"Vardis, what the hell do you want? The show is over. Either make a donation or get out." I force my voice to sound uninterested and less on edge than I feel. I wonder if I could remove his throat before his two guards, circling us, can stop me.

"I would be very cautious if I were you right now," he warns. "I'm paying you a professional courtesy. You owe me, and I'm putting you on notice that I will collect. You think you could keep her hidden? Charity?" He narrows his eyes. "Or is it, Rhea?"

I look at him impassively, then let my eyes roam over the room.

"I have no idea what you're talking about, old man. You're rambling." I reply dryly, doing my best to look uninterested in his words.

"Do not take me for a fool, Calahan Mitchell," he growls. "Your father promised that girl to me, then lied, telling me she was dead. I will take what I am owed. Seeing your interest in her only makes the taking sweeter. I'm sure she'll look even more beautiful, swollen with my child."

I feel my heartbeat quicken, but don't dare move a muscle, afraid I'll betray myself.

"Vardis, I don't have a clue as to what you're going on about." I finally turn and look him in the eyes. "And I don't care to find out. If you want to fuck the help, have at it. Just be warned—she spits." I give him a shrug. "I assure you, any arrangement you had with my bastard of a father has fuck all to do with me. Now, if you'll excuse me, I have guests to attend to."

I swallow down the last of my drink and methodically move away from him, my eyes slicing through the crowd.

Where the fuck is Raz? I need eyes on her NOW.

After many years of playing chess with my father, I know what I have to do.

An intermezzo.

Calculate your opponent's next move and disrupt it. Slide the piece out of reach before he can strike.

ELEVEN
Charity

The cool summer night air rushes over me, but does nothing to settle my nerves. I could sure use one of Sam's cigarettes now.

Asshole! I mutter, then start giggling to myself.

Part of me can't believe I spat in that man's drink—the other part wishes I'd worked up a full snot glob.

I look at the crumpled bills in my hand and quickly do the math. Dammit! With the rate I was quoted, I'm holding less than half of what I would've made if I'd kept my shit together. With the cost of the Uber rides factored in, which I won't be paid for now, I could've made more at the bar and not had to deal with that bullshit.

I pull my phone out of my pocket and groan. One bar of battery and no cell service. This night keeps getting better and better. I put the phone in low battery mode to save as much power as I can and start walking. Hopefully, once I get off the grounds, I can pick up a signal.

"You've got this, Charity," I tell myself. "This is nothing but a bump."

As I round the front of the building, headlights sweep across the drive. A sleek black car rolls toward the circular drop-off, slow and predatory.

Yes! Maybe they've got a phone I can borrow. Before I can second-guess myself, I throw up a hand to flag the driver down.

The car eases to a stop. The back door swings open.

And out steps Calahan "the bastard" Mitchell.

"You!" The word rips out of me before I can choke it back.

"Well, Miss Johnston, what an absolute pleasure seeing you again. Still hoping to find that rich fuck you were working so hard to score at my event?" The icy smile he gives me does nothing to cover his amusement at my predicament. I can see it in his eyes.

"Go to hell, asshole! I wasn't trying to score anything. I was doing my job. You know that thing that we poor folk are forced to perform so that you rich pricks can get richer? I would've been gone by now, but there's no cell service, and my phone is almost dead, so I can't call for my ride. Now, if you'll kindly get the hell out of my way— I have a long walk ahead of me."

I watch as he puts his hands in his pockets and looks me up and down, sizing me up and making me shift uncomfortably.

"Fine," he sighs, almost sounding bored. "Get in the car. I'll get you home."

I stare at him, bristling.

"Like hell I'm going anywhere with you," I snap at him.

I close my eyes for a heartbeat, knowing this is not the time for my temper to cause me more problems. Taking a deep breath, I muster up my sweetest smile.

"I'm sorry, Mr. Mitchell. That was rude of me. If you would be so kind as to let me borrow your phone, I'll call my Uber, and we can both forget about this unfortunate night and each other."

He lets out a short, sharp laugh, visibly amused by my shift in attitude.

"Interesting strategy." His voice drops an octave as he closes the gap between us. "If you think I'm going to trust you with my phone, you must take me for a complete idiot." He takes another step, crowding me further.

"No, Charity, you will get in the car, and I will escort you home. Don't be a fool. This location was chosen for its privacy. There's no cell service for at least two miles, and the chances that one of those 'rich pricks' will take pity on you are next to zero after your little performance in there. My friends don't make a habit of allowing feral strays in their vehicles. Besides, if anything happens on your way back to civilization, I don't need the bad press."

He sweeps his hand toward the open car door.

"Now check your very misplaced pride and get in the damned car before I lose what little is left of my patience."

I huff at him.

"If this is you being patient—"

"No more sass," he cuts me off. "Get in the car, tell my driver where we're going, and shut. the. fuck. up."

I catch the sharp bite in his words and force back a smile. Apparently, it doesn't take much to get under this man's skin.

I get into the car, flashing him a smug grin. I still hate him, but making him miserable on the way is the payback he deserves.

TWELVE
Cal

I watch her crawl into the car, and my traitorous eyes linger on the curve of her ass a bit longer than they should. She predictably sits in the rear-facing seat, forcing us to sit opposite, as if we're opponents in some twisted game.

"Seatbelt, Miss Johnston." My eyes cut to the belt at her side.

She looks at me with a challenge, the snark there before it ever leaves her lips.

"Don't trust your overpaid driver, Mr. Mitchell?"

"Does everything have to be a damn argument?" I drop my voice, deliberate and slow. "Put the belt on before I put it on you myself."

The little hurricane smiles to herself as she grabs the seat belt and pulls it across her body, calling attention to her perfect breasts.

Sweet fucking hell.

I avert my eyes and take in the darkness as we pass by, willing my cock to stay under control. This is not the time nor the circumstance. *Christ, Mitchell, you're not a hormone-drunk twenty-year-old kid. Control your damned self.*

I clear my throat and turn back to her. "Exactly how old are you, Miss Johnston?"

She looks at me with surprise.

"That's a weird question to be asking, Cal. I can call you Cal, right? I mean, I feel like we've gotten so close in the past..." She raises her wrist as if looking at an imaginary watch, "...twenty or so minutes."

I study her, amused.

So she thinks she's going to steer this conversation. Oh, you little fool.

"Well, Charity," I stress her name, and she shivers just a touch at my use. "Since you've already shared bodily fluids with me, I thought we'd dispense with the small talk."

"Touché, Cal." She smiles coolly at me.

I let her snark go because it's the first real smile I've seen all night, and it's stunning.

"If you must know," she continues, "I'm twenty-five. Prime of my life, or so they tell me." She turns her head toward the window, watching the lights blur by as we drive.

I study her for a heartbeat, and catch the flash of vulnerability she tries to hide. But I see through her.

"And you, Cal? What are you, forty? Forty-five?" Her eyes sparkle, and I know she's back to fucking with me.

I let out a low chuckle.

"Ouch," I wince. "Thirty-seven. Not quite ready for the nursing home." I give her a wink.

Color rises in her cheeks, and the temperature in the car climbs ten degrees.

I steady myself for my next question, already knowing the answer.

"And your parents," I prod gently. "Where are they?"

She narrows her eyes at me.

"Foster kid. Never knew my real parents. The people who raised me were more than happy to see me go after the checks stopped when I turned eighteen. Why are you asking me these questions, Mr. Mitchell? You have me kicked out of your fancy party. Now you're offering me a ride, and seem way too interested in my life. If you think you can snatch me and sell me like your old man did with all those girls, it'll be the last fucking thing you try!"

I sit back as if she just slapped me and feel the rage building again.

"First of all," I begin, "you chose to try to humiliate me in front of people who are very important to a cause I hold dear. Secondly, I do not trade in flesh as my father did, and don't you ever dare to compare me to him." I lean forward, invading the small space dividing us. "And lastly, do not ever talk to me in that way again, or I swear on everything someone like you—" My gaze roams over her dismissively to sharpen my point, "—holds dear, I will redden your ass until you can't sit for weeks. Do I make myself clear?" I snarl.

Panic flickers across her face, the fear radiating from her, but she says nothing.

"Words, Miss Johnston. Open that fucking mouth and use your words!"

"Yes, sir." It's a whisper, almost indistinguishable in the hum of the car.

"What was that?" I taunt.

"Yes, sir," she says louder this time, her voice unsteady.

I settle back into the seat and study her.

"Do you know who the man is that I was speaking with when you chose to put on your little display?"

She shakes her head, her gaze still locked on me like she's afraid I'm going to bite any minute.

Good. She should be.

"His name is Nikos Vardis," I tell her. "Unlike me, he does trade in flesh. In fact, he's one of the biggest traffickers in the world. Men, women, children—he has no limits, and what you did tonight, you stupid girl, was put yourself directly in his crosshairs. Oh yes, Charity, you have all the qualities a man like Vardis loves to break, and he will break you into a million fucking pieces."

She unsnaps the seatbelt in one movement and tries to bolt for the car door.

"Fuck you. Let me out of this car right now."

I don't flinch when she lunges for the door handle. The locks click down with a quiet finality before she can touch them.

"Sit. Back." I tell her, my voice flat.

Her chest rises and falls fast, eyes darting between the locked door and my face.

"You really think," I lean forward, slow and deliberate, "that running into the night is going to save you from a man like Vardis?"

She opens her mouth, but I'm already reaching across to her as if I'm about to buckle her back into her seat.

And with one tiny movement, I pierce her skin.

She jerks, eyes wide, and I feel the sharp inhale more than I hear it. I hate that it's come to this, but there's no other way.

"It's just a sedative," I murmur, holding her there as the fight drains out of her limbs. "You're about to make more trouble than either of us can afford."

Her head tips back, lolling against the seat. The last thing she sees before her eyes close is my face above hers.

"What the hell do I do with you now?" I mutter, more to myself than her.

THIRTEEN
Cal

The blank space where my father's portrait used to hang looms in front of me. It was the first thing I removed from this house. I couldn't stand to look at it. Even with it gone, I still see the old fucker looking down, mocking me.

I nurse my glass of bourbon while I watch her on the monitor in front of me, her chest rising and falling as she sleeps. Looking at the clock, I'm debating whether to give her another bump to keep her under a while longer.

She looks so peaceful, nestled under the white cloud of the comforter in the bed I've put her in. Her hair fanned around her like a fiery halo. Part of me wants to keep her this way. Peaceful and unbothered. I was careful with how much sedative I gave her, but it still took her under quicker than I expected. I remember the look of confusion, then fear, then fury, before her body had no choice but to give in to the poison working its way through her blood. Her small body so pliant and malleable as I carried her into the house and up to the guest room she will now occupy. I could've restrained her, probably should have, but I couldn't bring myself to do it.

She will not be peaceful when she wakes. My thumb pushes the syringe back and forth on the desk, the light reflecting on its glass barrel. I slip it into my desk drawer before I change my mind.

I hear a soft chime from the security panel. Raz and the men who were on duty tonight at the gala are back. Sighing, I scrub my hand over my jaw, preparing myself for a long-overdue conversation.

Raz's heavy footsteps echo in the hall before a light tap sounds on my office door, and it swings open.

"Boss," he smiles and settles in the chair in front of me.

"Everything wrapped up?" I ask.

"All good. The cleaning crew was just coming in when I left. The preliminary numbers for tonight were better than anticipated. We'll have the final numbers in by the end of the week," he reports.

"And Vardis?"

"Left at the end of the auction. The fucking hypocrite bid and won on two of the paintings. Everyone in that room knew where his money was coming from."

Raz cocks his head and almost squints at me.

"Cal, you okay?"

The concern in his voice would be touching if I didn't know how quickly I was about to turn it sour.

Without a word, I flip the screen around so it's facing him, and I watch his expression change.

"Is that Charity Johnston?" he asks, hesitation in his voice.

"It is," I say quietly.

"Cal, why does she look drugged?" his voice measured.

"Because she is," I reply as I watch his face, carefully gauging his reaction.

"What the fuck is going on, Cal. Why is Charity Johnston drugged and in the guest bedroom?"

"I didn't have a choice, Raz. She put herself on Vardis's radar. I can't allow him to take her." I lock eyes with him, praying that our years of friendship will help win the battle that's about to start.

Raz stands and paces. I can see him working through what I just said, trying to put together a puzzle that he doesn't have all the pieces for.

"Cal, we worked our asses off and waded through blood and gore to get out of that business. You need to tell me right the fuck now what is going on, or I swear to you I'm gone, and I'll burn this whole thing to the ground on my way out!"

I cock my eyebrow at him.

"Are you threatening me?" I ask.

"Do I need to?" he challenges back.

A soft moan filters in from the monitor, and I know we don't have a whole lot of time before she wakes.

I stand, walk around the desk, and sit in one of the club chairs. This isn't a conversation I want to have from behind my desk. I need to be across from him when I tell him the last of the secrets I'm holding.

"Raz, please sit," I ask him quietly. "Please."

I hear him let out a breath and walk over to the bar. The clinking of the glass and the sound of the bourbon being poured tell me he's willing to at least listen.

He settles down in front of me, his eyes darting to the screen and back to mine.

"Talk," he commands, and I let him.

"We thought we had cleaned up all of the old bastard's sins, Raz—but he hid one," I begin. "She was owed a debt. I thought I could keep her hidden. Safe from this life. She was just something to manage. I only wanted to make sure she had some sort of life. I know now that I wasn't the only one left who knew about her."

"Cal, you're rambling. What the fuck does this have to do with you having the girl drugged and in your fucking bed?"

He's losing patience, and I don't blame him, so I give him the last piece.

The night I learned exactly what kind of monster made me.

FOURTEEN
Cal

Twenty-two years ago...

"Cal, get up!" I feel someone kick my bed, and I roll over with a groan.

"I said, get up, you little shit. Your father's waiting for you." I pry my eyes open, working the blurry image of Finn into focus.

"Jesus Christ, Finn, it's 1 o'clock in the fucking morning! Get the fuck out!" I throw one of the extra pillows at him.

"Get the fuck up NOW!" He yanks me up and presses clothes into my chest. "Your Da is downstairs waiting in the car."

My blood turns to ice.

"Where are we going, Finn?" I ask. I steady my voice so as not to give away my fear. The last time my father woke me up in the middle of the night, it was the first time he put a gun in my hand, and I swore it would be the last.

"There's a problem with a rat. All I know is that your Da is requesting your presence," he smirks. "Try not to throw up this time."

The dread is like a rot in my belly as I pull on the black dress pants, black button-up shirt, and black tie. Rule #1: Don't wear white to a rat extermination; the blood never comes out.

Malcolm Mitchell, my father, is an exacting man. There is no room for mistakes. There is no room for weakness. As the head of our family and my only living relative since my mother's death, his word is law. I know not to cross that man.

A year ago, on my fourteenth birthday, he decided my childhood was over. I was a man now, he'd said. It's the way he was raised, he'd told me. His first kill at fourteen, his first woman at sixteen. It's the way things are done in this family. With that, a gun was pushed into my hand, and I was ordered to kill my first man.

I take one last look in the full-length mirror and straighten my tie. I hear my old man's voice in my head, "Death is no excuse for being sloppy." I take a deep breath and head out to the car.

I step into the cool night, look up for a moment, and marvel at the stars. It's been overcast for days, but tonight the sky is almost too clear, casting its light and shadows across my path.

The driver opens the door, and I slide into the seat next to my father. He doesn't say a word to me, just looks me over and gives me a nod, acknowledging his approval of my wardrobe choice. The car pulls out of the estate drive, the silence between us deafening.

I study my father for a moment, trying to find any clue as to where we're going or what this night is about.

His black three-piece bespoke suit, complete with a waistcoat, looks more like wedding attire than funeral wear. His wavy black hair is parted precisely, and his almost black eyes with their fine smile lines hide the monster locked inside.

"Calahan. How's school?" he asks nonchalantly.

I fight the urge to balk at his question.

"Going well, Sir. I have my last finals tomorrow, then summer break begins," I reply, working to keep my voice steady.

What the actual fuck?

"Very good. Seth will be expecting you at the warehouse on Monday. You'll be sixteen soon. It's time you start learning the run of the place. No piece of the business is more important than any other, Calahan. I expect you to earn your place and the respect of the men."

I nod, not bothering to look at him.

He never looks me in the eyes, anyhow. I have my mother's ice-blue eyes. I remember him telling her that he could see the entirety of the heavens in her eyes. I think he can't bear seeing her in me since her death.

The day she died, so did he in a way, or maybe that was the day the monster took over. Sometimes, it's hard to remember when he was ever any diffcrent.

Suffocating silence swallows the hum of the car as the trees rush by in a blur.

After some time, we turn onto another tree-lined single-lane drive, the palatial home coming into view. It's not as large as the one we live in, but it's not modest by any means. My stomach roils as I realize where we are. We drive around to the back of the house, where I notice three other cars that I recognize as part of my father's fleet.

For the first time since getting in the car, I turn and look directly at him. "Da?" my voice cracks—a symptom of my fifteen years. "Why are we at Uncle Cormack's house in the middle of the night?"

He peers out the window and sighs.

"Calahan, tonight is a lesson in trust and in betrayal. The man I thought of as a brother to me, and an uncle to you, has committed a grave sin against us. He's been lying to us, boy. He and his Greek bitch have been planning on sneaking away in the dead of night. I'm sure she put him up to it, but that's even more reason to deal with this brutally and completely." I watch him as he clenches his fist, "Women are a weakness, Calahan. A man who allows a woman to lead him is no man and has no place in our organization."

He turns to face me and swears under his breath.

"I won't make you take a life tonight, but you will be there to bear witness. It's not lost on me that this will be difficult for you, but sometimes difficult things are necessary. You will keep your mouth shut and your eyes and ears open. If you so much as blink a tear, I will end you. Do you understand me?"

I gulp down the rising bile and nod. He opens the car door and steps out, and I slowly follow behind him.

The coppery smell is the first thing that hits me as we enter the back of the house into the kitchen. I recognize the smell, and my racing heart threatens to jump out of my chest. Blood.

Without pausing, my father continues through the kitchen into the main dining area, where he's greeted by four of his men. The dining table has been moved, and there tied down in chairs, duct tape over his mouth, sits my father's longest friend, the man he's called brother my entire life. Cormack Brennan.

His dark red hair, usually slicked back, hangs partially down his forehead. Tears and sweat, mixing with blood from angry cuts, streak down his face. Next to him, his wife is seated, her head hanging, matted black hair covering her face and drifting across her shoulders. Her dress, once light blue, is now smeared in bright red and torn open in the front. Ropes wrapped around her torso make deep indentations across her chest, forcing her breasts to painfully bulge through the bindings. Her legs are strapped open to each leg of the chair, as if she's being presented to my father as some perverse gift. Red smears her thighs, evidence of the vile things that occurred before we arrived. She doesn't move, though, and if it weren't for the subtle rise of her chest, I would have taken her for dead.

Cormack's eyes focus, then widen when he sees my father. He struggles against his bindings and begins screaming through the tape, his eyes pleading. My father nods at Vinnie, who's leaning nonchalantly against the oversized fireplace. Without a word, Vinnie stalks over to Cormack and rips the tape from his face, and I wince as he lets out a painful scream.

"Malcolm, please," he pleads. "This is between you and me. Please let her go. Brother…please."

With no ceremony, my father walks over and backhands Cormack, his head snapping back from the force.

"Don't you fucking dare call me Brother, you traitorous piece of shit," my father snarls at him.

"Malcolm, I'm sorry, but it has to stop," Cormack continues, "I begged you to get out. I have a daughter. I couldn't watch those innocent girls get sold like worthless cattle. You tainted our money with your greed."

My father sneers but doesn't respond. He reaches over and grabs Eleni's hair, wrenching her head to the side, and a small moan escapes from her. The only indication that she's still alive.

"It was this Greek cunt, wasn't it?" I watch as my father's eyes roam over her once beautiful face. Her eyes are now swollen, and her cheeks are mottled with the shadows of bruises that I know will never fully develop.

He spits on her and roughly grabs her exposed breast and twists.

"Get your fucking hands off her!" Cormack screams.

My father lets out a sadistic chuckle.

"From the looks of it, my hands are the only ones that haven't been on her, brother." My father looks her over and scowls. He scans over his four men in the room, and when his eyes land on the scratches on Joey's face, he smiles.

"It looks like she put up a fight. The boys do love it when they fight. Don't you boys?" he asks.

Chuckles and muffles of agreement ripple through the men, but my gaze doesn't move from the scene playing out before me.

Everyone in this room knows how this will end. It's just a question of how long my psychopath of a father will drag it out.

My father sighs and steps back from Eleni, who still hasn't moved.

"Boys, move the guests of honor so that they're facing each other. Let them say their last goodbyes."

Without a word, two men move and swing Cormack and Eleni's chairs so that they sit across from one another. I watch as Cormack's eyes sweep over Eleni, seeing the full extent of the damage to her body and soul. His face contorts, and he lets out a guttural wail.

"Eleni, baby, I'm so sorry. I'm so, so sorry. I love you. Malcolm, please, let her go. Please," tears are streaming down his face, and I look down, unable to bear the intensity of the scene playing out before me.

My father's hand juts out before I feel the crack against the side of my head.

"Eyes up, boy!" he booms at me. I look up sharply and meet Cormack's torture-filled eyes.

It's then that I hear it, and I freeze. The small wail. A child's wail. I see Eleni's body jerk as if her primal instinct has taken over, and her soul knows she needs to go to her baby.

My father smiles, the reaction utterly vile in the wake of the scene before me.

"Oh, good," he claps his hands in sadistic delight. "The princess is awake!"

"Ryan, be a good lad and go get the princess for us."

No! She doesn't belong here.

Ryan gives a curt, "Yes, boss." He leaves the room, returning moments later holding a tiny, sobbing child. She couldn't have been more than three or four years old. Dressed in a thin nightgown, her cheeks red and wet with tears, snot trailing down to her trembling lips as her eyes find her father. Tiny arms stretch toward him, her sobs breaking into desperate, hiccupping wails.

My father pulls a perfectly folded handkerchief from his pocket and gently wipes the toddler's face.

"Shhh, little one. It's okay. You're okay," he soothes.

I've never seen this type of care from him, and my mouth goes dry. She seems to become mesmerized by the monster tending to her. She trusts this show of care, and for a moment, I almost do too. I fight my urge to push him away from the child and run with her.

God, please don't let him hurt her.

Cormack begins pleading again.

"Malcolm, not Rhea. Please not Rhea. Malcolm, please don't hurt her!"

My father takes the little girl in his arms and gives Cormack an almost sympathetic look.

"You didn't think through the consequences of your actions, did you, brother?" he growls. "Now, look at your beautiful—well," he chuckles as his eyes roam over Eleni once again, "—formerly, beautiful wife. Look at this precious child." He gently rubs his hand over the child's hair and kisses her on the forehead. "Lives, ruined. For what? Some newfound morality?" he asks. "Where was that morality when you were cashing the checks?" He holds the baby close, her body facing away from her beaten parents.

Small mercies.

"I'm going to show you the respect that you never showed me, Cormack Brennan. I'm going to tell you exactly what the consequences of your actions are and will be. I thought about taking your cunt of a wife, breaking her, selling her, but no. She's not worth the effort that her dried-up pussy would take. You will go to your grave knowing that your wife will be meeting you in hell, but your precious daughter?" He rubs his hand over the toddler's back as if he's trying to soothe her.

"Oh no, brother. She is mine now. She will help replenish the supply you worked so hard to deplete. You know who our clientele is. You know the vile perversities they enjoy. Know this, brother. Your precious Rhea? She will fetch me a price worth far more than your whore of a wife ever could."

He nods at Ryan, who pulls a gun out and fires one shot into Eleni's temple, blood spraying the wall.

Cormack's eyes go wild, his screams mixing with the wails of his daughter still in my father's arms. Vinnie slaps a fresh strip of gray tape over his face, muffling the sounds.

"This child…" my father continues, seemingly immune to the wails of the little girl struggling in his arms, "she will be raised never knowing who you are. When she comes of age, she will be groomed then she will be sold. Your 'legacy' will be nothing to her. It will be as if you never existed. Her sole purpose will be the pleasure she will bring to the men I rent her to."

My eyes snap to the child.

I watch my father give Ryan another nod, and another gunshot thunders through the air.

My father passes the small bundle to Vinnie and, with a curt nod, tells him, "Get rid of her, and" his hand sweeps around the room, "take care of this mess."

"Cal, let's go," he orders before stalking out of the room. Without a word, I follow, fighting the sickness threatening to fill my mouth.

We get into the car, and I can't bring myself to look at him. I know my eyes will betray my emotions. My anger, sadness, and the pure revulsion I feel at being connected to this man in any way.

As we drive down the road leading away from the house, I hear a boom and look back to see the structure engulfed in flames.

"You did well tonight, Son," my father says to me.

Without turning away from the flames getting smaller behind us, I ask, "What will happen to her? The girl?"

"I keep my promises. She will be given a new name, she will be raised, and when she reaches maturity, she will be sold," he shrugs. "Do you want to name her boy?"

I jolt, instantly enraged.

"She's not a fucking stray dog!" I spit at him.

He narrows his eyes at me, "Watch your fucking tone! What I just did was a show of fucking charity. I could've put a bullet in her head along with her parents. Or I could've put her back in her bed and let her burn. After what her father did to me, to us—I'm a goddamned saint!" he booms at me.

I can't breathe. I want out of this fucking car now, but there's nowhere to go.

I turn my head to look out the window, watching the trees flashing before my eyes, and feel a single tear fall down my cheek. I quickly wipe it away, knowing that showing any weakness right now will only invite more of his wrath. Closing my eyes, I try to shut out what I just witnessed, but all I can hear are the screams.

FIFTEEN
Cal

I study Raz as he takes in everything I've told him. He takes a deep breath, then drains what's left in his glass.

"Christ, Cal. You were just a kid." His eyes come back to me. It's not pity, I see, thank God, but something close.

He looks at the monitor again. Then back to me. The pieces click into place.

"So the baby… it was her."

I nod.

"All this time, since your father—"

"No." I cut him off. "I didn't know she was alive until she turned eighteen. My father never spoke of her again. I assumed she had died with her parents. There was no trace of her in any of his paperwork. You know how meticulous he was. A lawyer, whom I had no idea he had worked with, reached out seven years ago to inform me of an account that was closing since she was of age. I didn't know that the account existed before then. I didn't know she existed."

Raz's nostrils flare as he exhales. "He fucking named her Charity? Sick bastard."

"She was a name in a file, Raz. A photograph. A few reports. At first, I thought that if I put the right opportunities in front of her, she'd take them."

Raz huffs a humorless laugh. "Didn't expect her to be such a little fuck up, did you, my friend?"

"Raz—"

"Hey, I was there. You kept rearranging her life. The scholarship she blew off. The endless jobs she couldn't keep. The partying. Falling behind on rent when it was dirt cheap. It makes sense now why you wouldn't cut her loose. To be honest, I thought maybe she was a bastard sibling. I had no idea it was this fucked up." He pauses. "Cal, you do know she's not your responsibility, right? This isn't yours to fix."

I don't answer.

He shifts in his chair. "So the ping I saw on her records—Vardis?"

"He confirmed it tonight. Apparently, Charity's mother was promised to him before she ran off with Cormack. After my father executed them, he made a deal with Vardis. I still don't know the particulars. According to Vardis, my dear old dad, may he rot in hell, promised he could have Charity when she turned eighteen. Then, for some reason, Vardis was told she was dead right before Malcolm died."

Raz frowns. "Then how's he so sure she's the kid?"

"It makes sense that he would be monitoring us just like we watch him. I had no idea I was putting her in danger when I arranged for her to work the gala. I only wanted to see who she really was behind the reports."

Raz smirks, eyes flicking to the monitor. "From her performance tonight, I'd say my notes nailed it."

"It doesn't matter," I exhale. "After you dragged her out, Vardis said she looks like Eleni. Raz, he called her Rhea. That's when I knew I didn't have a choice. I had to act."

Raz studies me. "Act meaning…?"

"When I left, she was outside with no phone signal and no ride. I offered her one. I just failed to tell her she would be coming here."

I lean back. "That's it, Raz. That's all of it."

Raz lets out a breath.

"So what now?" he asks.

"Now, she stays here until I can neutralize the threat."

"Are you going to tell her?"

"Eventually. If I tell her now, it only puts her in more danger. She'll run, and Vardis will take her."

Raz nods, knowing I'm right. "I'll agree to help you, for now. What do you need from me?"

I release a silent breath of relief.

"I need you to help me keep her safe. She's reckless and irritatingly bold. She's going to do something rash and stupid, we both know it."

"Oh, brother," he smirks at me. "That woman spent five minutes with you and got your head all fucked up."

From my periphery, I see Charity start moving on the screen.

"Well, buckle up, my friend. Sleeping Beauty is about thirty minutes from turning into the banshee from hell when she realizes where she is and what you've done." He looks amused now, and it's pissing me off.

SIXTEEN
Charity

I try to will my arms to move, but they don't seem to be listening to me. There's an acrid taste in my mouth coating my tongue with sandpaper, making it almost impossible to swallow.

I groan as I force my body to shift, nothing under my control. Pain throbs in my head, keeping time with my heartbeat, and white light explodes behind my closed eyes. I try to force them open, but my lids feel impossibly heavy. The urge to give up and sink back into the dark and sleep is overwhelming, but I know I have to move. Something is wrong. I try to hoist myself up again, but fall back onto the pillow. It's wet from where I've drooled during my blackout, but I can't grasp how I blacked out. I search through the hazy memories of last night, trying to grab on to anything, but it's nothing but fog. The more I fight, the more it takes me back under until I finally give up.

I jolt back awake with a gasp, my eyes flying open, taking in the unfamiliar surroundings.

I don't know how much time has passed, but I feel more in control this time. The gray fog still clouds my mind, but I can feel it dissipating. I swipe at my mouth, wiping away the wetness, and finally rub my eyes, the room coming into focus.

What the hell?

There's no way the champagne affected me that much. I know my limits. Granted, I've been known to ignore them—but this is beyond any drunken night.

I search around me. The large room is clean, too clean. Its pale-yellow walls are too cheery. The weight of the white down comforter and the bed that is more comfortable than I've ever known almost soothes the terror inside. I note an open door to my right that looks like it leads to an ensuite bathroom. My whole apartment could nearly fit in this bedroom.

Do not panic, Charity.

I scold myself into calm, and take stock of the room again.

I spot a door. That must lead out.

I look to my right again, and as if on cue, my bladder screams to be emptied.

Feeling like a baby deer trying to stand for the first time, I wobble as I get out of the bed. The room seems to tilt as I try to catch my balance. I carefully make my way to the bathroom, hanging on to the room's furniture as I go.

Flipping on the light, I inch my way to the toilet and lower myself, thankful for the relief. The bathroom's white and chrome fixtures, accented with gray and yellow, carry the cool yet warm tones of the bedroom. I've certainly woken up in worse places.

I finish my business and flush, my head finally starting to clear. Turning to the double-sink vanity to wash my hands, I notice a fresh tube of toothpaste and a toothbrush still in the package.

Well, I'm not dead, so I might as well get this stink out of my mouth. I open the packages and add a liberal strip of toothpaste to the brush, relishing the minty feel and the cold water.

I start taking inventory. *Think, Charity.*

I'm still fully clothed in my uniform from last night, and I think I'd feel it if there'd been sex. I remember the gala, the temple, that asshole Cal Mitchell…

I stop short as it all starts coming back to me, and I spit in the sink, not bothering to rinse the bowl.

My almost-dead phone. Flagging down the car. *That motherfucker.*

I remember now. He was asking all those personal questions. I remember wanting to get out of the car, and then the piercing pain in the side of my neck. My hand flies to the spot, the skin still tender.

I feel myself becoming frantic, and I take a few deep breaths to fight it off.

I have to keep it together. I start opening the vanity drawers, looking for anything that might serve as a weapon. Every single drawer is empty.

I stand up straight and feel myself sway, still a bit woozy. I grab the cold marble to steady myself, turn on the faucet, and splash cold water on my face, forcing myself to stay alert.

The memory of what Sam told me about his father being a sex trafficker comes crashing down on me. Me calling him on it, and his denial. All the questions he asked. It was like he knew the answers before I gave them.

The realization hits. He's going to sell me.

I muster all the strength I have and straighten and stumble out of the bathroom. Frantic, I look around and head for the door. I pull, but it won't budge. I rush over to the windows and rip open the curtains.

Bars? Who puts bars on bedroom windows?

Assholes who steal women, that's who!

My eyes dart around the room again. That's when I see it. A small camera perched in the corner of the ceiling, the red light indicating that it's on.

He's watching me. That psycho is fucking watching me and getting his jollies off on my panic.

Oh, hell no!

SEVENTEEN
Cal

I watch the monitor as Charity starts coming to again. Raz stands next to me, just as invested.

When she finally sits up and makes her way to the bathroom, I let out a breath in relief. This is good. Movement is good. I don't have eyes in there, but if she falls, the camera's microphone will pick up the crash.

"Looks like your guest is awake. Mind if I hang out here and watch?"

I shoot him a look.

"Go make yourself useful. Get her food from the kitchen. She's going to need food." I growl at him.

He gawks at me.

"Why do I have to feed her? She's your pet!"

My eyes narrow, signaling that he's pushing me too far.

He holds up his hands in surrender.

"Fine. I'll get the brat some food. Can I make a suggestion?"

"What?" I snap, my patience fraying.

"Lose the gun before you walk in there and keep her away from sharp objects." He nods toward the screen, drawing my attention back to Charity, who's exited the bathroom and has now noticed the camera.

"That one," he continues, "she's going to slit your throat the first chance she gets."

As if to prove his point, Charity looks straight into the camera and lets loose, screaming every obscenity she can string together.

Raz grins. "This is gonna be fun." I hear a chuckle as he walks out.

Sighing, I take my gun out of my side holster and put it in my desk drawer. I lock it for good measure before I make my way up to her room.

When I unlock her bedroom door and step into the room, I'm not ready for the blur that slams into me. She's a flurry of curses and swinging fists.

For someone who's just coming out of a stupor, she doesn't seem at all fazed.

"You sick motherfucker! You drugged me!" she screams.

Her nails slice at my cheek, followed by the thud of her fists hitting me in the chest.

"Get out of my fucking way and let me go, or I swear I'll kill you!"

I grab her wrists and block an obvious attempt to knee me in the groin.

"Enough!" I shake her.

"Fuck you! Don't touch me!" she spits, twisting against my grip. She snaps her teeth at me, close enough to graze my arm.

I grab her wrists harder and force her to take a step back. She answers me with another kick.

For a brief moment, I almost admire her grit. Almost.

Her head jerks forward, trying to slam into my face, and that's it.

I'm done playing.

I drive her back, slamming her into the wall. One hand closes around her throat, pinning her in place, the other dragging her wrists above her head. Her body jerks, but her fight is useless. Her pulse races against my palm as she tries to catch her breath.

"You want to fight me? Fine, but understand this," I tighten my grip just enough to ensure I have her attention, breaking off her curses. "You will not win."

She stills for the briefest of moments, and I see her eyes searching mine, studying me for any sign of weakness. Her pulse is still hammering, her fight seeming to coil, ready to unleash if she sees any hesitation.

"That's better."

I peer down at her, my expression steel. "Now here's what is going to happen. I'm going to let you go. You are going to go and sit on the bed. I am going to sit in the chair, and we are going to have a conversation. Do you understand me?"

She doesn't blink.

"Charity, nod if you understand me."

She nods with a slight movement, her eyes never leaving mine.

"Good." I release her and nod to the bed. "Go."

She steps away from me, and I see her eyes dart to the door.

"Don't. If I need to tie you to that fucking bed, I will do it. Do not test me."

Straightening herself, she juts her chin out in defiance and stalks to the bed and drops, arms crossed, like she's daring me to push her again.

I follow her, turning one of the bedroom chairs to face her before I sit.

She glares at me, her expression dripping with venom, and I make a mental note to thank Raz for reminding me to lock up my gun before I came in here.

"You want to talk, then talk." Fury is coming off her in waves. "Why don't you start with why the fuck you drugged me and locked me in your damned house like some evil villain! Who's my buyer, Mitchell? Or are you just going to kill me and have Scarface hide my body?"

I don't flinch. "If I wanted you dead, you wouldn't have woken up. And to clarify, Raz doesn't hide bodies. He buries them where I tell him to."

Her eyes search mine, looking for the lies, but she won't find any.

"You're not here to be sold, Charity," I continue evenly. "That's all you've earned the right to know for now."

Her eyes flash, and I see the argument beginning to form, but I cut it off before she can start again.

"You will be staying here as my guest—" she interrupts me with a huff at the word guest, but I continue.

"There will be rules. You will be confined to this room until I deem that you are trustworthy enough to have access to the rest of the house. The better you behave, the more privileges you will be granted. If you misbehave, which I have no doubt you will, considering our recent history, there will be consequences." I watch as her eyes widen, but to her credit, she doesn't interrupt.

"Do you remember what I told you before I helped you sleep?" Even I know this is a stretch, but decide to go with it.

"Helped me sleep?" she sneers. "So that's what we're calling it?"

"Answer the question, Charity," I order, my patience thinning.

She tilts her head back, squeezing her eyes shut as if she's asking the universe for strength, and then her eyes snap back to me.

"I remember you telling me that you aren't like your father. That you don't sell women, but here we are now, aren't we?" she challenges.

She's baiting me, and it's working. I feel my anger rising, and I fight to keep control of the situation before it spins back out of control.

"Use your head," I snap, my voice razor sharp.

"Do you think that women who are snatched to be sold wake up in a room like this? Do you think they are supplied with a bed, let alone a toothbrush? No. They're not. IF they wake up—and many times that's a very big if—they wake up in their own piss and shit only to be hosed down, marked and tagged."

I can see by the change in her expression that I'm going too far, but I have to put a stop to, or at least a pause in, her fucking insolence.

"Now answer the fucking question. You can play nice, and maybe—just maybe—I'll give you some answers. Or," I growl, "and I do not recommend this course of action, you can keep up this act. I'll bind you to the bed, and we can try again tomorrow after you remember your fucking manners."

"You wouldn't dare!" she challenges.

I bolt out of my chair, my patience gone, grab her by the hair, and wrench her head back.

"I drugged you and put you in my villain lair, as you've called it. You think tying you to the bed is a stretch?"

I give her head a shake, daring her to challenge me further.

"There is one immovable rule—you will not disrespect me. Apologize! Now!" I command.

Our gazes are locked, hers in defiance and mine in control. I know I'm walking a fragile line with her, and I don't breathe until I see her swallow, and her eyes drop.

"I'm sorry," she whispers.

It's the first crack in her defenses, and I hate it.

I release her hair and step back to the chair. We both stare at each other, neither of us sure how to make the next move.

Finally, she clears her throat, and I wait to see what's coming next.

"I remember you mentioned someone who was at the gala. Someone dangerous. Someone like your father," she says, sounding unsure, which isn't surprising considering the drugs.

I answer her calmly. "Yes. Nikos Vardis. He's the reason I had to take you as I did."

Her eyes widen, but I put my hand up to stop her questions before they can start.

"I will explain everything eventually. Just know you are here for your safety. He is a bad man, Charity. Trust me when I tell you, this was the safest option."

A rap sounds on the door, and Raz enters the room, stopping the conversation before it can continue.

"Well, look who's up!" he says to Charity a bit too cheerily.

I watch as Charity glares at him, and I'm relieved to see her ire directed at him instead of me for a moment.

"The cook doesn't come in till the morning, but I was able to put together a sandwich. Since you're not a vegetarian, turkey should be fine for you. Got some chips and a bottle of water. Paper plate and no utensils, obviously. Wouldn't want you fashioning a shank."

"Raz," I warn.

"I'm not hungry. And how do you know I'm not a vegetarian?" she shoots back at him.

Raz grins. "Honey, the way you snapped your teeth at him," he jerks his chin toward me, "definitely a meat eater."

"Raz, get out." I sigh wearily.

He sets the paper plate down on the side table and winks at her before he leaves.

I stand and follow him to the door. Before I leave, I fix her with a look.

"You need to eat. Every bite. Then get some rest. The drugs are still working their way out of your system, and once the adrenaline of this wears off, you're going to need your strength."

I walk out of the room behind Raz, knowing that she's not done fighting me. Not by a long shot.

EIGHTEEN
Charity

I watch as he leaves and hear the click of the lock engaging from the outside.

There is no way that I will be some passive prisoner for Frankenstein and his monster. I scan the room while I try to plan my next move. I have to admit that it is a beautiful room, if not a bit generic. Besides the bed, there is a small sitting area with two high-backed dark gray library chairs, a small matching loveseat, and a dark, low-profile mahogany coffee table.

"A living room in a bedroom... pretentious fuck," I mutter to myself.

Directly across from the bed, which of course is framed in the same dark mahogany wood, is a chest of drawers again in the same wood. Everything is perfectly matched, but soulless.

My eyes roam until I spot another door next to the bathroom, and I walk over to investigate.

Opening the door, I see a walk-in closet. When I switch on the light, the space lights up. Empty clothes racks, the shelves, and built-in cabinets are individually lit throughout the oversized closet. Who has or even needs this many clothes? I walk in and start pulling open the doors and cabinets, looking for anything that might have been left behind. Nothing. Empty.

I flip off the light and close the closet door. I eye the dresser. Maybe there's a nail I can pry up somewhere. I've seen plenty of movies where small things were used as weapons. I only need one fraction of an opening to make my escape. I almost laugh at the visual of myself lunging at Calahan Mitchell and driving a nail through his eye like some badass action hero. *Focus, Charity!*

I open drawer after drawer, slamming each one shut harder as I work my way through. All of them empty.

I search the three windows again, pulling back the curtains. The black bars block my view, reinforcing the fact that I am a prisoner here.

Catching a red blur out of the corner of my eye, I narrow my eyes at the flashing red light of the camera in the corner of the room. I can't stand the thought of him watching me.

Stomping to the bedside table, I grab the plate and hurl it at the blinking red eye in the corner. Chips scatter across the floor, the sandwich splits mid-air, its contents smearing the wall before sliding down to join the rest of the mess.

"Fuck you, Calahan Mitchell! You bastard!"

I stomp to the bathroom, slam the door behind me, and sink to the floor. I put my face in my hands and feel the tears forming.

No longer able to fight it, I quietly sob.

NINETEEN

Cal

I should be working, but it's impossible to concentrate on the shipping manifests in front of me. My eyes keep drifting back to the monitor, watching my little captive. After I left her room and told Raz to get some sleep, I found myself back here needing to keep my eyes on her. I was curious to see whether she would follow my directive to eat and get some rest, knowing she wouldn't. I admit I wanted to see what her next move would be.

Predictably, she spent some time going through every inch of her cage, looking for escape. I knew she wouldn't find one. It was seeing her wildness that entranced me. The more she searched and came up empty, the wilder she got, and my God, her rage was beautiful.

Hearing her curse me and seeing her throw her food at the camera did nothing but act as a siren call. I wanted nothing more than to stalk up to her room, fling open the door, and fuck the disobedience out of her.

Instead, my concern got the best of me when she didn't come out of the bathroom. I went back to her room only to find her asleep on the bathroom floor. I picked her up and carefully tucked her back into bed. I watched her for a minute, brushing her stray brown locks out of her face before leaving and silently closing the door behind me.

I'm not sure when Charity Johnston changed from something to hide, something to protect, to someone I want to have. She tests my control, and I despise it.

I have no claim on this woman, and I've given her more than enough reason to hate me. That doesn't stop me from wanting her. Taking unwilling women has never been a need or a necessity. When you have money and power, sex is an inevitability. It's offered up, freely given. My tastes might venture into the darker side, but I have lines I will never cross. Still, the way she looked at me at the gala, before she knew who I am or discovered the lengths I will go... I want to see that look again. Her curiosity disguising her hunger. Fucking Vardis. This was not how I wanted our introduction to happen.

No, I tell myself again, forcing those thoughts away. I brought her here for her safety. I told her that this is the safest option for her right now, and it is the truth. I will keep her safe, even from myself.

I close my eyes and, despite myself, drift off.

I wake with a start and instinctively reach for my gun, my holster empty.

"Easy, Cal. It's just me. I brought coffee." My eyes snap to Raz sitting on my office sofa.

I rub my face, trying to wipe away the sleep.

"Did you sleep in here last night?" he asks, handing me a cup.

I take it, still trying to get my bearings.

"I must have dozed off. What time is it?"

"Just before seven. She's still out." He nods toward the monitor, Charity's sleeping form filling the screen.

"I'm surprised, to be honest. I thought she'd still be yowling. I could hear her cursing you out all the way in my room."

"Yeah, about that," I start, letting the bitter liquid coat my tongue. "I need a favor. Our guest destroyed her quarters last night. Get someone to clean it up, and while you're at it, bring her some decent clothes and whatever else women need."

He cocks his eyebrow at me.

"What kind of damage are we talking about? And how the hell am I supposed to know what to get her?"

I close my eyes, still exhausted, and let out a breath.

"Nothing major. She decided your sandwich skills were lacking and chose to show her disfavor by throwing it at the camera. Ask Marie to clean it up, but you need to be there with her. I don't want her trying to convince any of the staff to help her escape."

Raz nods.

"I've already talked to Marie and Cora. They understand the situation. Cora's fixing her breakfast. I'll have Marie accompany me when I deliver it. Speaking of—you need to eat something, Cal." There's concern in his expression.

"I will. I need to attend to some things first. The shipment with the Fabergé egg is expected this morning for Nathan Riggs. Another gift for his wife."

"Nate's dick get him into trouble again?" Raz asks with amusement.

Nathan Riggs has been a client for years. His wife is especially fond of Fabergé and other Russian antiquities. Anytime he gets caught cheating, Ann receives another treasure, and I get another money transfer.

Raz's phone vibrates. He looks down at the message, and I see him furiously type back a reply.

"Problem?" I ask.

He holds up his phone, and I see a video of the exterior of Charity's apartment. Four men, dressed in black, get out of a dark SUV and enter her building.

"I've had Trey watching her building. This was from a few hours ago. He says they showed up, were there for about thirty minutes, and then left. When Trey went in, they had turned her apartment inside out." He watches my face. He's waiting for my next move.

"Ask Trey to take pictures and videos of the damage and send them to me along with the video of the car. It might come in handy for my conversation with her later."

I watch as he sends another text to Trey and tucks his phone back into his suit pocket.

"I'll send it all over to you as soon as I get it. In the meantime, I guess I need to get breakfast for your pet and clean her pen. Oh, and then there's the personal shopping." His voice is dripping with sarcasm.

"Raz, quit referring to her as my pet, or I swear," I threaten him.

"Relax, I'm fucking with you. You make it too easy." His cocky grin gives away how pleased he is with himself.

TWENTY
Charity

The door opens, and I bolt upright. I look around, confused as to how I'm back in the bed, but before I can spend too much time questioning it, a woman enters carrying a tray, Cal's henchman following close behind her.

"Good morning, Brat. Sleep well? Marie, you can put the tray there." Raz nods at the coffee table.

The woman, not much older than I am, soundlessly places the tray on the table and lifts the silver lid, revealing a plate of scrambled eggs, bacon, and toast. Without being told, she walks across the room and begins filling the lid with the scattered chips and remnants of the sandwich that I now remember flinging at the camera.

She's dressed in a simple black uniform pantsuit, her dark brown hair pulled back in a severe bun, with little to no makeup. When I catch her eyes, I see a flash of what looks like sympathy pass over her face.

I can feel Raz studying me, so I turn to look at him as he sets a small duffel bag in one of the chairs.

"I'm a little disappointed, but not surprised, that you made a mess of the sandwich I made you. Lucky for you, I don't take tantrums personally." I can hear the teasing in his voice.

I should be furious, but his teasing throws me off balance.

"Now, Cora made you a delicious breakfast, and I need you to come over here and eat it. No argument. No more theatrics. Don't make Marie clean up after your tantrums—it's rude, and I don't like people being rude to our employees. Understand?" Raz holds out a bottle of water, and I take it without argument.

The water slides down my parched throat, relief washing over me despite my determination to resist anything he offers.

"How did I get here?" I ask Raz.

He raises an eyebrow at me.

"You don't remember? The gala? Cal? Vardis?" He studies me with concern.

"No, no, I mean here in the bed. I was in the bathroom. How did I get here?"

"Ah. That. Most likely Cal. For some ungodly reason, he was worried about you—even after your fit." His smugness re-sparks the fight in me.

I glare at him, ready to unleash on him when I see his face soften a touch.

"Hey, I get it. This has been a lot to take in, but I need you to listen to what I'm saying. Vardis is no empty threat. Cal's tactics weren't ideal, but think about it—if he'd told you what was going on, would you have believed him?" He arches a brow at me and continues.

"Cal is a decent man. I won't say he's good, but he's honest. His reasons aren't mine to tell. You need to accept that he's doing this to keep you safe."

His words feel like a bolt of lightning entering my body, and it snaps me out of my fog.

"Safe? Fucking Safe?" I yell at him. "Your boss drugged me and is holding me fucking prisoner in a room with bars on the damned windows! People are going to look for me. They're going to notice I'm gone. Where's my phone? Where is the almighty Cal Mitchell? Why isn't he here himself?"

Out of the corner of my eye, I see I've startled Marie with my yelling, and for a millisecond, I almost feel a twinge of guilt.

"You need to calm down!" Raz directs sternly. "Cal has some things to take care of, and then he'll be up to talk to you. In the meantime, eat your breakfast. Take a shower." He nods toward the bag. "Marie was kind enough to lend you some clothes until we can get you some things of your own. There's soap, shampoo, and probably other girly shit in there too. If there's anything specific you want, tell me, and I'll make sure it gets to you. Now don't be a bitch and tell her thank you."

A growl festers from my throat, and I catch the slightest curve of a smile on Marie's face, but the monster isn't fazed.

"Marie, finish up. I have things to do today, and babysitting this one isn't on the list."

Marie nods. Taking the silver lid now filled with the mess I left for her, she heads for the door, Raz on her heels.

They both leave the room without another word, the click of the lock reminding me that I have nowhere to go.

I clench the bottle of water still in my hand, fighting the urge to hurl it at the door, but I think of Marie cleaning up the sandwich. I won't make another mess for her. This isn't her fault. She's probably a victim like me.

The smell of the bacon causes my stomach to growl again, and I grudgingly get out of bed and walk over to the tray of food. I take a bite, and despite myself, I moan at the taste of the salty meat. Unable to fight my hunger any longer, I devour the breakfast, wishing they'd included coffee. Who doesn't offer their guests coffee in the morning? I huff dryly at that thought. *Yeah, Charity, you're a guest.*

Eyeing up the duffel bag, curiosity gets the better of me. I walk over and begin rummaging through it.

Two pairs of black leggings, a few T-shirts, some fuzzy socks, and a soft light gray hoodie. I'm surprised to find a package of new underwear and two sports bras. Marie and I are about the same size, from what I could tell, so I'm sure everything will fit well enough. I dig deeper into the bag to find brand-new travel-sized deodorant, shampoo, conditioner, and body wash in a neat zip-lock bag, as well as a comb and brush—all the essentials a woman in captivity needs to feel at home.

Raz definitely did not put this together, and now I feel like a heel. I need to thank Marie when I see her. Not only did she lend me clothes and pack me the essentials, but she also cleaned up after me. Hopefully, someone reimbursed her for this.

Gathering my new-to-me gifts, I make my way to the bathroom. When I turn on the shower to let the water heat up, hot water immediately flows from the wide showerhead. A luxury I didn't have at home. I adjust the temperature, strip off the uniform I'm still wearing, and step in.

I scrub my skin with the floral-scented body soap and wash my hair twice with the expensive shampoo before applying the matching conditioner. I almost forget that I'm not in a high-end hotel for a minute and close my eyes, letting the hot water pound my body, releasing some of the pent-up tension.

Freshly showered and dressed in my borrowed wardrobe, I curl up on the sofa, my wet hair tied up in a scrunchie. I don't know how long it's been, but I'm starting to feel a bit stir-crazy when I hear a knock at the door. Startled, I sit up straighter.

The door swings open, and Marie steps in, one arm loaded with bedding, a bucket with cleaning supplies hanging from the other. She looks at me and smiles.

"Hi, Miss. I'm here to change your bedding and finish cleaning the wall." She nods at the spot on the wall where the sandwich landed during my lame act of defiance.

I look past her, but before I can ask, she continues, "It's just me. I assured Mr. Verrick that we'd be fine without him." She tilts her head at me. "We will be fine, right? You won't cause me any reason to call in the guard standing outside the door?"

Her gentle challenge makes me smile, and I find myself instantly liking this woman.

"Yes," I assure her. "I won't do anything to get you into trouble."

She sets the bucket down, places the bedding on the dresser, and begins tearing the used sheets and blanket off the bed. I can't sit while she waits on me, so I join her to help.

"You know I only slept in here one night. There's no need—" she cuts me off with a look.

"Telling me how to do my job already?"

I shake my head and go silent.

We work on reassembling the bed for a minute. Neither of us speaks until I can't stand the quiet any longer.

"Marie, do you need help? Is Cal holding you like he is me?" I ask, my voice full of concern.

She stops for a minute and then laughs.

"Oh my, you are sweet. No, Charity, Mr. Mitchell is my employer. I'm in no danger. I'm well paid, and I come and go as I please."

I step back, angry with her and her answers.

"You do know he's holding me against my will, right? How the hell can you work for someone like that? You think bringing me breakfast and some clothes washes away your part in this?"

She narrows her eyes at me, drops the sheet, and crosses her arms.

"You hold it right there. You do not know anything about me, so you can stop making judgments. Let me clue you in on something, Sunshine." Her voice drips with sarcasm.

"Calahan Mitchell is the only reason I'm alive. Three years ago, I was locked in a basement on the other side of the world, dirty, hungry, and abused. Mr. Verrick rescued me. Cal Mitchell rescued me. That breakfast that you enjoyed this morning? Cora is the woman who cooked that for you. Why don't you ask her about Vardis when you get the chance? She can tell you better than others what a real monster looks like. She was in his stable—yes, Charity, they're called stables. It's where monsters like Vardis keep the women he steals to be trained as their slaves. She was in his stable for almost ten years. If Mr. Mitchell hadn't rescued her when he did, she'd be dead. I don't know your story, but how dare you presume to know mine. What I do know is that if Mr. Verrick and Mr. Mitchell say this is the safest place for you, then believe them."

Stunned, I'm not sure what to say.

"Now, you can help me, or you can sit your ass over there and watch. What you will not do is trash-talk the only people in this world who gave a damn enough to pull me out of that life and offer me a new one. Do we understand each other?"

I nod and watch as she grabs the fitted sheet and begins remaking the bed.

"I'm sorry," I whisper. I fight back the tears that well in my eyes.

Marie drops the sheet and sighs.

"Look, I'm not saying I agree with his tactics, but from what I've seen, you didn't give him much of a choice. This," she sweeps her hand around the room, "is temporary. How long the temporary lasts is up to you. Now, let's get your room back together, yeah?"

I nod again, and we silently finish making the bed.

After the wall has been cleaned, she gathers the used linens, puts them in the bucket, and starts to leave. She turns back to me before she reaches the door.

"I'll be up with lunch in a few hours. If you need anything, knock on the door, and Lem will pass it along. I'll talk to Mr. Verrick about getting you some magazines or something to pass the time. Mr. Mitchell should be back later tonight." She pauses, really looking at me, her brown eyes softer now but steady. "I know this isn't easy. Try to remember, Charity, no one here is your enemy."

She looks me over one more time, knocks on the door, and disappears.

TWENTY-ONE
Charity

I must have fallen asleep after Marie left, because the next thing I know, the room is darker. There's a cold bowl of soup with a grilled cheese sandwich sitting on the coffee table in front of me, a stack of magazines next to the tray. I'm not sure what time it is or when lunch was brought, but the shadows tell me that it's long past lunchtime.

Getting up, I stretch my body, stiff from being curled in the same position too long. Moving to the window, I push the curtains open to look outside. My heart hitches. I'm surprised to see the bars are gone. I try to push up on the sash, but it doesn't budge. Wishful thinking on my part, I guess.

The view outside my window is what I'd expect from someone of Cal's status. The grounds are a long rectangle, lined by tall evergreens, perfectly landscaped. Off to the side, below my window, I can see a stone patio leading to a pool. Next to it, an almost grotto-looking hot tub, with white wisps of steam rising from the swirling water.

Flowering purple and white hydrangeas separate the pool area from the rest of the grounds with a stone path leading to a flower-covered gazebo. I can still see the breathtaking blooms in the twilight.

I hear the door to my prison open and abruptly turn around to see Cal Mitchell standing in front of me. He studies me like I'm an artifact he's trying to catalog.

Dressed casually in slim-fitting black jeans and a pale blue linen shirt open at the collar, the color makes his already striking, icy eyes seem more intense. His black hair is a bit disheveled, but still impeccable. If the devil does have minions to tempt us mortals, they look like Calahan Mitchell.

He nods toward the sofa.

"Let's sit."

"Is that a request or a command, Cal?" I ask, refusing to be the timid houseguest I think he expects me to be.

He cocks an eyebrow at me.

"Does it matter?" he asks, sinking into the sofa.

Sighing, I walk over. Instead of taking a seat next to him, I lower myself into one of the chairs facing him.

He leans back, taking me in, putting me on edge.

"I hear you had a chat with Marie. Try not to take my actions out on her. She's had a rough go of it. She deserves your respect," he begins.

I scowl at him.

"Are you here to lecture me on how to treat your staff, or is there a point to this conversation?" I ask, my patience thin.

His face darkens, and I think I might have pushed him too far, but then I see him force his expression to relax.

"Okay, we're not doing small talk. I can't tell you everything right now, but I will tell you what I can. Let's try to handle this with a modicum of civility. I'm tired, and I'm admittedly a bit grumpy, so don't push me, Hurricane."

He leans forward, his forearms on his knees.

"So, ask your questions."

I'm taken aback by the openness I see in him, but I try to hide my suspicion.

"Really?" I ask again.

"Really," he confirms.

My mind races, deciding which of the million questions to ask first.

"For starters, what happened to the bars?" I ask, my eyes moving to the windows.

"They're a safety feature," he says with a shrug. "I can retract them when I want. Last night, I didn't know how you'd react to the drugs. I didn't want you throwing yourself out a third-story window, hence the bars. Raz assured me you weren't stupid enough for that." There's the faintest spark in his eyes. He's teasing me. And damn him, I don't hate it.

Testing him again, I ask, "What's with the nickname? Hurricane?" I cock a brow at him and stick my chin out.

This brings out a laugh, the sound warming my insides. *What in the Stockholm Syndrome?*

"Oh, Charity, you are definitely a hurricane," he beams. "You are a force of nature, whipping everything in your path into a frenzy. You have absolutely no regard for your own safety, and God knows, no respect for authority. You leave destruction in your wake. It's not intentional, it's not personal—it's just what hurricanes do."

I search him for any signs of judgment or the disappointment I'm used to from most people, but I don't find any. Somehow, this makes me braver.

I take a deep breath and let it out slowly.

I lock eyes with him again and ask the real question I need answered. "Why me? Why take me? I'm no one." I feel the tears stinging my eyes and force them back down.

He reaches into his back jeans pocket and pulls out his phone, taps something, and then he places it on the coffee table in front of me.

My eyes go wide with recognition at what's on the screen.

The video starts playing from a street view, my street. Four men dressed in black enter my apartment building. A moment later, I see my apartment lights turn on. Their shadows move in the windows, but I can't make out what they're doing. The next images show the inside of my apartment. The place is in shambles. My poor half-dead plant tipped over, the pot's contents scattered on the floor. There's broken glass everywhere. The couch tipped over, and the cushions ripped, as if someone were looking for something. The video continues showing me images of my bedroom and bathroom, both in worse condition than the previous rooms. My chest tightens as I see the few things I have in this world broken and discarded. None of it was worth anything, but it was mine.

"I suspected Vardis would have someone pay you a visit, so I had someone watching your apartment. As you can see, I was right. Regardless of what you think, you are somebody. You are someone to him. If I hadn't taken you when I did, he would have. I couldn't let that happen." I can feel him studying me again, and I throw my walls up, refusing to let him see how much it hurts.

I finally lift my eyes and meet his.

"So, should I thank you now? Is that what you're expecting?" I'm provoking him, and I don't care.

He shakes his head and rubs his jaw.

"Jesus Christ Charity. I'm not looking for your goddamned gratitude. I'm trying to keep you alive. What other proof do I need to show you?" It almost sounds like a plea.

"Okay, fine. Let's pretend I believe you." I fire back. I throw the phone on the table, stand, and start pacing around the room. Something like claustrophobia overtaking me.

"What happens now, Cal. How long are you going to keep me here? Can't we call the police or something? I can't stay in this locked room, like your damned pet forever." I throw my hands up in the air, the frustration seeping out of every pore.

"Agreed. You can't," he retorts, amused. "You make a terrible pet, barely housebroken." The bastard gives me a teasing wink.

I shoot a glare at him, and he lets go of a low chuckle before he continues.

"As to your question of contacting the police, not wise. I can't be sure of who he has on his payroll. I know this is an impossible ask for someone with your," he pauses, "tenacity, but if you can prove to me over the next, say, three days, that you can be trusted. I'll consider giving you more freedom within the house and grounds."

My mind starts racing. Three days. I can work with that. I just need to play whatever fucked up game this is for three days.

"I agree to the terms," I tell him as if I have a choice. This earns me another dark smirk.

He stands, crossing over to where I'm sitting. He towers over me, forcing me to look up at him, my neck craning.

"I see those wheels turning, Charity. Cross me, try to manipulate my staff, or any more outbursts will result in additional time in this room. You may not believe me, but neither of us wants that to happen." He nods at my untouched dinner. "I'll have Marie bring you a fresh plate. Your soup's gone cold."

He doesn't wait for any acknowledgment. He just turns and walks out the door like someone who knows he rules his world and everyone in it.

TWENTY-TWO
Charity

It's the second day I've woken up in Calahan Mitchell's house. Marie has already been in with breakfast. I've showered, put on my borrowed clothes, and paced the room a few hundred times. I need to start forming a plan to get out of here, but since I've been in solitary confinement, I have no idea what's happening outside this bedroom door. The few guards I've caught glimpses of when the door has opened seem to rotate on shifts. He promised me three days. I have no choice but to hope he keeps his word.

There's a sharp knock at the door, and an older woman in a crisp white coat steps into the room. Her dark, gray-streaked hair is cut short, and she looks all business.

"Hi Charity, I'm Dr. Miller. I'm here to see how you're doing." She offers me a smile, but it doesn't reach her eyes.

"He brought in a shrink? Are you serious right now? You can tell him that I'm not getting my head shrunk by one of his lackeys."

She laughs, and I can see that she is genuinely amused.

"No, I'm not that type of doctor. I'm also not here as one of Mr. Mitchell's 'lackeys', as you put it." She moves closer to me and sits on the far end of the couch.

"He keeps me on retainer, yes, but I don't answer to him. Whatever we discuss is between you and me, period. Normally, I'm called in to help with the women that his organization has rescued. As I understand it, you may have been subject to some unorthodox means of sedation."

I narrow my eyes at her. "You people are incredible. He drugged me and brought me here against my will. Aren't you bound by some oath to report it when people are in danger?"

She nods. "Yes, I do have a duty to report. Personally, I permit myself to bend that oath when reporting it would be the more dangerous choice. I've had experience with women who've escaped Vardis. Unfortunately, men like him have the money and means to avoid the consequences they deserve." I see a slight tremor go through her. She clears her throat and continues.

"Now, let's get back to the immediate reason I'm here. I'd like to give you a cursory exam, make sure there are no lingering side effects from the sedation." She opens her bag and pulls out a stethoscope, draping it around her neck. She holds her hand out to me and smiles warmly, trying to put me at ease.

"May I? Just a pulse, blood pressure, and check your breathing. All painless, I swear."

I don't move.

"Charity, Mr. Mitchell may pay me, but I am your doctor. That part of my oath, I don't waver on. Unless you give me explicit permission, anything that happens in this room stays between us."

I hesitantly reach my hand out to her.

"I don't even know what he gave me."

She takes my wrist and eyes her watch.

"You were given 4 milligrams of midazolam," she states without looking up. "It's a drug that's typically used for outpatient procedures and anxiety. Fast-acting and quickly metabolized, with few side effects. You probably woke up feeling a bit hungover, wobbly most likely?"

I nod.

She drops my wrist and grabs the stethoscope from around her neck. I watch as she methodically adjusts them in her ears, places the disk just inside my hoodie, and listens. We go through the typical breathing instructions, followed by her taking my blood pressure.

"All good," she pronounces.

"When was your last period? Do you need birth control?"

My eyes go wide.

"Oh no, Charity," she quickly corrects herself. "I know you came here unprepared. Abruptly stopping birth control can have its own side effects."

I relax a little.

"I have an IUD. I'm one of the lucky ones who rarely get a period. I think it's been a year."

She nods. "Not so uncommon."

"Anything else we should chat about? Do I have your permission to tell Mr. Mitchell that your vitals are fine and there are no residual effects we need to be concerned about?"

"Fine. But nothing else. If he wants to know anything else, he can ask me himself." At least I get a choice in this.

She nods again, packs her equipment, and stands to leave.

"If you need anything, you let anyone here know, and they'll call me. Understood?"

I murmur my agreement. I should thank her, but I don't know what I'd be thanking her for.

She turns and walks out of the room, leaving me alone again with my thoughts.

I'm not sure how much time has passed before another knock, and the door swings open. Marie brings in my lunch, and we chat while I eat. I appreciate her company. In our brief exchanges, she's open and kind. Always careful to avoid answering any of my questions with too much detail, but I'm also careful not to ask her anything that may put her in an awkward position.

After I've finished the chicken salad, she picks up the tray to leave. "Oh, I almost forgot, Mr. Mitchell wanted me to let you know that he'll be joining you after dinner this evening."

My heart rate kicks up at the announcement. "Why?" I ask suspiciously.

She sighs. "I guess you'll need to ask him that yourself." With a small smile, she turns and leaves.

The afternoon drags on, but I use the time to plan. I rehash everything I know about Cal. It's not much, but it might be enough to work with. If I show interest, get him to let his guard down, maybe I can find a weakness. By the time Marie brings my dinner, I've talked myself into it. Cal wants a malleable, agreeable captive—I can be that. I think. I push the food around on the plate. My nerves are on edge, and I can't force myself to eat. I finally give up, and I set it aside. Like clockwork, Marie's back to take the tray away, only this time Cal is on her heels. He's in a dark pinstriped suit, a crisp white dress shirt open at the collar, a rectangular wooden box under one arm.

As Marie picks up the tray and wipes the table down, I see him notice the uneaten food. Is that concern in his eyes?

"Not hungry?" he asks.

I catch myself before I say something snarky and shake my head. "Not a lot to do to burn off the calories." I shrug.

"Marie, can you please ask one of the guards to bring us some beverages and maybe some pretzels. Then go ahead and leave for the evening. Thank you."

"Absolutely, Mr. Mitchell. Good night to you both," she nods and leaves us alone.

He sits down across from me, opens the box, and lays out what looks like a checkerboard on the table.

I raise my eyes in surprise. "Checkers, Cal?"

He doesn't look up at me, but I see the hint of a smile on his face as he continues setting up the pieces on the board. It's then that I recognize the pieces are part of a chess set.

"I don't know how to play chess," I argue, even though he hasn't said a word yet.

When the black and white pieces are arranged, he turns the board so the white side is in front of me. He finally looks up at me, challenge in his eyes.

"So, you'll learn. Your move."

TWENTY-THREE
Charity

I gape at him.

"People don't learn chess in an evening, Cal. I don't even know the rules."

"Charity," he says calmly, "the only rule is to survive longer than your opponent. Chess is about strategy. It's not about winning, it's learning how the other thinks, reacts, and countering those reactions with logic."

This isn't about the game at all. The bastard wants to get into my head.

He quickly gives me an overview of the pieces and how they can and can't move on the board. I'm overwhelmed, but I refuse to let him see it. When he's finished, he nods at the board, letting me know it's time for my first move.

I bite my lip and move a pawn forward two squares. He gives me no reaction, just reaches across the board and shifts one of the carved horses into place.

I move another pawn. I look at him, but he's still looking at the board, still giving me nothing.

Unable to stand his silence, "Who taught you how to play?" I ask.

"My father," he states flatly before moving the same piece toward my pawn.

He finally meets my eyes. "Your move."

I move one more pawn, putting it in front of the king, recalling Cal telling me that the king needs to be protected.

"So where's Raz tonight? I haven't seen him today." Cal looks up, and the air shifts.

"Attending to business," his voice still flat. He moves another piece.

"What kind of business?"

Cal leans back and raises an eyebrow. "Awfully curious tonight, Hurricane."

I shrug. "If I'm going to be living here for the foreseeable future, I should get to know him too, I guess." I nudge the piece with the cross, having no idea if I'm doing any of this right.

He takes me in, and I do my best to hide how his intensity affects me.

"Okay, I'll bite," he says cautiously. "Raz and I are partners in several ventures. The Phoenix Group, of which you are aware. We also specialize in curating antiquities, a few social clubs, other imports, and exports."

I remember what Sam told me, and so far, everything he's told me has tracked.

I watch as he takes his own cross piece and moves it toward my king. He gives me a smug wink, and I narrow my eyes at him.

A knock at the door interrupts us, and Cal calls for them to enter. A guard enters carrying a tray with two bottles of water and a bowl of pretzels, sets them down on the table, and exits without a word. "Thank you," I holler to him as he leaves.

"Now she finds her manners," I hear Cal mutter under his breath.

I roll my eyes at him as I move another piece. I want this game over.

"You left yourself exposed." He tilts his head at the board, offering no further explanation. Moving his queen behind the bishop, he states flatly, "Checkmate." I watch with irritation as his manicured hand reaches across the board and pushes my king over, making it topple with a clatter.

I sit back and offer him a slow clap. "Well, congratulations, Cal, you beat me. All my experience, and you still beat me," my voice full of snark and contempt. I'm being a bitch, and I know it.

A slow smile spreads across his face, and I feel my face flush.

"Well, that didn't take long. Welcome back, Charity."

My temper flares. "You set me up," I accuse. "You're going to create situations to frustrate me so that you can keep me in this fucking room longer?" I watch the amusement fill his eyes, and it makes my anger grow hotter.

"In what reality did you think you stood a chance at winning this game? You said yourself, you've never played. You don't know the rules." He sits back, completely at ease. One ankle crossed over the other knee, arms relaxed and draped over the arms of the chair. "Or are you pissed because now that the game is over, so is our time together tonight?" The bastard is teasing me again.

Setting my jaw, I glare at him, refusing to play whatever game this is. I've played enough games tonight, and they've gotten me nowhere.

"Answer the question, Charity," he baits. "You agreed to the rules. Not answering me is disrespectful and will earn you more time in here." His eyes drift over the room that's been my prison. "I've heard of captives getting so used to their cages that when the door is open, or they find a means to escape, they choose to stay. Scared to leave, scared to stay." His attention snaps back to me. "I didn't think it would settle in you so quickly."

"You are out of your goddamn mind, Calahan Mitchell." I stand up, put my hands on my hips, and force him to look up at me. It feels good to look down at him for once. "I didn't want to play your silly war game. It's boring, and I don't understand it. Most of all, I hate fucking losing. That's all. Open the door, and I'll show you how easily I'll walk through it." It all comes out in an angry rush.

He shakes his head, then he stands up. Still smiling, he meets my challenge. When he's at his full height, I fight the urge to take a swing at his smug face.

His eyes, still playful, lock onto mine, and he grabs my chin, stopping me from looking away.

"You hate to lose?" he growls. "Then win. Everything you need to beat me is on that board. Your instincts are sharp, but your lack of discipline makes you a danger to yourself. In here," he nods at the door, "and out there. Now sit down, shut up, and beat me, dammit."

I wrench my face from his hand, sit down, and start slamming the pieces into place.

TWENTY-FOUR
Cal

It's mid-morning before I finally make it to my office, my hair still damp from the shower. My routine has been completely disrupted since taking in my guest.

It was almost two in the morning before I finally left Charity's room. She was intent on beating me last night. To her credit, she didn't give up, and I could see her mind working as she studied the board, looking for my weaknesses. After each loss, she set her jaw and growled "*again*," like an angry kitten who just missed her first kill. If she keeps up the practice when this is over, she might become a formidable opponent someday.

I feel an unfamiliar pang at the thought of her playing with anyone else, and I scowl. I remind myself that she is not mine to keep. I flip on the monitor to check on her, half expecting her to be sleeping in, but no. She is wide awake, coffee in hand, studying our last unfinished game. A smile creeps over my face as I watch her pick up a piece, move it, shake her head, and place it back. I can see her mind working, looking at the whole board, not just the easiest move.

There's a sharp knock before Raz enters, his eyes clock the image on the monitor, and a slow grin takes over his face.

He moves closer and tilts his head. "Is she playing chess?"

"Apparently," I reply dismissively while I shuffle the papers on my desk. "Where are we on the shipment from Bosnia? Any issues with customs?"

He crosses in front of my desk and makes himself comfortable in one of the chairs across from me. "Where'd she get the chess set?"

He's not going to let this go.

"Fine," I huff. "Marie was worried that she was getting too restless. I gave her the board. We played a few games last night." My eyes drift back to the monitor for a moment. "She was actually a very adept student once she got out of her own way."

"Hmm. Interesting."

I slam the papers down on my desk and glare at Raz, my irritation making my shoulders stiff.

"Verrick, say what you need to say. Then leave it alone."

This draws a bark from Raz.

"Wow. Okay then," he starts. "You haven't played chess with me or anyone else since—" his eyes look up at the blank space above the fireplace.

"Don't you dare say his name, Raz." I snarl.

"Cal, snarl and snap all you need to, brother. I know you. You're letting yourself get too deep. It's not going to be good for either of you—especially her."

I narrow my eyes at him.

"Let me call the club, arrange one of the girls. Go let off some steam. Get your head straight."

"Stop right there, Raz. I appreciate what you're doing, but you're coming dangerously close to overstepping. If I decide I need to fuck, I sure as hell don't need you to arrange it." Normally, a club visit clears my head. I center my control, and a nameless woman gets off. Everyone wins. Now, the idea does nothing for me.

I cock my head at the smug bastard. "Now, can we please take care of our business?"

He grins again. "Customs is all set. There won't be any issues. I checked on the clubs last night. Angel sends her regards." He adjusts himself, making sure I get his point.

I shake my head at him. Usually, I appreciate his inability to be serious. Today is not the day.

"Charity's wardrobe will be ready in the morning. I need you to pick it up. I'd have it delivered, but I'm not keen on any unfamiliar faces near the compound right now. I'm letting her out tomorrow."

That gets a reaction from him, and now it's my turn to be smug.

His forehead wrinkles in confusion, but I stop him before he can start protesting. "She'll have free run of the house and inside the grounds." I continue. "As both of you have correctly pointed out, she is not a house pet. The longer she's kept in that room, the more restless she'll get. Restless Charity will return to being reckless Charity, and I don't have the patience for it. Alert the guards. Make sure that they all know who she is—and exactly where her boundaries are."

Raz rubs a hand over his face and sighs. "I think it's too soon, but it's your decision. I'll let the men know." He stands to leave, giving me another incredulous look. I think he's about to say something, but he stops himself, tips his head in acknowledgment, and heads out the door.

I settle in to finish my calls and paperwork, allowing myself one more glance at the monitor before hitting the off button. The sooner I get things done, the quicker I can return to our game.

It's late afternoon when I'm finally able to wrap for the day. I make a quick call to the kitchen to let Marie know that I'll be dining with Charity. There's no reason for us to eat alone in separate rooms.

When I reach her room, her guard opens the door without hesitating. I'm not surprised when I find her still in front of the chessboard. She's studying it like it holds the answers to all of her questions.

"You know, Marie knocks," she sasses, not looking up.

"Yeah, well, this isn't Marie's house," I snark back.

I take my jacket off, drape it across the back of the other chair, and settle in across from her. I catch her watching my movements beneath her thick lashes, and I swear I see her lick her lips.

"So, have you figured out the move?" I ask.

A tiny rumble of frustration leaves her chest, my body reacting to the unexpected sound. Her eyes lift, and I see the fire dancing—she's at her wits' end, and it delights me.

"I've been coming back to this all damned day, and no matter where I move, you've got me trapped," she complains. "The irony isn't lost on me. What are you doing here so early anyhow? Don't you have work to do?"

I arch a brow at her audacity. Still untamed, definitely unbroken. "I finished up early and found myself unable to resist your charming company. Now watch your tone and look at the board. The opening is there. Be brave enough to take it."

She props her elbow on her knee, cupping her chin as if getting closer to the board will make the next move clearer. She reaches for her knight, but before she can make a move that will cost her, Marie's familiar knock stops her.

"Come in," we both echo. Her eyes narrow at me as if I've crossed a line, and I have to stifle a grin.

As Marie wheels the dinner cart in, I study Charity's face. The fading lights from the sunset outside her windows catch the auburn in her brown hair and the gold flecks in her eyes. It looks like tiny tendrils of fire, reaching out, ready to singe anything that gets too close.

"Thank you, Marie. You can leave it there. Have a good evening."

Marie dips her chin, and I catch the silent exchange between her and Charity.

Hmmm, curious.

"We're eating here tonight. Together," I tell her.

Her disbelieving look as I get up, lift the lid on the cart, and reveal the box of pizza is all I need to know this was the right decision. I grab two of the four bottles of beer I requested and walk them over to the far side of the coffee table. Setting the pizza down, I twist the cap off one of the bottles, hold it out to her, then pull it back.

"Can I trust you, or do I need to be concerned that you'll slice my throat with this bottle?"

She scoots herself down the couch and grabs the bottle from me. "You watch too many movies. Besides, that would be a horrible mess for Marie to clean up."

I fight the twitch of a smile and motion toward the pizza, encouraging her to dig in. She grabs a slice, and I watch her mouth as she takes a bite, unconsciously licking my own lips. When she lets out a soft moan, my cock gives an involuntary jerk. I cough and adjust myself.

"So, can I still ask any questions I want?" She bats her lashes at me before taking another bite.

"Within reason," I concede. I take a swig of my beer, bracing myself for what might be coming.

"Tell me about your BDSM clubs."

I nearly choke.

Pulling the bottle from my lips, I clear my throat. Tilting my head at her, I'm more than curious where she's going with this.

"What do you want to know, Hurricane?"

"Well, is it all whips and chains and walking women around on leashes? It's obvious both you and Raz are doms," she rolls her eyes. "Control freaks," she mutters under her breath. "I'm just curious... what's your kink?" She deepens her voice and almost whispers, "What depravity are you two into that you had to form your own clubhouses?"

I bark out a laugh.

"Those questions aren't in the 'within reason' threshold."

"Oh, c'mon, Cal," she pushes. "Give me something."

There's almost a whine in her tone, and I know she's playing with me. "Finish your pizza and then the game."

Her eyes light up. "Oh, about that." She wipes her mouth and hands before reaching over to the chessboard. She moves her knight, plucks my queen from the board, and places it triumphantly next to her on the table.

My eyes shoot up.

"I was thinking about what you said—how sometimes you have to sacrifice the queen to win the game. If I'm seeing this correctly, you can probably take my knight, but it still leaves your king open. I think you're out of moves,

Mr. Mitchell." Her self-delight is making her glow, and I've never seen anything more stunning.

I offer her a smile. "Well played, Miss Johnston. You know I'll need a rematch."

"Fine," she sighs with mock annoyance. "But you'll need to find another set, because I'm keeping this." She picks the queen up and slips it into her pocket. "Now we had an agreement," she stands as if she needs courage for the next part of her conversation. "I've done what you've asked. You told me three days, and I'd get more freedom."

"Agreed," I reply, not arguing. "The guard outside your room stays, but you won't be locked in anymore."

Her eyes sparkle at my concession.

"Don't get any ideas," I continue. "During the day, whoever is on duty is your shadow. Wherever you go, he goes. Understood?"

She nods, and I can feel her excitement at the thought of getting out of this room.

"At night, you do not leave the room. Under NO circumstances do you leave the property unless Raz or I are with you. You try it, I will catch you and those consequences I mentioned before? You don't want those, Charity, trust me on this."

"Fine," she agrees, nodding, a little too quickly. I throw her a look of suspicion.

I stand and walk over to her, gently grab her arms, and look into her eyes. The intensity between us is palpable, and I see her breath hitch. I fight the urge to lean down and brush her lips with mine.

"Charity, I make you this promise: as long as you do what I say, Vardis will never touch you. Once the danger has been cleared, I'll help you return to your life. Understood?"

She nods again, and I take a breath. I'm so close that I can smell the floral scent of her shampoo and body wash. Dropping her arms, I force myself to step away from her.

"Breakfast is at seven. I'll have your guard escort you down. After, I'll give you a tour of the house and the grounds. Good night, Hurricane."

Grabbing my jacket, I leave her before I change my mind.

TWENTY-FIVE
Charity

Sunrise is just starting to crest the horizon when I open my eyes. It's my only indication of the time. I need to ask Cal for my phone. Probably a long shot, but worth a try.

I jump out of bed and race to my bedroom door, flinging it open to find a red-haired man, dressed in black, standing guard, arms folded in front of him. He looks young. He can't be more than nineteen or twenty.

"Good morning!" I practically sing.

His eyes shoot up in surprise.

"Good morning, ma'am," he replies politely.

"Ugh, no. No ma'am shit," I tell him. "You call me Charity, got it?"

"Yes, ma'am - er, I mean Charity. Miss," he shuffles his feet.

"Good," I nod to him. "Now what should I call you? Oh, and what time is it, and how long before breakfast?"

He glances at his watch.

"I'm Tommy. I usually take night watch. It's just before six a.m. You have about an hour before breakfast service."

"Fantastic! Plenty of time." I exclaim.

"Miss Charity, would you like me to have coffee brought up to you?"

"Coffee would be amazing!" I pause. "On second thought, Cora and Marie are probably busy. I don't want to bother them."

This earns a smile from the overly polite young man.

"It's no bother, Miss. I can have one of the guards bring it up. They're probably in the kitchen eating breakfast anyhow. It's almost time for shift change."

I watch as Tommy presses something on his ear and requests coffee be brought up to my room.

"Oh, so you're leaving me?" I ask, batting my eyes at him. I can't help flirting with him a little. The red flush almost matches his red hair, and it's adorable.

He nods shyly.

"I'm to escort you to breakfast, and then one of the other guards will take over from there.

I sigh dramatically.

"Fine. Leave me on my first day of freedom. Although I have to tell you, Tommy, I'm a little heartbroken. We spend the night, and now you're passing me off to the next guy."

"Brat, leave the boy alone." I hear Raz rumble.

Leaning around Tommy, I see Raz stalking toward us.

"Not even sunrise and already causing trouble?"

"Oh, Raz, settle down. We were just getting to know each other, weren't we, Tommy?" I give him a mischievous smile. "What are you doing here anyway, Raz? Didn't you hear? I'm getting sprung today!" I grin at him.

"Against my better judgment," Raz growls. "I heard the radio call and thought I'd check to make sure you aren't breaking rules already." He looks me up and down with narrowed eyes. "Go put some clothes on. I'll make sure your coffee gets to you."

I look down and realize what caused Raz to look at me like that.

In my excitement, I'd forgotten I'd gone to bed in only a low-cut t-shirt and underwear. The shirt is barely long enough to cover me.

I giggle. "Do my breasts make you uncomfortable, Razzie?" I tease.

Tommy's eyes go wide.

"Get in your room. And you," he points a finger at Tommy, "you keep your eyes to yourself, or Mr. Mitchell might decide you're better off without them."

Before I have a chance to ask what that statement meant, Raz pushes me back into my room and slams the door.

TWENTY-SIX
Cal

I'm sitting at the dining table, drinking my coffee and reading the morning newspaper, when Raz comes in and sits down with a heavy sigh.

I lower the paper and glance over at him, annoyance written all over his face.

"Problem?" I ask.

He scrubs a hand across his jaw.

"Are you sure letting her out this soon is a good idea? I just caught her flirting with Tommy in her underwear. I thought the poor kid was going to come in his pants."

A laugh escapes me before I can stop it. Poor Tommy. The kid is as green as they come, and putting him outside her door is proving to be a mistake.

"Is he okay?" I ask.

Raz smirks.

"He's fine. I warned him to keep his eyes to himself, or you'd mount them on your desk. The kid went from almost coming to shitting himself with a quickness."

I shake my head, setting my coffee down.

"Take Tommy off her detail. He doesn't deserve that torment." I think for a moment and grin. "Replace him with Freddy."

Raz looks up, brows raised. "Cal, Freddy doesn't have a tongue. He can't talk."

"Exactly," I grin wider.

Raz meets my grin with his own.

"You got it, boss!" he chuckles.

"She's testing," I say, more to myself than to him. "She'll continue to test until she finds her limits. I intend to show her where those limits are."

As if on cue, Charity bounds into the room, Tommy on her heels, looking like he's being dragged to his own funeral.

"Good morning, Monsters," she sings, overly pleased with herself.

I watch as she glides into the room, takes a seat across from Raz, and dramatically drapes her napkin across her lap.

She's dressed in black leggings and a light blue hoodie. The blue suits her. Her dark auburn hair is still wet from the shower, tied up in a messy bun.

I look up at Tommy and nod at the door.

"Go get some breakfast, kid, then knock off for the day. Check with Lem at the start of your shift tonight. I've decided to reassign you."

"Thank you, Mr. Mitchell!" he blurts, nearly tripping over himself in his rush to leave the room.

Charity scrunches up her face.

"What do you mean he's being reassigned? I like Tommy."

"That's exactly why he's being reassigned," Raz growls at her. "He's a good kid. He doesn't need you pulling any bullshit on him and getting into trouble."

Charity waves him off as she reaches for the coffee carafe.

"Whatever."

"So, Cal," she begins, and I look at her over my paper. "When do we start the tour? Do I get to use the pool? I was looking out my window—are there woods beyond the gazebo? Can I go hiking?" She's chattering away, and I find myself both delighted and annoyed at the same time.

Raz, clearly not up for her prattling, grabs a pastry from the plate and starts heading for the door.

"I'm out. Text me if anything comes up," he announces dryly.

"Wait, Razzie," an impish grin crosses her face. "Can I go with you? Cal said that I can go out if I'm with one of you."

"Absolutely not!" he scoffs at her gruffly. He leaves without a backward glance.

"Razzie?" I raise an eyebrow at her. "Do you think it's wise to be baiting him like that?"

She grins widely.

"Don't let him fool you. He's learning to love me. Besides, what's he going to do, spank me?"

I grip the newspaper tighter, feeling it crinkle in my hands, and pin her with a look.

"Careful, Hurricane," I warn. "Eat your breakfast, I have things to do."

I return to my newspaper, not seeing the words. My mind too clouded with the vision of her bent over before me.

Dammit.

TWENTY-SEVEN
Charity

Cal leads me down the hallway, his palm at the small of my back, steering me where he wants me to go. He points out paintings by people that I've never heard of, telling me stories of how he acquired them and why they matter to him. Some are sweeping scenic views, while others look like messy splashes of paint.

When I point out that he should get some toddlers on his payroll to fill out his collection, he scowls at me and playfully swats my ass.

I freeze, but he keeps walking like it never happened.

Stunned, I realize I didn't hate it. I give myself a shake and hurry to catch up with him.

Along the way, we pass numerous staff and guards. They all nod politely, and Cal greets them by name, asking personal details about each one—how's your mother doing? Any new pictures of the little one? If you need help with the move, be sure to let Raz know, and we'll arrange it.

I'm not prepared for how approachable he is and the genuine affection he shows them. His smile is easy with them, and I want those smiles for myself.

We reach the kitchen, and I see Marie's familiar face.

"Marie," I exclaim.

"Miss Charity. Mr. Mitchell," she responds warmly.

"Hello, Marie. I'm giving Charity a tour of the house and grounds."

She returns his smile, then turns to me. "Good to see you out and about, Charity."

Just then, a woman comes into the kitchen carrying a tray of fresh bread. She has beautiful chocolate eyes, and her dark hair is pulled back in a messy knot. A single white streak frames the left side of her face. I watch as she sets the tray down and wipes her hands on her apron before turning to us.

"Ah, Mr. Mitchell. What brings you to my kitchen this fine morning? And who's this you've brought with you?"

I think I hear a slight Irish lilt in her voice.

"Cora, you've been with me for over ten years now. When are you going to stop with the Mister business?"

I watch as Cal's face softens, the ice in his blue eyes melting. The love in his eyes for this woman stirs something warm in me.

She snorts. "As long as you sign my checks, you'll be Mr. Mitchell when I address you."

He shakes his head but lets it go. "Cora, this is Charity."

Cora walks around the kitchen island and wraps me in a hug, throwing me completely off balance.

Tears spring to my eyes from the pure affection as she whispers. "You're safe here."

Then, with a quick squeeze, she sets me back.

"If there's anything special you'll be wanting, you let me or Marie know. Green smoothies?" She cocks her head.

"Ugh!" I wrinkle my face. "I mean, thank you, but no. I'll stick to my coffee."

Cora barks a laugh and looks over at Cal.

"This one will do," she says smugly.

Cal shakes his head and leads me out of the kitchen.

"Ladies, if you'll excuse us."

I study him for a moment, wanting to know the story behind that exchange.

"What was that about?" I ask.

He smirks at me. "Nothing for you to be concerned with, Hurricane. Let's go. Still lots to see and then I have some work to do."

He shows me around the grounds, making it clear that I'm not allowed past the gazebo.

"I mean it, Charity. Do not test me or—"

I cut him off, "Yeah, yeah, yeah, consequences!" I reply dramatically.

He ignores my cheekiness, and we continue on the tour.

Cal explains that guest bedrooms take up the second floor, the third has Cal's wing to the left, Raz's wing to the right, and my room in the middle. He shows me the workout room, separate weight room, and sauna on the lower level. The kitchen, dining, and other receiving rooms are on the main level, along with his office and the reading room.

We reach a large mahogany door, and he leads me into his office. I'm almost knocked back. I can smell him in the wood and the leather. It's the clean, sharp smell of Calahan Mitchell. An oversized mahogany desk sits at one end, with two leather club chairs facing his place of power. My eyes instantly land on the computer taking up a corner of the desk.

"All of the computers are locked with biometrics, so don't even think about it. Any unidentified attempt at access causes an immediate shutdown of all electronics, doors and windows lock, and the perpetrator is dealt with severely." He pins me with a glare.

"Noted," I reply with an innocent shrug.

My eyes wander over a large leather sofa and two comfortable-looking chairs positioned around a low-profile center table. Everything in the room is as imposing as the man himself.

I walk around the office studying the antique maps encased in ornate frames along the walls. I can feel him watching me, his gaze making my temperature rise. I stop at one map, a large dragon-like monster in the center.

"So, is that where you found Raz?" I quip, trying to lighten the air in the room.

I catch his smirk out of the corner of my eye. "You can't help yourself, can you?" he chuckles. "Raz isn't even here, and you still bust his chops."

I turn my head and flash him a smile. "He's easy prey."

This gets me an actual laugh, and I can't help but feel pleased with myself.

It's then that I spot the bare space over the fireplace. I can see the outline of whatever was there. The emptiness looks out of sync with the rest of the room.

"What was there?" I ask.

I feel the air in the room shift, and I immediately regret asking.

"It was a portrait. I got rid of it." His tone makes it clear that the subject is closed.

He walks to the end of the room and throws open the double doors, and my eyes go wide.

"You have your own library?" I make my way into the expansive space.

"I prefer *reading room*, but yes," he agrees, looking around like he's seeing it for the first time. "I guess you could call it a library."

Bookshelves line every wall with more volumes locked behind glass doors like precious artifacts. In the center of the room, display cases house open books, their pages spread showing off their contents.

"Wow," is all I can manage, my eyes taking everything in.

"Charity Johnston, have I finally managed to make you speechless?" I can hear the teasing in his voice, and I narrow my eyes at him.

I walk over to the first display case and see a single tattered page placed on a deep burgundy velvet riser. Miniature figures are painted on the page in vivid blues and gold, a beast curling around the margins. It's breathtaking.

"Revelation. The Apocalypse," he begins. "Late fourteenth century, Latin Vulgate. The seven-headed beast with its ten horns represents the fall of empires and the corruption of power. Medieval monks were as fascinated by their demons as they were devoted to their saints."

"Shouldn't this be in a museum?" I ask in disbelief.

"Pieces like this disappear into archives. A museum would keep it locked away, safe, yes, but unseen. These pieces are available for any institution to study upon request. I don't make a secret of its existence."

"So you're not hoarding treasures like some ogre?" I sass back.

"Oh, I hoard my treasures, and I am an ogre," he quips. The way he looks at me tells me he's not talking about his books.

I walk over to the next display case, and I gasp. The open book displays an image of a man on his knees, gripping the woman in front of him, her body arched over embroidered cushions. The colors are still so vibrant they seem to shift on the page. There's no mistaking what the image is depicting.

"Antique porn, Cal?" I tease, unable to tear my eyes from the image.

I feel Cal move behind me, almost pressing himself against my back. He leans forward, and I can feel his breath on my neck.

"The Bahname. Late sixteenth-century Ottoman. It's an instruction manual of sorts."

He leans in closer, and my pulse spikes. I swallow, my throat suddenly dry.

"The Ottomans believed it was a holy missive to ensure the pleasure of women. This book was studied to ensure that any man given the gift of a woman's body was equipped to master it. Every position, foreplay technique, and rhythm, specifically aimed at prolonging and ensuring her repeated orgasms. Anything less, and the man was considered a failure."

I lean back into him, his lips grazing my neck, and I feel myself go wet.

The door on the other end of the library opens, and we jump away from each other, my face growing hot.

"Cal?" I hear Raz before I see him.

"Raz," his voice rough. I catch him adjusting himself and bite back a smile.

Raz's eyes dart between us, registering what he just interrupted.

He clears his throat, noticeably uncomfortable.

"There's a call. You need to take this one. It can't wait." He fixes Cal with a look, and I hear the edge in his voice.

Cal turns to me, all warmth gone.

"Dinner is at six. Don't be late. I'll see you then."

Without another glance, he walks into his office and shuts the door.

I look up and see Raz's eyes locked on me.

"I put some things in your room. Why don't you go up and check them out?"

I narrow my eyes at him suspiciously.

"What things, and why are you being nice to me?" I ask.

"Don't get it twisted, they're not from me." He nods toward the office door. "He's going to be tied up for a while. Go, make yourself scarce. Freddy's waiting outside. He's not much of a conversationalist, but he'll make sure you don't go far."

Raz gives me one last look, then disappears through the doorway, his footsteps fading down the hall.

TWENTY-EIGHT
Cal

Settling behind my desk, I wait for Raz to join me before I answer the waiting call.

"What do I need to know?"

"It's Vardis," Raz says, his jaw clenching.

I press my tongue to the back of my teeth, steadying myself for the incoming confrontation, and hit the line.

"Vardis."

"You have something of mine, Mitchell. I want it. Today."

"I reviewed the manifests from the auction," I say evenly. "Your paintings will be in your hands in three days. Thank you again for your generous bids," I reply, giving him nothing.

"Fuck the paintings, Calahan. Where is Rhea?"

I let out a low breath.

"Nikos, we went over this. I don't know any Rhea. Maybe the grief of losing your son is still fucking with your head, but you need to quit fucking with me and seek help, old man."

Without another word, I hang up the phone.

Raz grimaces and shifts in his seat.

"Cal, are you trying to start another war?"

I let out a sharp laugh.

"I'm not worried about that prick. His men have been abandoning him in droves. We've taken on how many, including Freddy? He's old and weak."

Raz tilts his head at me.

"If he's so old and weak, why is she here?"

"Because she belongs here," I blurt out.

I run my hands through my hair.

Where the hell did that come from?

"You hear yourself, right?"

"Raz, leave it. What else do you have for me?" I give him a look that I hope makes it clear that I'm done discussing it.

"You're the boss." Raz lets out a breath and continues.

"I had Lem take Charity's shopping bags up to her room. Freddy's escorting her up so she can go through them. Looks like you bought out the store."

"Also, Samantha Kellogg came at me in the parking lot at Club Lilith. She is spitting fire. I think we need to arrange a playdate or, at the minimum, a call. She threatened to go to the FBI," he says, amused. "Damn, she's cute as hell."

I raise an eyebrow.

"Is she going to be a problem?" I ask.

"Naw," he replies dismissively. "She wants what she called 'proof of life.'" He grins. "It's your call, but if you want to convince Charity that she's not a prisoner here, best bet is to let the sprite visit."

"Fine, arrange it."

"Otherwise, boss, everything's good. Business as usual at the clubs. Deliveries from the auction are all set for the end of the week. I've got a line on a few items that just hit the black market. If anything pans out, I'll let you know."

I nod.

Raz gets up and starts moving toward the door.

"Hey, Raz," I call to him.

"Yeah, Cal?"

"Sam's visit—for Charity, right? Nothing to do with you wanting to see her?" I needle.

"Things to do, Cal. Later."

I smirk as he shuts the door. Raz doesn't fool me for a second.

TWENTY-NINE
Charity

When I exit the library, I'm met with an older, bald, broody-looking man waiting for me outside the door. I instinctively take a step back. He puts his hands up, indicating he's not a threat, but I'm not so convinced. I eye him warily.

In response, he hands me a small notebook with neat writing:

My name is Freddy. I'll be your escort for the rest of the day. I cannot talk, but my hearing is fine. I'm here to keep you safe.

I huff and hand it back to him.

"He assigned me a mute? No offense, Freddy. I'm sure you are delightful, but c'mon. Who am I going to talk to?" I know I sound whiny. I don't care.

Freddy smiles. I watch him quickly write something; then he holds it up for me to read.

I am delightful :)

I laugh, and Freddy shrugs.

"Okay, Freddy. I hear I have gifts waiting for me in my room. Let's go."

We make our way up to the third floor. Like the good soldier he is, Freddy opens the door for me and gestures me inside.

The door shuts, and I stop short.

Bags and boxes with Calista & CO written on them clutter the room.

I slowly walk over, peek in one of the bags, and see tissue wrapping hiding various boxes.

What the hell?

I reach in and pull out a box. Lifting the lid, I see another box inside with the words "Christian Louboutin" in fancy script. I recognize the red soles immediately.

I break out in a cold sweat.

Nope.

A knock sounds at the door, and Raz's heavy footsteps sound behind me.

"Raz, what the hell is all of this?" I ask, without turning around.

"What's it look like?" His voice is gruff but amused. "You need stuff. Cal made a call."

I instantly turn on him.

"Take it back. Take it all back. I don't want it." Even I can hear the panic in my voice.

Raz lifts an eyebrow and looks at me like I have three heads. It would be comical if I weren't on the verge of losing my shit.

"What the hell is the matter with you? I thought all girls like this kind of shit," he says, exasperated.

I take a step toward him, ready to launch.

"In case you haven't noticed, I'm not like 'all' girls, you neanderthal! Take. It. Back! You think I can be bought with this shit?" I yell at him.

"Settle down, or do I need to tell Cal that you aren't ready for visitors?" he arches a brow.

I stop.

"What visitor?" I ask, hesitantly.

He grins.

"Well, that worked better than I expected." He hands me his phone, numbers already entered on the screen, the green call button ready.

"Call Sam. Let her know you're okay. Tell her I'll pick her up tomorrow, seven p.m. You two can do whatever you two do for a few hours." He waves his hand at me dismissively.

Shocked, it takes me a minute to digest what he just said.

Before I can stop myself, I fling my arms around his torso.

"Oh my God, Raz! Really? Thank you, thank you, thank you."

"Yeah. Yeah." He doesn't return the hug. Instead, he grabs me by the arms and peels me off. "Don't thank me. It was Cal's decision. Thank him. Now call before I change my mind."

I clutch the phone and hit the green button.

As soon as I hear Sam's voice answer the phone, my eyes fill with tears, relief flooding my chest.

"Sam?"

"Charity? Oh, thank God! Where are you? Whose number is this? Are you okay?" I can hear the worry in her voice as she peppers me with questions.

"I'm fine. Well, fine is subjective." I look up at Raz.

"Careful, Brat," he warns, his voice low.

"I'm at Calahan Mitchell's house, well, mansion actually. This is Raz's phone. Remember the beast?"

I wink at Raz, and he huffs.

"I knew they had you!" she exclaims. "I warned that asshole that if he didn't give me proof you were okay, I was going to the cops. You are okay, right? Why are you there, Charity?"

"It's a long story. Just know that I'm safe and I'll explain everything later. Cal said you can visit. Tell me you can visit Sam, please, I'm going out of my mind here."

Raz is watching me like he's anticipating Sam's answer as much as I am.

"Tell me when and where, and I'll be there."

When she says it, my knees almost buckle. For the first time since this nightmare started, I don't feel completely alone.

"Raz says he'll pick you up—" The phone is torn from my hand.

"Hey!" I protest.

"Sprite. I'll pick you up tomorrow. Seven p.m.—Of course, I know where you live—Never mind that."

I'm only getting Raz's part of the conversation, but I don't care. I'm so happy I feel like I'll explode.

"One more thing. Not a word to anyone about her, about me. You don't know where she is or what she's doing. Got it? (pause) Oh yeah, well, we can cancel the visit and—good girl."

I snicker. Raz doesn't know he just hit Sam's sweet spot with that "good girl."

"Fine. Tomorrow." He hangs up the phone and stuffs it back in his pocket.

"Put this shit away," he points his finger around the room, "then get your ass down to dinner."

"Yes, sir." I give him a smile and salute.

"Christ," he mutters as he goes to leave.

"Hey, Raz."

He turns back to me.

"Yeah?"

"Thank you."

"I'll tell you what. You can thank me by taking it easy on Cal, okay? His methods might need work, but trust me—he's different with you. He's trying to do right by you. Deal?"

I blink at him.

"O-o-okay." I stutter, not sure how to respond to that admission.

In usual Raz fashion, he leaves without another word.

THIRTY
Cal

I turn the speed of the treadmill up and increase the incline. My heart races and sweat drips from my forehead, but I don't bother trying to wipe it away. I push harder, keeping time with the music pounding through the speakers. I need to feel the burn—to exhaust myself until I can turn off the thoughts of her.

It was far past late when I finally shut down my computer. I should have joined Charity for dinner, but I didn't. She's a distraction. Things have been put off since she's been here, and it has to stop. I have businesses to run, obligations that must be met.

When I dismantled my father's ties to the trafficking organizations, we re-tooled those supply lines. Debts were cleared. New alliances were formed. The few who chose loyalty to Malcolm over this new order were eliminated. Syndicates. Families. Cartels. Different names for the same rot. They can have their old rules as long as they don't interfere with mine. I just do business with them.

Being in imports and exports gives us and our business partners the cover needed. To anyone on the outside, we are simple entrepreneurs and philanthropists, giving back to the community to the tune of millions every year. They get the story, while we manage reality.

My mind drifts back to her again, and I stumble. Swearing, I jam the stop button, stalk over to the weight rack, and load the bar heavier than I should. My forearms burn, but I keep counting through each curl. I try to focus on my movements, my breathing, anything but her. Her scent as I leaned in, the way her eyes lit on fire as I told her the story of the Bahname, the way her body leaned back into mine.

Because she belongs here.

Fuck!

I let the weight bar drop, and it hits the mat with a thud.

I'm not a fucking predator. I am not my father. I will not become HIM.

I pace the length of the room, squeezing my eyes shut, trying to get control of myself.

Grabbing my phone, I stab at the security app. I need to see her. It's about her safety, I lie to myself. Watching her has become a reflex—like breathing.

I scroll through the cameras, stopping on her room, and there she is.

Blankets kicked off, dressed in nothing but her usual t-shirt and panties, she's completely oblivious to the torment she's causing me.

I see her eyelashes flutter, and my pulse jumps as she begins rubbing her thighs together. When I see her lips move, I turn up the volume and swipe the screen, zooming in, but I can't make out her words.

When I zoom back out and see her hand start to drift, her breathing getting heavier, I can't look away. She slips her hand into her panties, and when her fingers reach where she needs them, I hear a soft moan. Her hips buck, grinding herself harder into her hand.

Gripping my phone tighter, I swallow hard, my cock straining against my sweats.

I should shut it off. I should look away. But I don't.

Unfamiliar jealousy twists in my gut.

Who's making you feel so good, Hurricane?

Her tongue darts over her parted lips and—fuck me. She's getting closer, her moans getting louder, and her hips rising higher.

Her back arches, and I hear it.

"Cal," she moans, sending a jolt through me.

"Say it again, Charity. Say my name," I command her.

As if she can hear me, she obeys.

"Cal—yes," she breathes as her body shudders.

I watch as she relaxes back into the mattress, her breath returning to normal. I zoom in again and stroke her cheek through the glass.

"I'm here, Hurricane. You just made your choice, and now, I can't let you go."

THIRTY-ONE
Charity

Dinner last night was uneventful. Cal locked himself in the office, and Raz was nowhere to be found either. Determined not to risk my visit with Sam, I arrived promptly at six p.m. as directed, only to end up eating alone. That won't be happening again. I'd rather eat in the kitchen with Cora and Marie.

I hung up the new clothes and placed the shoes on their lighted shelves, feeling dread with every new discovery. Some of the labels I recognized, and some I didn't. All of the pieces cost more than I make in a month, hustling drinks. They're beautiful, but they're not me. I can't afford to get used to this world. Eventually, I'm going to go back to my life and back to my thrift store finds.

When I woke up this morning, Marie brought breakfast as has become usual. I showered, and with no other options, had to choose something from the new wardrobe. I'm falling into a routine, and it's unsettling. My life unraveled so fast, I'm only now feeling the weight of everything that's happened.

I spent the rest of the morning aimlessly wandering around the estate, finding myself back here in the library. I've decided it's my favorite room in the house.

The smell of the books is comforting, reminding me of the hours I'd spend hidden at the public library growing up. I always felt like a burden, constantly being reminded of how lucky I was that someone would take in the orphaned girl.

When I was lost in the pages of a book, I could be whoever I wanted to be and go wherever I wanted to go.

Grabbing one of the worn covers, I settle into the overstuffed couch and try to get lost, finding it hard to focus.

I keep replaying the scene from yesterday. Cal's body hovering over mine, his breath on my neck, stirring up feelings I have no business feeling. In that moment, I wanted nothing more than for him to kiss me. Maybe even bend me over like the woman in the book. To forget that he's my kidnapper and pretend it might be something more. I picture his lips and wonder what it would've felt like to lose myself for just a moment.

For fuck's sake, what is wrong with you, Charity!

I'm not sure how much time has passed when I hear the door open, startling me. I sense him before I see him and sit up straight, like I've been caught doing something I shouldn't.

"Well, here you are." He smiles warmly and sits down on the couch next to me.

Turning toward him, I fold my legs protectively underneath me as I clutch the book in my hands.

"You said I could come in here anytime I wanted," I reply defensively.

His eyes flick to the book I'm holding.

"Interesting choice."

"I can put it back," I shoot back, moving to get up before his hand lands on my leg to stop me. Heat shooting through me at his contact.

"Charity, it's fine. You're welcome to read anything you'd like," he soothes. "I was only commenting that out of all of the books in here, you chose that one."

His eyes sweep over me.

"I hear you were less than pleased with your new wardrobe. I have to hand it to you. I've seen Raz deal with many situations. You have him completely baffled." The playfulness is back in his eyes, and I feel my heart stutter.

"I need to give Stephanie a bonus. She picked well."

I bristle at hearing another woman's name on his lips, but ignore it, looking down at my outfit.

"Oh, I can only imagine the bonus you have in mind for Stephanie," I reply dryly.

Cal cocks an eyebrow and smirks.

"That almost sounded like jealousy, Hurricane."

I huff.

"Jealous of what?" I sneer. "You can fuck all the Stephanies and Helenas you want, Cal. I'm just your captive, remember?"

"Helena?" He looks thoroughly confused, and I feel myself getting pissed on behalf of a woman I don't even know.

"Helena…the woman from the Gala. Gorgeous, green dress, she introduced you? I can't believe you. It was obvious that she has a thing for you. I knew you were the type." I shoot back.

"The type?" He's looking at me like he doesn't have a clue what I'm referring to, and it's just frustrating me more.

I roll my eyes at him.

"The type… the guy that fucks a woman and then moves on to the next, not giving a shit about any damage he's done."

"Charity," he sighs, but there's still a slight smirk. "Have I fucked women? Of course. Plenty of women. Helena? Absolutely not. That woman is a viper."

His gaze holds mine. "Stephanie is on my payroll. I don't fuck the women on my payroll. She handles clothing and essentials when women come out of situations with nothing. That's it."

He reaches out and tucks a stray stand of hair behind my ear, his hand grazing my cheek as he pulls back. I involuntarily shiver.

"Now tell me why you almost took Raz's head off when you saw the clothes."

There's no judgment in his eyes, and it makes me feel off balance.

I clear my throat.

"I am no one's charity case." I see the amusement flash across his face. "Don't you dare laugh at me, Calahan Mitchell! I don't need you buying me clothes or shoes or—God knows what else you have planned. If you'd let me go to my apartment, I could get my own damned clothes. It's bad enough that I'm living here, without consent, I might add. I'm not going to fuck you as some kind of payoff."

Cal's eyes darken, and he sits back, peering at me.

"Did you not see what Vardis's men did to your apartment? As much as I would love to see you walk around naked, for the safety of the men who work here for me, I need you covered. If any of them lay eyes on your body, I'll have to eliminate them. Training new men is something I don't have time to do while I'm trying to keep you safe."

He leans forward again and grabs my chin in his hand.

"Do I seem like the type of man who needs to use sex as a transaction? When I fuck you—and I will fuck you, Charity Johnston—you'll fuck me right back." His eyes flare, and I shiver at his words.

"It won't be because of some false obligation. It will be because you're aching so much for my cock you can't imagine your next breath without having it—without having me. The only price is the cum I'll rip out of your body when I make you scream. Understood?"

I swallow hard and nod.

"Good." He leans closer, places a soft kiss on my lips, and I feel myself melting into him.

Before I can say a word, Cal stands and tilts his head toward the book, still in my hand.

"You know," he says, his voice low, "Fanny Hill thinks she's making her own choices. That she's in control." His eyes lock on mine. "But in the end, she only ends up where she was always meant to be."

Unable to move, I just watch as he walks out of the room.

THIRTY-TWO
Charity

I'm in a daze the rest of the day, unable to untangle what happened with Cal. He, of course, has gone MIA again. I spend dinner in the kitchen with Cora, barely picking at my food when I notice the time.

Sam should be here soon. Thank God.

"So, Miss Charity," Cora begins, "I've made a batch of margaritas for you and your friend when she gets here. Do you want to sit outside, or up in your room? I can take them to the theatre room if you'd like."

I look up at her with surprise.

"There's a theatre? Never mind, of course he has a theatre in his lair. Wouldn't want to mix with the lowly public to watch a movie. Don't worry about it, Cora. We can grab them ourselves when Sam gets here. You don't need to wait on us."

Cora laughs.

"It looked like maybe you were softening a bit on Cal. Something happen?" Her eyes twinkle with curiosity. I can tell by her quiet amusement that she doesn't miss a thing that happens in this house.

"You mean besides drugging, kidnapping me, and holding me against my will?" I shoot back at her, and I'm immediately sorry.

She nods, accepting the edge in my words.

"Marie mentioned that she told you a bit of my history. I'm not going to go into any details. I don't like reliving it, and you don't need the burden of it. You look around, and you see a rich, evil man in a big, fancy house with big, scary guards. You're right to be angry. He did all those things," she nods, and then looks me in the eyes. "And I'm glad he did. What do you know about Calahan Mitchell, Charity?"

I huff.

"You about summed it up. He's a rich, evil man in a big evil lair who sells expensive things to other evil men."

"Oh, come, girl. You can't fool me. I see the way you look at him and the way he watches you … whew." She smiles and fans herself. "You know as well as I do that Cal isn't evil. He lives in an unconventional world and has unconventional rules. Now, Nikos Vardis," she spits out his name. "That man is evil personified. For whatever reason, he's got his sights on you. I'm not telling you that how Calahan went about this is right, but if he thought this was the only way to protect you, then it was the only way." She peers at me, making sure she's made her point, and I nod reluctantly in recognition.

Out of the window, I see a black SUV pull up along the side of the house, and my heart leaps.

Raz and Sam exit the car. From the looks of it, she's giving him hell, and he looks like he regrets agreeing to pick her up. I laugh at the sight of them. Scary Raz getting dragged is the second-best thing so far today.

She's in mid-rant when she looks up, sees me through the glass door, and barrels into the kitchen, the door slamming in Raz's face.

She grabs me and hugs me so tight I can't breathe. She pulls back, scanning over me.

"Charity, I'm so fucking relieved. You're okay."

She throws a look over her shoulder at Raz.

"Thanks for the ride, Beast. You're dismissed."

He narrows his eyes at her, and I can see that his control is hanging by a thread.

"Sprite, you and I are going to tangle," he growls.

"Yeah, probably," she laughs, "but it won't be today. Today I'm getting caught up with my girl."

She waves a hand at him, and with an exasperated huff, he stomps out of the room.

I hear Cora bark a laugh behind us and remember my manners.

"Cora, this is Sam. Sam, this is Cora. She works for Cal," I introduce the two women.

Sam arches an eyebrow.

"Are you being kept here, too? Do I need to spring both of you?"

Cora laughs and shakes her head.

"I can see why you two are friends. No, Miss. I'm Mr. Mitchell's employee. No need for rescuing. Now, the margaritas are in the fridge. There are chips and dip in the pantry. I'll be taking my leave for the evening. Charity, leave the dishes. I'll clean up in the morning." With a head tilt, she takes her apron off, grabs her purse from the cupboard, and leaves.

"Well, she seems amazing," Sam says appreciatively.

"She is." I nod, knowing I don't need to go into detail. I give Sam a nudge. "Now help me grab the drinks and chips, and let's go sit by the pool. Margaritas!"

We make our way out to the pool area and settle in. I pour each of us a glass, Sam looking around like she's trying to take in every detail. Wait until she sees the inside, I think to myself.

"So, leave it to you to get kidnapped and held in a mansion," she huffs. "This place is amazing."

She looks over at me, suddenly serious. "Charity, you're really okay?"

I sigh and take a long pull from my straw, drinking down the tart sweetness.

"So much better now that I've got a drink. My God, these are good."

Sam narrows her eyes at my deflection.

"I'm fine, Sam. Better now that you're here." I smile at her, trying to reassure her.

"Cut the bullshit, Charity. What's going on? Raz wouldn't tell me anything. Trust me, I tried to get him to talk. That man is a fucking vault."

"To be honest, I don't know how much to tell you. I don't know all that much myself, and I don't want to put you in danger with what I do. All I know is that the guy that Cal was talking to when I made that scene at the gala, well, he made some comment that made Cal think that he was going to snatch me. Cal decided to snatch me first." I shrug.

Her eyes go wide.

"Are you talking about Nikos Vardis?" There's genuine panic in her voice.

I blink at her. "You know him?"

She rolls her eyes at me and sucks in a breath.

"Remind me to thank Calahan Mitchell. Fuck, Charity. When I saw him at the gala, I thought some shit was going to go down. It never dawned on me that you would be the shit. Why the hell did he set his sights on you?"

"My stunning personality?" I shrug and wink at her.

"Charity, no jokes. That man is the monster that monsters tell their kids about to get them to behave."

I go still and stare at her, gripping my glass tighter.

"You're serious."

"As a fucking heart attack." She shakes her head. "I'm starting to understand why Cal nabbed you. I don't like it, but if he's keeping you out of Vardis's hands," she locks onto my eyes, "then he's my new best friend."

I look down, not knowing what to say.

She cocks her head at me.

"So, what's he like?"

I feel my face flush. "Who?" I ask innocently.

"Cal Mitchell, that's who," she barks a laugh.

"Oh my God. Are you fucking him? You're fucking him," she accuses.

"What? Jesus, Sam. He kidnapped me, remember?" My voice cracks, which I know makes me sound guilty.

"Uh-huh. Didn't answer the question." She tilts her head, studying me. "Maybe you haven't fucked him, but something happened."

I roll my eyes, swinging my head around to her.

"There might have been a kiss. It was no big deal."

Sam cackles.

"Oh, this is too fucking good. I couldn't make this up! You get kidnapped by the son of a former trafficker who's saving you from a trafficker, and now you're sucking face? How the fuck do you do it?"

"Oh, fuck off, Sam," I say, smiling. I lean over and refill her drink. "Now drink up! I've got to give you the tour, and I can't wait to hear about the car ride with Raz."

THIRTY-THREE
Cal

I'm sitting at my desk watching the pool area through the cameras when Raz walks into my office.

"What, you don't knock anymore?" I ask him.

"I know you saw that she was here, which means you knew I was home. The natural progression of events is that I'd be coming to your office." He shrugs.

He leans around my desk to see the image on the screen.

"What, no volume?" he smirks.

"I thought I'd give them their privacy. You were right. She needs this." My gaze stays locked on the woman in question. Her face is lit up with laughter, and I'm a little resentful that it was Raz who knew what my hurricane needed before I did.

I am so fucked.

"Any news on Vardis?" I ask.

"No, nothing. He's been suspiciously quiet," he replies. "I had Tommy's girlfriend fly to LA like we discussed. It took some magic, but our tech guys are good. The credit card will look like it's got a few years of history, and she looks enough like Charity that if cameras are checked, she should pass. We've got two men and Tommy on the same flight in case they take the bait too soon."

"Good." I nod. "And Samantha?" I look up at him. "Anything I need to be concerned about?"

"Nope," he replies too quickly.

"She's a pain in the ass, that one," he shakes his head. "She has a lot of questions. I do admire her loyalty, though."

This piques my interest.

"What kind of questions?"

"Nothing to worry about. She's just worried about her," he nods toward the two women drinking and laughing on the screen. "I handled it."

I narrow my eyes at him.

"Raz, what exactly do we know about Samantha Kellogg? If she's going to be a problem, I can't have you thinking with your cock." I growl.

He straightens.

"Cal, with respect, it wasn't me grinding against Sam's ass yesterday in the library, now was it?" he growls back. "Again, I've got it handled."

I lean back in my chair and give him a nod. Charity has me on edge, and I don't fucking like it.

Raz lowers himself into one of the chairs in front of my desk, arms crossed over his chest.

"Are you going to tell me what's going on between you two? And don't tell me it's nothing. Everyone in this house can feel it."

I pull my shoulders down, trying to release some of the tension that's trapped.

"I kissed her." I close my eyes, forcing the image of her out of my mind. "I didn't mean to, but I kissed her, and now, I'm walking around my own house avoiding a woman that I'm technically holding captive."

Raz barks out a laugh.

"You didn't see this coming? C'mon Cal. I've known you for years, and I've seen you two together. It wasn't *if* you would, it was *when*. Manifest destiny, my friend. So, did she slap you, spit at you, what? What was so catastrophic that you're hiding in here like a teenager?"

"Don't mock me, asshole," I glare at him, which just causes another laugh.

Raz forces his face to go serious, but still can't hide his amusement. "I'm sorry. The teenager line—too far. Seriously, how'd she react?"

I lean back in my chair and look at the ceiling.

"She kissed me back," I say, cringing.

Raz is full-throated laughing now, and if I were a lesser man, I would get up from this chair and punch him in the face.

"Go ahead, get it out," I say flatly.

"What the fuck is the matter, man? You are two consenting adults. I've spent enough time with her to know if she didn't want that kiss, you'd be choking on your teeth right now."

Before I can respond, there's a knock on my door.

"Come in," I answer.

Paul, one of the perimeter guards, comes through the door looking nervous as hell.

"Sir, we might have a situation with the girls."

Raz and I look over to the monitor to see Charity and Sam in the hot tub. Stripped down to nothing but their t-shirts and underwear, each of them is holding a bottle of something I can't make out, and they're…singing?

I turn up the volume and hear the caterwauling of a song I don't recognize. I'm barely able to make out the words, "boss bitch."

"Well fuck." I curse. "Paul, grab some towels and a hoodie from the pool house. Meet us by the hot tub."

He nods and retreats.

Raz lets out a heavy sigh.

"You get yours—I'll get mine. This party is over," he says gruffly. I decide to let his own possessive response go, for now.

We head out to the patio where the girls are still yowling.

"Charity, come out of the hot tub," I command.

Grinning from ear to ear, she ignores me and points at Raz.

"Razzie! Come join us!" she exclaims.

"Yeah, Razzie," Sam mimics, "Come play in the hot tub."

"Charity," I repeat, "party's over. Come here."

Paul appears with an armful of towels and a hoodie for Sam. He drops them on the table and quickly moves to leave.

"You!" Sam hollers at him. "You're cute. Come play with us!"

Raz lets loose a low growl, and I have to stifle a laugh. "Sprite, out. Now!"

Charity splashes water at both of us.

"You two need to lighten up. You're killing our buzz!"

Sam stumbles and falls back into the water in a fit of giggles, still clutching her bottle.

"That's it," Raz declares. He stalks forward, scoops her out like she weighs nothing, takes the bottle from her, and slams it on the table. Pushing the hoodie over her head like she's an errant toddler, he steers her toward the door. "Let's go," he orders. "Say goodnight to your friend."

"Aww, come on, Beast," she teases. "I thought you'd like me wet." She waggles her ass, earning her a sharp smack, making her yelp. "Move it!"

I tilt my head at Charity. "Your turn." I curl two fingers, beckoning her to me.

She meets my gaze and the stubborn thing takes a swig from her bottle, juts her chin out, and replies, "Nope." The *p* snapping.

I stalk toward Charity. Instead of giggling, I see her eyes spark with mischief a second before her hand cuts through the water, soaking me with a splash.

I stop, steeling myself. Without another word, I haul her out of the water, throw her over my shoulder, and stalk toward the house, straight for her room.

She kicks her feet, laughter bubbling out of her. I adjust her on my shoulder as I climb the stairs, gripping her hip tighter. When I reach her room, I nod to her guard, who swings the door open for me. Ignoring her giggles, I dump her on her bed.

"Stay," I command. I'm soaking wet, and my patience is gone. I stomp to her closet, rummaging through lacy lingerie—no fucking way is she putting these on—until I find something closer to pajamas. I throw them at her with a grunt. "Get out of those wet clothes and put those on."

I regret the words as soon as they leave my mouth.

As if on a dare, Charity sways to her feet and grabs the hem of her shirt. In one sharp tug, she peels it off along with her sports bra, leaving her bare. Locking eyes with me, she cups her breasts and begins thumbing her nipples.

"Charity," I warn.

"Cal," she fires back in the same tone, her eyes blazing.

Not dropping my eyes, I make my way toward her and move her hand out of the way, replacing it with mine. I grip her beautiful, full breast, kneading her stiff nipple, nuzzling her neck until a groan escapes her lips. I grind my cock against her pussy.

"Is this what you want?" I breathe into her ear, my cock straining.

"Oh God, yes, please, Cal," she moans.

I search her face for a moment, and lean in, my lips almost brushing hers.

"Too bad, Hurricane. I don't fuck drunk women,"

I spin her around and shove her face forward onto the bed as she gasps. Before she has time to retaliate, my palm cracks across her ass with a series of swift blows, making it clear that I'm done playing her games tonight.

"Put those clothes on and sleep it off."

Without another word, I stomp out of her room, slamming the door behind me.

I'm vibrating with frustration as I head to my room. I strip out of my wet clothes before I even reach the bathroom. I turn the shower on and step in, still seeing that fuck-me look in her eyes. I grab my stiff cock and start pumping hard and fast, each stroke echoing the sounds of her moans until thick, white ropes of come splash against the shower wall. When the edge finally blurs, I lean my forehead against the tile, still breathing heavily, and groan her name. It's not enough. It will never be enough until she's mine.

THIRTY-FOUR
Charity

I wake up as the curtains are torn open, morning light pouring in, and I wince.

Marie stands beside my bed, holding out a glass of water and two ibuprofen.

"Oh God, my head." I take the pills and squint up at her. "Please tell me you brought a pound of greasy bacon and some of Cora's cheesy eggs?"

She smirks, passing me a cup of steaming coffee.

"No such luck this morning, kid. I don't know what you did, but Mr. Mitchell is in a mood. His exact words were, *'Tell her she will be eating with me in the dining room, and if I have to retrieve her, there will be a repeat of last night's activity.'*"

Confused, I shift in bed, and my body reminds me. *Oh, oww.*

I watch her move around the room, picking up my discarded clothes.

"I laid some fresh clothes out for you. I thought a dress would be more comfortable." She tries to hide her smirk. "I wouldn't take too long getting down there if I were you. The last time I saw him this on edge, Freddy lost his tongue."

I gape at her.

She bursts out laughing, but her smile fades. "I'm kidding. Freddy's tongue was gone before he came here. Don't test him, Charity. I'm serious about that."

"Ha, ha. Hilarious, Marie," I say dryly as I heave out of bed and make my way to the bathroom.

After a shower that was quicker than I'd like, I head down to the dining room. Cal is in his usual seat at the head of the table. He's in a crisp white dress shirt and dark tie, not a hair out of place. Raz, seated to his right, looks just as put together as Cal.

Cal looks up, his expression unreadable.

"You. Sit there." He points to the chair on his left.

My eyes dart to Raz, who's smirking, and I know I'm in for a fun breakfast.

I walk around the table and gingerly lower myself. I hear Raz chuckle.

"Problem?" he asks, eyebrow cocked.

"Fuck off, Raz."

"Enough," Cal barks. "I've had it with you two bickering like siblings."

Glowering, I reach for the carafe of coffee, trying not to look at either one of them.

Raz's mouth twitches.

"In case you're wondering, I got Samantha home safe and sound. I'm betting she's not in any better shape this morning than you are."

"Why? Did she get her ass beat last night, too?" I throw Cal a glare.

Raz laughs. "No, but she probably should have."

Cal clears his throat, drawing my attention.

"Charity, if you think that was an ass-beating then I suggest you watch yourself going forward. I won't be so easy on you next time."

Raz tosses a phone on the table. "There are four numbers programmed into that phone: Cal, Sam, mine, and the guard shack. It's monitored, and there's no internet."

I stare at the phone as if it will burn me if I touch it.

He takes a final swallow from his coffee cup, wipes his mouth, and gets up.

"I'll call you later when I have news."

Cal answers with a grunt as Raz makes his way to leave.

The silence hangs heavy in the room until Cal moves his chair away from the table, startling me.

"Stand up and come here."

I look at him blankly.

"Charity, that's not a request."

I stand slowly and inch my way forward until he grabs my wrist, pulling me to him and spinning me around so that I'm facing away from him.

Putting his hand on my back, he forces me forward until I'm bent at the waist, elbows on the table. I suck in a breath.

"I appreciate the dress. It makes this easier."

I jolt up.

He slaps my ass. "Bend. Now," he commands.

I slowly lean forward and feel him flip the back of my dress up, waiting for another onslaught of his hand.

"No panties." It's not a question.

"They were uncomfortable," I respond, still holding my breath.

Instead of the pain I'm bracing for, I feel his hand rub something cool and soothing over one cheek, then the other. I sigh at the relief.

"Not bad for your first. You pink up nicely."

The heat from my bruised ass travels to my face.

He lowers my dress and grabs his napkin to wipe his hands.

"Sit. We're going to have a conversation, and I don't want to hear one word of your shit talk." He's leaving no room for argument.

My mind is whirling, screaming for me to run, but instead I do as I'm told and lower myself back into my chair.

"Did you enjoy yourself last night?" he asks, eyes locked to mine.

I swallow and nod. "For the most part."

His face is stony, and I feel uneasy at what might come next.

"Which part didn't you enjoy, Charity? Be specific. Sam's visit? Getting drunk in the hot tub? Flirting with Paul and almost getting him killed? Or was it the not getting fucked? I need you to clarify that."

I reach for my cup and take a sip of coffee, trying to measure my response. I can feel his eyes boring into me.

I tilt my head, returning his challenge.

"I did not put Paul in any danger," I respond steadily, careful to keep the snark out of my tone.

His fist comes down on the table with a bang, and I jump.

"Did I or did I not tell you that I would put a bullet in any man—including my men—who dared to look at you? Yet, you try me by inviting him to join you in *my* hot tub?" I hear a low, guttural growl come from him. In that instant, I realize I may have underestimated how angry he is.

"I'm sorry, okay? We were drunk, and we got carried away. It won't happen again—we were just blowing off some steam." I take a breath. "And about what happened in my room, that was total bullshit, but I get it. I forgive you." I tell him, keeping my voice steady.

His jaw clenches, and I see his hand twitch. "You forgive *me*?" he asks, his tone lethal. Leaning forward, he encroaches on my space. "You. Forgive. Me? You were playing a very dangerous game with me last night, little girl. What you got was only a tease of how dark my tastes can go. Don't think for a second that I didn't see how wet it got you—how wet it's getting you now. Hell, I can smell you from here."

My eyes widen, and I catch my breath. I press my knees together under the table.

"Oh, you are a filthy thing, aren't you?" he taunts. "Look at you, cheeks flushed, pupils dilated, clenching your knees together like that'll stop you from dripping all over my chair—and I haven't even touched you." He's staring at me so intently that I feel like I'll burst into flames right here.

"The games stop now. When you're ready to explore what this is—" his eyes sweep over me—"you will come to me, and we'll discuss it. There are rules, Charity. Rules that keep us both safe. Until then, keep your fucking clothes on." He pushes his chair back, the scraping sound grating against my nerves, and stalks out.

THIRTY-FIVE
Charity

I haven't moved from the table, my fingers still wrapped around the cold coffee cup, when Marie pushes through the door to collect the morning dishes.

"Charity?" I can hear the concern in her voice. My head snaps up, and hot tears start streaming down my face. "Oh, Honey," she says as she sits down in the chair next to me and pulls me into her arms. "It can't be as bad as all that. What happened?"

"I fucked up, Marie. I almost let him pull me in. Dammit. I'm so angry with myself. I let my guard down, and look where it got me." I wipe my face, furious at my own weakness. "I should have known better. I'm just another toy to him."

She gives me a stern look. "So that's what this is about, the argument with Cal?"

I look at her, surprised. "You heard?"

She huffs. "These walls have ears, girl, no matter how thick they are. The question I have is, did you hear him?

Not his bluster, you'll get used to that. Did you hear what he said underneath that anger?"

I'm looking at her blankly. Of course I heard him. Before I can answer, she cuts me off. "Charity, how can someone as street smart as you still be so damned stupid?" She sighs and returns to placing dirty dishes on her cart.

"You don't play with a man like Calahan Mitchell. From what it sounded like, you dangled yourself like bait and then acted shocked when the shark snapped. He's been holding himself back from you with everything he's got, and you go and throw it in his face? What kind of reaction did you think you were going to get? You throw a party in his hot tub, taunt him with one of his guards, and you're surprised that he reacted like that? It's time you grow up."

Her words hit me like a slap.

She grabs the coffee cup out of my hand and looks down at me.

"Maybe you should stop wallowing and start wondering why he walked away when you were throwing yourself at him. Most men in his position would've taken what was offered." She shakes her head with disappointment, her lips pressed into a thin line, and wheels her cart toward the door.

I grab the phone that's still on the table and head outside. I need to call Sam and make sure she's okay. Talking to her about this disaster is just a bonus.

I pull up the contacts. True to Raz's word, there are only four numbers programmed. I check the rest of the phone just to be sure, and of course, everything else is disabled.

I hit Sam's name, and she picks up on the first ring.

"Charity?" She sounds as rough as I still feel.

"How'd you know it was me?"

"Raz programmed your number last night when he dropped me off. He said it would probably be a few days before you'd call. How bad was the damage?"

"Oh, Sam. I fucked up." I sigh.

"Oh shit, what did you do?"

"Before we get into all that, are you okay? How're you feeling? I guess things got a bit out of hand."

"I'm feeling like hell, but that's expected. Beast brought me home. Made sure I got into my apartment. Growled a lot. Told me I was lucky I wasn't his woman... and then growled some more." A tiny laugh slips through.

I sit up straighter. "Did you just fucking giggle?"

"Hey, he's cute when he growls," she giggles again.

"Unfuckingbelievable."

"Says the woman falling for her kidnapper," she snaps back. "Now tell me what happened after I got dragged out of there."

I groan.

"Before or after he beat my ass? And NO, I am not falling for Cal Mitchell."

"He whaaat?" she practically screams in the phone.

"The worst part is, I think I kind of deserved it."

"Charity, no one deserves hands put on them like that," she argues back.

"You might want to hear the whole story before you make that call."

I tell her the entire ugly sequence of events, and there's nothing but silence on the other end of the line.

"Sam? Say something, please," I groan again, running a hand through my hair.

"Well," she takes a deep breath. "It sounds more like he gave you a spanking and, honestly, you did kind of earn it."

"Sam, what the fuck? You're supposed to be on my side!" I whine.

"Charity, I love you, but be real for a second. You tried treating a man who owns BDSM clubs like one of your fuck boys for Christ's sake. What did you think would happen?"

"I thought he'd fuck me into the fucking mattress, not spank my ass and leave me a panting mess!" I exclaim. "I certainly wasn't expecting him to be so pissed off about it!"

I hear Sam burst into laughter on the other end of the line. "Oh my God, you're gone for that man! I mean, I get it, but Charity, you've got to see the irony in this. You decided to taunt a grown man like a horny schoolgirl, so he treated you like one."

"Ugh, why did I even call you?"

"Okay, okay, I'm sorry. Cal Mitchell is a mean, terrible man. He spanked you, and it was so wrong, even if you liked it." She starts laughing again.

"Sam, I swear I'll hang up on you," I warn.

I hear her take a breath to stifle her snickers.

"So, what are you going to do?"

"I have no idea. He's so pissed at me right now."

"Well, he can't be too pissed if he put cream on his handprints," she snickers again. "I'm almost jealous— almost! Here's what I think," she continues. "You put on your big girl panties—when you're able to wear them, that is—and you have the very adult conversation of where you two stand. If Vardis is the threat to you that they say he is, who knows how long you'll be there. Or you can ask to stay at one of his safe houses. Maybe put some space between the two of you."

"You think he has safe houses?"

"Charity," she says, exasperated with me, "men like Cal Mitchell always have safe houses. The question is, where would you rather be? I hate to cut this short, but I'm already three hours late to work. My boss is going to kill me. Love you—go talk to him!"

She hangs up, and I sigh. My stomach twists because I know what I have to do. I need to have a grown-up conversation with Cal Mitchell.

I slip the phone into my dress pocket and make my way to Cal's office. I hesitate outside his door, my heart ricocheting off my chest. I knock once and hear his voice on the other side.

"Enter."

When I step into the room, I see Cal behind his desk, the sleeves of his pristine dress shirt rolled neatly up his forearms. Raz stands next to him, the two of them poring over papers. Cal doesn't look up at me right away. He takes his time, finishing whatever notes he's making before finally lifting his expressionless eyes, as if he's already bored with my presence.

He gestures toward the chair in front of him. "Sit."

"I'd rather stand, if you don't mind."

I see the slightest shadow of amusement in his eyes before he replies. "Suit yourself."

"I was wondering if we could talk." I give Raz a pointed look. "Alone."

Raz looks between us before clearing his throat. "If you'll excuse me, I need to be anywhere but here."

Cal and I don't look away from each other, and when the click of the door sounds, he raises an eyebrow. "You wanted me alone, Charity. We're alone."

He's not going to make this easy.

I take a breath and lower my eyes, deciding to start at the most logical place.

"I owe you an apology. A real apology this time. I am sorry, Cal. I treated your house disrespectfully, and what I did to you, well, that was pretty disrespectful too."

When I raise my eyes, he's looking passively at me.

"Accepted. Anything else?"

"Cal, I'm trying here," I say quietly, my stomach in knots.

He leans back in his chair, fingers drumming on the armrest. "Charity, forgive me if I don't fall all over you with gratitude at your apology. You were looking for a reaction, and you got one. You were testing me, and I don't like being fucking tested."

"I don't know how to do this, Cal. All of this feels so fucked up. I'm not supposed to have feelings for you— you fucking kidnapped me! I just wanted to take back a little bit of my power. Don't you get that?"

Cal gets up, walks around, and leans against the front of his desk. Crossing his arms, he peers at me.

"You think seducing a man gives you power?" His voice is calm—too calm. "No," he shakes his head, "I don't think that was it. That was such a poor display of seduction that it pissed me off. It infuriates me that you think for one fucking second that whatever that was would be enough."

His words sting, but I can see from his expression that he's not done. His jaw flexes, and for a moment, the fire I see in his eyes looks less like anger and something more… tender.

I draw in a breath.

"If I ever take you, it won't be because you were drunk and waving yourself in my face like some cheap whore. I don't fuck drunk women, and I sure as hell don't fuck whores. What I want from you isn't that shallow. And for you to think it is—" he breaks off, shaking his head, the muscle in his jaw ticking.

His eyes lock onto mine, cutting into me.

"You're not the only one who's found themselves feeling things, Charity. But if you ever think you can turn that into a game, I'll walk away before I let you waste this."

I'm shaken by his admission, but I don't let myself react.

"So where does that leave us?" I ask, my voice sounding smaller than I mean it to.

His eyes soften, but his body stays still.

"I don't know, Charity. You say you want power." He slowly reaches out and gently brushes away a tear that's slipped down my face. "You don't see that I've given you the power to ruin me. And the fucked-up thing is, I think I'll let you."

His words hang between us, and I don't know what to say.

Cal studies me for a beat, and in almost a whisper, I hear, "Just go…"

I nod and slip silently out of his office, my chest tight, my hands shaking as I try to process his words. By the time I reach my room, I'm unable to stop the tears. I catch Freddy's concern. Thankfully, he only opens the door for me, leaving me to unravel what just happened.

THIRTY-SIX
Cal

The words on the pages in front of me blur as I struggle to stay focused, last night's conversation repeating over and over in my head. The condemnation in my voice. The hurt I saw in her eyes. The things I said…the things I should've said. I admitted too much, yet I still didn't say enough. I was too harsh, my voice too much like my father's.

Raz walks in and quietly sets a plate of food on the corner of my desk before lowering himself into the chair in front of me. I look up and see genuine worry for me on his face.

"Did you sleep at all?"

I rub a hand over my face, trying to center myself.

"I think I got a few hours. Have you checked on her this morning?" I ask.

"Of course. She hasn't come out of her room yet. Freddy said he could hear her crying most of the night.

Poor guy is beside himself over it. You're not the only one she's wrapped around her finger."

I huff a laugh.

Raz clears his throat.

"So, I put a man on Samantha. Figured it wouldn't hurt to keep an eye on her since she'll probably be around more. She's already slipped past him twice." He grins.

I lean on my desk, my fists keeping my head steady.

"Maybe it's better if we move Charity to a safe house. Vardis hasn't made a move, and we can still keep her protected. Bringing her here was a mistake. It was a rash decision, and I fucked us both by doing it."

Raz narrows his eyes at me.

"You're joking. You think a safe house is the answer?" I can hear the challenge in his voice, but he's being careful to keep his face neutral. "She got under your skin, acted like the twenty-five-year-old she is, and you're going to ship her off. That's your answer?"

"Raz—" A sharp knock on my door cuts me off.

"What?" I bark.

Lem enters, looking pale, carrying an envelope and a long box. "Sorry, Sir. This just arrived at the gatehouse. It's been cleared, but you'll want to see this."

Raz stands and reaches for the items. "I'll take it."

When he opens the box, the first thing that hits me is a familiar coppery smell. Inside, a single white rose, blood drying on its delicate petals—a card bearing the name Rhea lying on top.

My heart stops. I stand and rip the brown envelope out of his hand, photos scattering over my desk. Images of Tommy and his girlfriend, covered in blood, mutilated. A recent photo of Charity lying on top of the girl's ripped-up corpse. Her face is so much like Charity's that bile rises, burning my throat. I can't tear my eyes away from the images.

"Lock this place the fuck down, NOW." Raz orders. "You call every goddamn man we have, and you make sure that every one of them is at their posts. No one comes in, no one goes out. I want every property covered, got it?" I hear a "yes, sir" before the door closes.

"Cal, I think it's time you tell her the truth. She needs to, no, she deserves to know what the stakes are here." I barely hear him, my mind racing.

I have one more card to play. It's the only way to keep her safe and keep her with me. It's desperate, and when it all comes out, she will probably never forgive me, but I have to take that chance.

"Call Freddy. Have him bring Charity here." I answer, still unable to tear my eyes from the photos. I hear Raz's voice, but the words aren't registering.

Stacking the photos in a neat pile and slipping the card into my pocket, I brace myself for what's coming. I don't pray. If there is a God, he gave up on my soul twenty-two years ago in Cormack Brennan's home. Still, I send a plea to the heavens. *Let this work.*

A few minutes later, I'm sitting on the sofa, the cool leather sending chills up my spine. The photos flipped upside down in front of me, waiting.

There's a quiet knock on the door, and she enters. I see her red, puffy eyes, her face tired and drawn. It guts me that I'm the cause.

"You wanted to see me." Her voice is so timid that it almost breaks me.

I straighten myself and brace for what comes next. "Charity. Please come sit."

I see the concern wash over her face, the seriousness of this day choking the air.

She swallows hard before walking toward the sofa and timidly sitting on the edge of the cushion.

"Look, Cal, about last night. Maybe it would be better—" I cut her off.

"There's been an escalation with Vardis." I start.

Panic flashes over her face. "What kind of escalation? Is it Sam? Is she okay?" She searches our faces for answers.

"Sam's fine, Charity. I've got men protecting her," Raz assures her.

I reach for her hand, and she pulls away like my touch burns. Her face is full of confusion.

"It's Tommy."

"Tommy? The guard?"

I clear my throat. "Tommy had a girlfriend. From a distance, her features are similar to yours. Same height, same build, same hair color. We asked Tommy to take her on a trip, to be a decoy of sorts. It worked for a few days, but Vardis found them."

The color drains from her face, her eyes lock on the photos, face down on the table. Before I can stop her, she grabs them and gasps at the images.

"No. No. No," she shakes her head in disbelief. I can see if I don't stop this, she's going to spiral.

I grab her face in my hands and look into her eyes.

"Charity, look at me," I command.

Her eyes meet mine, and I can see her start to center.

"Good." I soothe.

Releasing her but keeping my eyes still locked on her, I continue.

"We have one more option. Vardis believes he has a right to you. Somehow, in his twisted mind, he already sees you as his. There is one way to quell that."

She wrinkles her face in confusion.

I clock Raz out of the corner of my eye, just as confused as Charity.

"Tomorrow, you and I will be married. He'll have no claim on you because I claim you." Her eyes go wide, and I can see her wheels turning. I know I have seconds to get this out before she unleashes hell on me. "Men like Vardis live by the old rules. I can call on people who live by those rules—men who don't abide other men taking what isn't theirs to take."

"You are out of your fucking mind!" she says in a whisper.

I look over at Raz, and his expression repeats Charity's words.

"Marry you?" her voice rising. "You don't deem me worthy to fuck, but you want to marry me?"

There she is. I exhale a small sigh of relief.

"You drugged me and kidnapped me using that same excuse. Do you hear yourself right now?" she turns to Raz. "Tell me you hear how insane this is."

Raz throws me a look but then straightens himself and shrugs.

"It makes sense. You lose your shine to Vardis if he thinks you're fucking someone else—especially him." He nods over to me. I throw a glare back at him.

"Charity, this is happening. The only other option is to wait and risk Vardis's next move." I hold up the picture of Tommy and his woman to drive my point. "This will not be you!" I vow to her.

She stands and straightens her shoulders. "We'll see about that," she huffs.

As she heads for the door, I call to her, and she stops.

"When we say those vows, I will make you mine in every way."

She slowly turns around, her eyes going wild, and Raz quickly steps in between us.

"Go. Call Sam," he directs her. "You'll want her here for this." I hear her mutter something, but I can't make it out.

What's not missed is the thunder of her steps and the slam of the door.

After she leaves, Raz lowers himself into the chair across from me.

"A little warning next time, brother."

"There's no other way."

He nods. "Fair. But what happened to telling her the truth?"

I lock eyes with him.

"That's what I thought," he shakes his head. I can see he's measuring his words carefully. "You always have my loyalty, you know this, but hear me. I'll wait until this wedding is done, only because it does make some twisted sense. But if you don't come clean with her after—I will."

He gets up and walks out of my office, leaving me alone with the gruesome picture of a woman who could be her, empty eyes staring lifelessly back at me.

THIRTY-SEVEN
Cal

I spend the rest of the day watching my properties and making preparations. The clubs are closed for now, and the girls working there are under guard at various safehouses. Every man and woman I employ is on high alert, directed to report anything suspicious or even slightly out of place.

Raz had Sam brought to the house. He used the wedding as the excuse, but I think he knows she's safer here. Whether he'll admit it or not, he's invested in her safety.

Charity, as I expected, has been avoiding me. Tucked away in her room or surrounding herself with staff, with Sam acting as some sort of buffer. It's amusing that she thinks that will work.

I grab the contract I've had drawn up, along with the small box in front of me, and make my way to her room. There is one more detail to work out before tomorrow.

I nod at Freddy before entering. I don't knock.

The women are seated on the floor, Charity puffy-eyed and Sam looking concerned. Charity's eyes fly up to me.

"Still not knocking, I see," she snipes.

"Still my house," I quip back.

"Samantha," I say, not taking my eyes off my soon-to-be wife, "I'd like a word with Charity if you don't mind. Raz is down in the kitchen. Go join him, would you?"

Sam nods and rises, brushing the wrinkles from her clothes.

Charity narrows her eyes at me. "She can stay," she challenges.

"Samantha," I say again, keeping my voice even.

"Okay, you two obviously have some things to work out." She reaches down and squeezes Charity's shoulder. "I'll be with Raz. It'll be okay." I wait until I hear the door close.

"If you'd please," I motion toward the sofa in her room.

"I'm fine where I am."

"Charity," I say with a hint of warning.

"Fine," she huffs. She hoists herself up from the floor and plops onto the sofa. "What do you want, Cal?" her voice dripping with annoyance.

I sit next to her and place the box and contract on the table in front of her.

"Read it."

Her hands slightly shaking, she carefully moves the box over and picks up the paper.

"A contract, Cal?" She looks at me with disbelief. "Of course, you have a contract ready. Boilerplate, I assume?"

I ignore her sass. "I assure you, there is nothing boilerplate about this situation."

I watch her as she begins scanning the document.

"I believe the terms are fair and reasonable," I continue. "You fulfill it, you walk away with enough money to keep you in comfort for the rest of your life. You will be protected for the rest of your life. Make no mistake, this marriage will be a true marriage in every sense of the word." I let my eyes roam over her body to ensure that she doesn't mistake my meaning. "If a child is conceived, you will carry to term. Whether you want to be part of its life will be up to you. Either way, I will acknowledge the child and ensure he or she wants for nothing."

She narrows her eyes at me. "I have an IUD. Unless you plan on ripping it from my body, children will not be a possibility."

"No infidelity," I continue, ignoring the fight she's trying to instigate. "No one touches you but me."

Her scoff is soft. "Fine. But you're not screwing around either. That includes whatever happens in your little clubs."

"Charity," I say her name roughly. "You're not listening. This isn't about my clubs. This is about you. Any man who touches you will die before you take your next breath. You'll be standing right there when I make him pay the price for touching what's mine. I want that perfectly clear before you plan any of your games."

Her bravado flickers, but I see it.

She leans forward, and I think for a moment she might bite. "Crystal. But the same rules apply to you, Mitchell. If I see so much as a finger on another woman, I walk. Vardis can have me."

The sound of that name makes my control snap, and I grab her by the chin, forcing her to look at me.

"This isn't a game. The minute you take my name, you will be mine, body and soul. You will obey me because anything less puts you in danger, and I refuse to allow that."

"Six months." She grits out, unfazed by my words.

I raise an eyebrow. "Excuse me?"

She wrenches away from my grip. "I'll agree to being married to you for six months." She straightens herself and stubbornly sets her jaw, and I have to fight to keep the smile from my face. I admire her obstinacy as much as it annoys me.

"You're telling me that this is for my safety. You have six months to take Vardis down."

I cock my head at her, letting her believe I'm mulling over her terms.

"Agreed, with a few conditions and caveats. If, when those six months end, our separation jeopardizes that operation, the contract automatically renews for another six months. Also, if your birth control fails and you become pregnant with my heir, we stay married until the child is born. I will not have you making my heir a bastard over your stupid pride. That is non-negotiable."

She thinks for a moment and nods.

"Write it in and sign it," I say, my chin jerking toward the paper.

"And if I don't?"

I close my eyes, gathering every ounce of my patience, not caring that she sees how far she's pushing. I lock eyes with her, hoping my words deliver the weight they intend.

"If you don't, I'm not sure I can protect you. This isn't your world, Charity. The rules are different. Even though I don't immerse myself in my father's old channels, his name still carries clout. The Mitchell name will protect you, even from Vardis."

"Maybe I'll just go to the police. Tell them everything I know. It should get someone's attention."

I bark a laugh. "The police?" I pull out my phone and open my contacts to make my point. "Would you like to call the chief, lead detective, or maybe go straight to the mayor? Senator Gordon attended the gala—perhaps you met her? You do not understand how this game is played, Hurricane. Whether we are on the fringes of legality or in the black, we all pad their pockets in exchange for their blindness. Maybe if this were an election year, you might get someone to grow a conscience. Sadly, that is not now."

Her eyes drop, her expression unreadable for a moment before she looks back up at me.

"I never really thought about marriage all that much, but when I did, this isn't how I imagined it. It feels so dirty—like a back-door deal." She tries to hide it, but I can see her vulnerability, and somehow, I know what she needs.

I grab her chin, gently this time, and look into her eyes.

"Charity Dawn Johnston, I can't promise you love. I'm not sure a man like me knows what that truly is. What I can promise is that I will protect you with my life. I will honor you with my actions. I will worship you—because, my God, you are worthy of it. Tomorrow, I want to make you my wife. Say that you'll agree."

She searches my face for a minute, and I see the second she decides.

I watch as she scribbles her name, and then I do the same.

"I want a copy of that contract, Cal. And I'll need a safety deposit box or something that you can't touch."

I don't try to hide my smile. "One step at a time, Hurricane. I'll have it notarized tonight and in your hands before our vows."

I pick up the box, take the ring out, and push it on her left ring finger.

She gasps.

"That doesn't come off. It was my mother's. The only other woman I've ever loved."

I pick up the paper and pen and leave, shutting the door behind me.

THIRTY-EIGHT
Charity

I'm woken by a small nudge.

Groggy, I roll over and see Sam lying next to me in my bed.

"Good morning, Sunshine. It's your wedding day." She gives me a small smile.

I groan. "Don't remind me." I sit up in bed and rub my face, the weight on my finger reminding me of last night.

Sam lets out a small gasp and grabs my hand. "Wow, it's beautiful."

"Yeah, after you left, he made me sign a contract and slapped it on my finger." I study it in the morning light, remembering what he said about love. "He said it was his mother's."

The platinum bespoke Claddagh ring holds a heart-shaped aquamarine beneath a small crown set with diamonds. Two marquise-cut emerald stones serve as the hands, with delicate, subtle engraving. It's not gaudy or flashy. It's almost perfect.

"Charity," she starts carefully, "if it was his mother's and he gave it to you, that says a lot. I was talking to Raz—" I interrupt her before she can continue.

"What's the deal with you two? Are you fucking him?" I narrow my eyes at her.

She arches a brow. "Really? That's where your head goes? You're about to get married off to save yourself from the devil, and you're worried about my sex life?"

I groan. "I'm sorry, Sam. I need someone who is entirely in my corner. If Raz gets his hooks into you—"

"Oh my God, listen to yourself! The only one getting hooked is you!" she huffs. "As I was saying, I know this isn't how you wanted your wedding day, but Raz thinks that Cal really does care about you. Even if he won't admit it to himself."

I eye her suspiciously. "He said that?"

"Well, not in so many words, but—" Sam mimics Raz's deep voice, "the man's lost his fucking mind over her." Despite the seriousness of today, her impression cracks me up. She grabs my hand and squeezes it. "I'm in your corner, babe, and if marrying Cal Mitchell keeps you safe, then I'll hogtie you and drag you to the altar myself!"

Marie comes hurriedly into the room carrying a tray with coffee and pastries.

"Morning, Ladies," she says, setting the tray on the coffee table and rattling off details as she hurries around the room.

"Hair and makeup will be here in three hours. Dresses will arrive soon, so you'll have plenty of time to choose what you want to wear. The ceremony is at noon, and I don't have to tell you, Mr. Mitchell will not be happy if you keep him waiting."

"Hair and makeup? Marie, this is just a formality. And if security is so tight—"

She stops and puts her hands on her hips in her no-nonsense fashion.

"Charity Mitchell, if you think your future husband is going to let you get married in a street dress, you underestimate him. That man doesn't miss a detail."

It's the first time I hear my married name, and my stomach bottoms out.

"Johnston," I whisper. "My name is Johnston."

She gives me an understanding nod. "I know, hon. I thought you'd rather try it on now before hearing it at the ceremony. A little less jarring."

Sam squeezes my hand. "It's got a nice sound to it. Very Irish to match that gorgeous ring."

"Okay, no more dawdling," Marie says, breaking the tension. "You need to eat so you don't pass out at the altar. If you need anything tonight, pack a separate bag. We'll be moving your things into the master bedroom, but we won't have time to unpack them."

I gawk at her. My head starts spinning. This is all happening too fast.

"You thought you'd be staying in this room?" She shakes her head. "Samantha, you're welcome to use this room as long as you'd like. Just put your things on the bed, and I'll make sure they don't get packed with Charity's things." With a click of the door, she's gone.

I look at Sam and break out in a sob.

With no hesitation, Sam pulls me in. "Shhhh, I've got you," she soothes. We stay like that for a minute until I get myself under control. When I pull away from her, she wipes the tears from my eyes. "For what it's worth, I think this marriage might surprise you." Her words are meant to encourage, but the dread knots tighter. I nod and head for the shower.

When I come out of the bathroom, I'm greeted by two racks of dresses. While Sam oohs and ahhs over the design and the labels, I can't decide.

"He might be an asshole, but there's no denying the man's choices in fashion." I can't disagree with her, but the sound of awe in her voice annoys me. I decide to let her enjoy herself and let it go.

After some debate, I choose a champagne-colored slip dress. Simple with clean lines. The delicate shoulder straps and low neckline feel more elegant than sexy. It's understated, and that's what I need this day to be.

Sam settles on a light blue curve-fitting dress with delicate lace flowers scattered in tulle. She looks gorgeous, and I can't help wishing she was the bride today, not me.

Make-up and hair arrive, and we both decide to wear our hair down. They're skilled, but I can't stand the feel of all the hands on me. When the dress is in place, I look in the mirror at my reflection, wondering if I'll feel like the same person in a few hours.

Marie sweeps into the room, arms full of flowers, and stops in her tracks.

"You look beautiful, both of you!"

She hands a bouquet to Sam and then to me.

"Mr. Mitchell had precise requests."

Sam's bouquet is made up of pale blue baby roses, perfectly matching her dress. I look at the bundle of champagne-colored roses in my hand, my stomach tightening. The bastard knew exactly which dress I'd pick.

"It's time. The gentlemen are already in the garden, waiting with the officiant." She gives me an encouraging nod, and I steel myself.

"Well," I take a deep breath. "Let's get this over with."

The garden is covered in flowers. The smell of the roses and jasmine twisting around the trellis permeates the air. Petals are intentionally scattered, making a path to where Cal and Raz are standing.

Standing along the side, I see Marie and Cora, along with many of the faces I've come to know since being brought here.

And then there he is.

Cal stands at the far end of the pathway, a black three-piece suit cutting sharp lines over his frame, the faintest sheen on his shoes catching the noon sun. He's not smiling, but his eyes hold mine with an intensity that makes my stomach flip as I take the first step toward him.

Raz is at his right, looking unfairly good in a dark suit that does nothing to soften the brutal beauty of his scars. His hair's been neatly trimmed, and he's looking at Sam like she's the only person he sees.

Sam walks beside me, bouquet in hand, the pale blue of her gown catching the light.

As we close the distance, Raz leans in toward her, voice low enough I barely catch it.

"You look smokin', Sprite."

She laughs under her breath, a little flush on her cheeks. "Cal's got great taste."

Raz's mouth quirks.

"What makes you think he picked that out for you?"

She freezes mid-step. I glance at her, then at him, but he's only got eyes for her, the air between them crackling.

The officiant clears his throat, gesturing us into place. There's no preamble; he goes right into the vows.

Cal doesn't take his eyes off me as he promises to honor and cherish me. The word love glaringly absent. I let his words wash over me, trying to pretend that this isn't an arrangement and that maybe he truly means them.

When it's my turn, the words are different. The officiant asks if I will take this man as my lawful husband, to cherish him, honor him… and obey him.

My mouth goes dry. *Obey?* I glance at Sam. Her brows pull together, a question flashing across her face. Out of the corner of my eye, I see Raz's lips curve in a knowing smirk.

Cal tilts his head, one brow lifting just enough to say, *Your move.*

I swallow. "I will," I mutter.

His smile is slow, satisfaction radiating off him.

The officiant turns toward our witnesses for the rings.

Sam places Cal's wedding band into my palm. He doesn't look away from me as I slide it onto his finger.

Cal takes my band from Raz and slides it onto my hand, his thumb caressing my knuckle like he's trying to soothe me.

The officiant opens his mouth to pronounce us, but Cal doesn't wait. His hand is in my hair, pulling me into a deep, claiming kiss. He leaves no doubt that I belong to him now.

I hear Sam's surprised laugh, Raz's low chuckle, and the clapping of the witnesses behind us.

When Cal pulls back, his mouth is curved in quiet triumph.

"Come, wife." Grasping my hand, he leads me back down the path. A man stands with a camera snapping photos, documenting every moment. Champagne is poured, and cake is passed. To anyone looking in on us, we look like the perfect newlyweds. Any hesitation Cal had about touching me is gone now. His hand never leaves the small of my back as he leans in, nuzzles my neck, and lightly kisses the top of my head. So affectionate, or maybe it's just lust.

I look over at Raz and Sam, and they almost mirror us. Raz seems protective of her, like she's become precious to him. Tenderness shines in his eyes when he looks at her.

Eventually, Cal takes the champagne flute from my hand and, setting it on one of the small tables, pronounces, "We're done here."

Nodding at Raz, who joins us, I hear him say, "I want those pictures delivered tonight."

He grasps my hand tighter and drags me from the reception.

He stalks through the house like he's on a mission, and I tug my hand from his.

"Where are we going?"

It's a question I don't need him to answer. I know exactly where he's taking me.

Cupping my face, he leans in and gives me a gentle kiss that makes my pulse kick. "It's time to make you truly mine, Mrs. Mitchell." He takes my hand and leads me up the stairs.

THIRTY-NINE
Charity

With his hand on the small of my back, he opens the door of his bedroom and waits for me to step in. I step through and am instantly hit by his scent. Like his office, his bedroom smells sharp and clean with hints of firewood. Everything about the room feels like Cal. The walls are covered in dark wood, and a massive bed takes up the center of the room, the dark fire-honed wood swirling with scorch marks. Dark wine-colored sheets peek out from the satin comforter, matching pillows piled at the head.

I feel him behind me, studying me while I study his room. I tilt my head over my shoulder and give him a look. I have the urge to ask him how many women have stood in this exact spot, looking at the room like I'm doing now, but I don't want the answer.

He moves in behind me, closing the gap, and I feel a single finger tracing along my spine before gliding up the side of my neck. I shiver even though the heat is already pooling low, my skin buzzing for more.

"Before we go any further, I need your consent, Charity. I've never taken a woman against her will, and my wife will not be the first."

I lift my hand, ready to tug the strap of my dress down, desperate to speed this up, but his hand closes over mine, stopping me.

"I need your words. Tell me you want this."

I take a breath, "I want this, Cal." It's not a lie.

His breath ghosts over the shell of my ear, lips brushing my skin, and I hear him whisper, "We have all night. Let me look at my wife on our wedding day."

The word wife lands like lightning, searing through me. It's too much. The heat, the weight of him behind me, the quiet claim in his voice, it's overpowering. I should step forward, create space, but instead I lean back into him, feeling the fire.

I feel his arm wrap around me, pulling me back and grinding me into him. His arousal is evident in the hardness, and a moan escapes my lips.

"Yes, Hurricane," he growls against my ear. "That's all for you. Every goddamn inch."

Turning me around, his hands in my hair, he pulls my lips to his. The kiss is deep and possessive, and I want more. His hand slides down and he cups my breast, never releasing my lips, just taking more. He tweaks my nipple, making me ache, and presses against him harder, and I reach for him through his pants, wanting him.

"Wife, you're making a mess of your wedding dress. I've barely touched you, and I can already smell how wet you are," he says against my lips.

On instinct, I nip at his lower lip and look up with him teasingly.

His growl vibrates against my mouth. The sharp crack of his palm lands on my ass, making me gasp into his kiss. "Keep it up, and I'll be painting your ass with more than my cum," he threatens, and it somehow makes me wetter.

"Do you remember what I told you, Charity? How'd I'd only give you my cock when you begged for it?" He grabs me and grinds harder, and I gasp. I nod, licking my lips.

"I'm prepared to make you beg, Wife."

His hands skim my shoulders, finding the thin straps of my dress. He doesn't tug them down right away, just strokes the silk against my skin, teasing us both. His eyes are heavy on mine, pinning me in place. He pushes one strap down, then the other, the fabric sliding over my breasts, my nipples aching for his touch. The cool air hits my skin, causing another shiver, but it's his stare that makes me flush. Pushing the silky fabric over my hips until it pools on the floor, he looks me over and hums his approval.

"My God," he breathes. "You are fucking beautiful."

"Jesus, Cal," my voice desperate, "just fuck me, or let me fuck you, but do something!"

His mouth curves in a wicked grin. "Impatient little hurricane."

Leaning down, he snatches a nipple in his mouth and bites until I groan. The pleasure and pain mix into a new sensation. "Fuck...Cal," I moan. He lets it go with a pop.

"Step out of the dress. The shoes stay on," he commands, his voice low and needy.

I do as I'm told, afraid he'll stop if I defy him.

He gently pushes me back into the bed until my knees hit. "Lay back," he commands.

I lay back and prop myself up on my elbows. "Are you always going to be so bossy, husband?" I ask with a grin. It's the first time I've used his new title, and I like the feel of it on my lips. The smile on his face tells me that he liked hearing it.

He cocks his head at me, "Forgotten your vow to obey already?" he smirks.

"About that—" I start.

"Charity, do I need to gag you?" he interrupts. I press my lips together with a giggle.

He shrugs out of his suit jacket, tossing it over a chair, and begins working the buttons of his shirt, one by one. His eyes sweep over me, taking his time. My smirk fades. It hits me at that moment—I've never seen Calahan Mitchell without a shirt, never mind naked.

"Three."

"Three?" I question.

"That's how many orgasms you'll give me before my cock touches you."

His shirt lands somewhere behind him, followed by his pants, and for the first time, I see all of him.

My eyes wander over his broad shoulders and wide chest. He's lean-muscled with faint lines that ripple as he moves. A trail of dark hair trails down his stomach, disappearing below his hips, and then—

Oh.

My mouth goes dry. His hard cock stands rigid and proud, and I know he's going to fill me in all the right ways. I see a bead of precome glisten on the tip, and I lick my lips.

He watches me taking him in, "Pleased, wife?"

Heat spikes low in my belly. I shift on the bed, squeezing my thighs together, but it doesn't help.

"Jesus, Cal…" I mutter before I can stop myself.

He pushes me back against the bed, his body caging mine. I feel the thick press of him against my thigh, but instead of giving me what I want, his hand slides lower. Fingers part me, slow, deliberate, stroking through how wet I already am.

I buck against him, desperate. "Cal, please—"

His mouth curves into a dark smile. "Please, what? Say it."

I want to spit a retort, but his thumb circles my clit, and my voice breaks into a moan instead. "Please…fuck me."

"Not yet." His tone is silk over steel. "You'll give the first one by my hand."

He pushes two fingers inside, knuckles deep, curling until my back bows. The stretch burns, but his thumb doesn't stop, grinding my clit until I'm writhing beneath him.

"God, Cal…fuck—" My hands claw at his shoulders. I'm too close already, humiliatingly fast.

"That's it," he growls, his breath hot against my ear. "So greedy. Drench my fingers, wife. Show me how badly you need my cock."

I break, crying out as the orgasm rips through me, every nerve on fire. He keeps moving, unrelenting, dragging it out until I'm trembling and gasping his name.

When he finally eases his hand away, he doesn't wipe it off. He lifts his fingers to my mouth. "Open."

I glare, but my lips part anyway, and he pushes them in, letting me taste myself. My cheeks heat.

"Good girl," he murmurs, pulling his fingers free. His grin is wicked. "One down."

He slides down my body, lips grazing my stomach, then lower. I know where he's going, and my thighs twitch closed, instinct to hide how much I want it.

He forces them apart with his hands, pinning me wide. "Don't you dare," he warns. "I'll spend all night between your legs if I want to. You gave me vows, Hurricane. You will obey."

"Cal—" My protest dies in a gasp when his tongue flicks over my clit, devastatingly slow.

I fist the sheets, my hips jerking. "Jesus…fuck."

He hums against me, the vibrations making me shudder. His tongue is deliberate, teasing circles, then sudden pressure that makes me cry out. He pulls back just long enough to look up at me, his mouth slick, his eyes black with hunger.

"Such a sweet pussy," he murmurs before diving back in, sucking my clit hard enough I almost scream.

"Cal, I can't—"

"You can." His fingers slide inside me, curling until they hit that spot that makes me see stars. "You're going to come for me again. Right now."

I thrash, caught between wanting to hold it back and needing to give in. "Please," I choke out, half-begging, half-demanding.

"Beg prettier," he growls against me, tongue relentless.

"I'm begging!" My voice cracks. "Cal—fuck—don't stop, I'm coming—"

The orgasm tears through me, a blinding rush that arches my spine off the bed. He doesn't let up, licking me through it, swallowing everything I give him until I collapse into a shaking mess.

When he finally pulls back, his mouth is wet, his chin slick. He wipes it with the back of his hand and smirks.

"Two," he says simply, his voice dark with satisfaction.

His grin is wicked as I watch him slide down until he's between my thighs again. The sight of Calahan Mitchell on his knees for me makes my breath stutter.

"Number three," he growls.

His tongue is relentless, rough strokes against my clit while two fingers thrust deep inside me, curling to that spot that makes me see stars. I cry out, my hips jerking, but he pins me with one arm across my belly, holding me down, forcing me to take what he's giving.

"Cal—I can't—"

"Yes, you can. You will." His voice is muffled against my skin, low and commanding. "You'll come until you're dripping, until you can't breathe without choking on my name."

The pressure builds sharp and fast, my body quaking against him. I thrash again, desperate. He only drives harder, fingers ruthless, tongue merciless, dragging me right to the edge until I shatter a third time. My scream rips out of me, hoarse and raw, as wave after wave crashes through me.

By the time he eases off, I'm a mess. Slick, trembling, my hair stuck to my damp cheeks. He crawls up my body, bracing over me, his chest heaving.

"Three," he rasps, his mouth curving in a feral smile. "I told you, wife. Now beg for my cock."

I can barely breathe, but I find his eyes. "Please, Cal… I need you. I need to feel your cock inside me. Please," I beg.

His pupils blow wide, hunger sparking as he lines himself up. The thick head of his cock slides against my soaked folds. He pushes in slowly at first, savoring the way my body stretches around him, then thrusts deep with a guttural growl that rattles through my bones.

I gasp, clutching at his shoulders, the sensations overwhelming. He fills me completely, owning me from the inside out.

"Fuck, yes," he snarls against my neck, his thrusts sharp and punishing. "You feel that? That's mine. Every moan, every shiver, every drop your sweet pussy weeps— you fucking belong to me now."

I arch into him, clinging, giving him what he wants. "Yours, Cal. All yours."

His pace turns brutal, each thrust driving me deeper into the mattress. Between our bodies, his fingers find my swollen clit, circling with merciless precision until I'm climbing toward that high again. My vision blurs as the pressure builds, my body clenching around him like a vise. He falters for just a moment, his rhythm breaking as my muscles grip him.

"Fuuuck—" he roars.

His pupils swallow the color of his eyes as he convulses above me, his release flooding me in hot waves. He stays buried deep, neither of us able to move. Sweat dripping from his temple, his eyes locked on mine, refusing to let go.

"Fucking perfect. And fucking mine."

FORTY
Charity

I wake to a wet, relentless pressure dragging me from sleep. My legs twitch, trying to clamp shut, but they're already spread wide, hands pinning me open once again.

"Cal…" It comes out half-whimper, half-warning.

He doesn't answer, just groans against me, tongue pressing harder, sucking my clit until I jolt awake.

"My God. Again?" I gasp.

The crack of his palm on my pussy makes me yelp. The sting blooms hot, only to be soothed instantly by his tongue.

"Don't test me, wife," he growls into me, voice muffled and hungry. "I'll take you whenever I want. Now quit interrupting my breakfast."

He dives back in, unrelenting. My hips buck, torn between writhing away and arching in to offer him more.

I twist my fingers through his hair, anchoring myself against the sensation.

The edge of his teeth grazes my clit just enough to draw a sharp cry, and he hums with pleasure at the sound. His tongue works me over mercilessly, circling, sucking, each flick and press of his tongue torture and pleasure. My thighs tremble, my breath sharp gasps. I'm so close it hurts.

"Cal—please—"

He pulls back suddenly, lips slick, eyes black with hunger. "Not yet."

Before I can protest, his hands flip me onto my stomach, spreading me wide. He drags me up onto my knees, my face pressed into the sheets as he lines himself up.

The first thrust is brutal, driving him deep, stealing my breath. I cry out, clutching the bedding, my body sore but still starving for him.

"Take it, wife," he commands, one hand fisting in my hair as he pounds into me. "And give me what's mine!"

The sting of his palm lands sharply on my ass, setting my skin on fire. His slick finger teases lower, pressing at that forbidden place until I jolt, clenching around him.

"Cal—" I try to squirm away from the invasion.

He bends over me, his voice a growl in my ear. "I will have every part of you. Let me in."

The stretch burns, sharp and shocking, but with his cock driving deep at the same time, it tips me over the edge. The orgasm rips through me raw and violent, and I scream against the sheets.

"Good girl," he growls, his pace turning feral. He slams into me, punishing me and worshipping me all at once.

His rhythm breaks, his roar tearing through the room as he buries himself to the hilt, spilling hot and deep. He holds me there, trembling with the force of it, his chest pressed to my back, his hand still locked in my hair. He kisses my neck tenderly and whispers, "Good morning, Mrs. Mitchell."

He takes me again just as ferociously in the shower, and I'm afraid I won't live to see the end of that six-month contract. The man is relentless.

When we finally make it to the dining room for breakfast, I'm surprised to see Sam sitting at the table, across from Raz, chattering away. I ease into the chair beside her, wincing slightly. Sam's eyebrows shoot up, a conspiratorial smile playing at her lips as she leans in. "That good, huh?"

"Seriously?" I hiss, but can't help the flush creeping up my neck. I know my satisfied smile betrays me.

"So did you spend the night?" I ask. She nods and looks down at her food.

I look over at Raz, who's talking with Cal. He pauses briefly, turning to Sam, grinning from ear to ear.

My eyebrows shoot up. "Samantha!"

"Hey," Sam says, voice low like she's telling me a secret, "he picked out a dress for me. It would've been rude not to thank him. And, by the way? He has officially proven his nickname. That man is a fucking beast."

"Oh, ewwww, Sam!" I groan, half-laughing, half-horrified.

"If the maid of honor and best man are both single, it's obligatory that they fuck. It's in the handbook. Bad luck for you if we hadn't," she insists. "You and Cal are in for so much good luck."

Her giggle sets me off, and soon we're both laughing.

"Oh, before I forget, I found these in the library when I was snooping. Have you seen these?"

She pulls out a weathered photo album, sets it on the table, and flips the first page open. I smile at a young Cal, looking back at me. He can't be more than nine or ten. He's dressed in a baseball uniform, wearing the same serious look he still wears today.

I flip the page and let out a surprised gasp. "What the—I know him."

Sam looks at me, confused. "Charity?"

I point to the man standing next to Cal in the photo, his arm possessively on Cal's shoulder.

"Cal," I hold the picture up, "who is this man?"

Cal and Raz both turn to look at the picture, and I see a look I can't read flash across their faces.

"Where did you find that?" Cal asks. I can hear in his tone that he's hiding something.

"Sam found it in the library. Why is the man who used to visit me standing next to you, Cal?" I can't name why, but I feel panic rising inside of me.

I watch as Raz looks pointedly at Cal, something passing between them.

"You must be mistaken."

"No, Cal, I'm not mistaken. This man visited me every year on my birthday. I remember because he would bring me a gift on each visit. It was the only gift I got."

"Cal." I catch the warning in Raz's voice.

Lem rushes into the room.

"Sirs, Lilith has been hit. There was an explosion about 15 minutes ago," he says in a rush.

"Goddamn it!" Cal yells as he gets up from the table. Raz follows suit.

"Charity, you stay here. We'll talk when I get home, I promise." He leans down and presses a kiss to the top of my head before heading for the door.

Raz points his finger at Sam. "You too, Sprite. Stay."

They stalk out of the room, leaving me with my questions.

"Charity," Sam says, hesitation in her voice. "I'm pretty sure that's Cal's father. That's Malcolm Mitchell."

"That doesn't make any sense." I shake my head. "Why would Cal's father be visiting me, and why would Cal not tell me that his father knew me?"

Sam shrugs. "Maybe he didn't know."

She narrows her eyes at me. "I see that, look, Charity. Don't spin out on this. If Cal says he'll talk to you, you need to trust that."

"Since when did you become Cal Mitchell's cheer squad?"

"Since you walked in here looking like a woman smitten with her husband. I watched the way he looked at you during the wedding. That wedding wasn't just about Vardis, Charity. Raz is right, he's got it bad. And I think you do too." She grabs my hand. "Come on. Let's go see what other secrets we can find." She gives my shoulder a playful shove, and I let her lead me from the dining room.

After wandering around the house, avoiding the overrun of guards making their rounds, we settle in the theatre room to watch a movie. I must have dozed off because the next thing I hear is my phone ringing. I pick it up and see an incoming call.

Sam?

It doesn't make any sense until I see the note lying in the seat beside me where she had been.

Need to get some things from my apartment. Don't worry, Freddy is taking me. bbs.

I hit the green button and answer, "Raz is going to kill you for leaving Sam!"

"Rhea. Finally. Nikos Vardis. You're a very hard woman to contact."

I hear a voice on the other end of the line, and I immediately recognize the thick accent from the night of the gala.

Terror floods my veins.

"Who the fuck is Rhea? What are you doing with Sam's phone? Where is she?"

"Samantha is here. She's fine for now. It will be up to you if she stays that way. She's pretty, this, Sam of yours. I already have a few very interested buyers."

I hear a ping as a text comes through, and when I click on it, an image of Sam fills the screen. Her blond hair is matted with blood and hanging in her face. Her arms and legs are bound to the chair. I can see a bruise on the side of her face, but her eyes are wild with a mix of fear and anger.

"What do you want with her? Why are you doing this?" My voice is a mix of desperation and fury.

"Oh, come now, Rhea, let's dispense with the games. We both know it's not Samantha that I want. She was simply a fortunate means to find you. You know I've been looking for you. My patience thins. I've waited long enough for what is mine. You will come to me now, or I will get to you eventually. The question is, will you let Samantha pay for your disobedience to me in the meantime?"

"Why do you keep calling me by that name? Cal is going to kill you, Vardis, mark my words. Let her go!"

"Enough," he snaps. "You will find a way out of Mitchell's house. There is a service road in the back. My men wait there. You have twenty minutes. For each minute beyond that, I take a piece of your friend."

"You motherfucker!" I scream into the phone, my voice breaking. "How can I trust you'll let her go?"

"Twenty minutes, Rhea." The phone goes dead.

"No," I scream. My hands shaking, I pull up my contacts and stab at Cal's name. Voicemail.

I try Raz next. Voicemail.

FUCK!

Think Charity, think.

I stand and feel the chess piece shift in my pocket. I know what I need to do.

I slip my rings off and place them on the arm of the lounger. No matter what happens, Vardis doesn't get these. I pull the chess piece from my pocket. I've carried it since I took it from him, and I put it with the rings.

Sometimes you have to sacrifice the queen to save the board.

I bolt from the theatre room and head to the kitchen. Cora and Marie are nowhere to be found, and I do the only thing I can. Ripping the towel from the oven door handle, I turn on the back burner and lay it on the flame. Flames shoot up, and smoke begins to fill the kitchen.

The alarms start blaring, and I head for the service entrance. I can hear the three men stationed nearby thudding toward the kitchen. I cut through the laundry corridor and slam my shoulder into the door, and it gives with a groan.

The cool night air hits my face, and I run, heading toward the wall that surrounds the back of the house. I creep in the shadows, hiding among the hedges, when I see one of the guards heading toward me. I tuck myself into a shadow and hold my breath as he stops, lights a cigarette, and finally moves on. I follow the wall until I reach the back entrance, and I slip out, heading for the road beyond the boundary of the property. My heart is pounding, and my lungs burn, but I don't stop.

Ducking in between the trees, I wind my way toward the road. The terrain is unfamiliar, and I feel my feet slipping, but I can't take the time to get my bearings. I keep running blindly until I see a break in the trees. I surge forward, but before I can make it, pain explodes at the base of my skull. Everything goes black.

When I come to, the back of my head is screaming in pain. I open my eyes, but all I see is black. I try to move my hands and feel ropes digging into my wrists. My legs are met with the same resistance. The picture of Sam's face flashes in front of my eyes, tied and bloody.

In one swift motion, the blackness is ripped away, and I'm met with blinding lights, making me wince.

"Hello, Rhea. Welcome home."

FORTY-ONE
Cal

It's almost midnight before Raz and I finally make our way home. It wasn't only Club Lilith that was hit—Vardis attempted the same carnage on Club Eden, as well as one of my warehouses. It was a coordinated attack. Luckily, my men are well-trained, thanks to Raz, and the losses were few.

I know instantly that something is wrong. The house is too quiet. Something is missing. The men are looking at each other nervously, but not one of them will look Raz or me in the eye.

We share a look, and I nod toward Lem, silently directing him before making my way to my bedroom to check on my wife. When I approach, the first thing I notice is the lack of a guard, my ire rising. I'll deal with Freddy tomorrow. Right now, I need to crawl into bed, wrap my arms around her, and take in her sweet scent.

Before I reach for the door handle, Raz calls to me from behind.

"Cal, she's not in there. She's gone."

I feel my heart rate spike, the walls closing in on me the instant I hear his words. Turning around to face him, I fight to keep myself under control. "What do you mean she's gone?"

"Freddy took Sam to her apartment to grab some things," I hear Raz's voice crack, and dread washes over me. "When he didn't return with her and didn't answer his phone, a few of the men tracked him. He's dead, Cal. They found him in her apartment. Sam wasn't there. Whoever got to him—they were waiting."

"And Charity?"

"The men have searched the house and the grounds. She's not here. It's like she's vanished. They found these in the theatre room." Raz holds out his hand, and in it are her wedding rings and the tiny black chess piece—the queen.

"Vanished?" I roar. "How the fuck does my wife vanish from a fucking compound with armed guards and cameras in every fucking corner?" I make my way to my office, my fists clenched, screaming orders at anyone in my path. "Get whoever was on the cameras in my office right the fuck now! I want every piece of footage."

Raz is following behind me, muttering into his earpiece as he puts my demands into action. I know he's got his own concerns about Samantha, but all I can focus on right now is my wife.

I barge into my office, turning my computer on. Raz is on my heels, fingers flying over his phone.

"I've got a ping from her cell outside of the back perimeter. It's a few hours old. I'm pulling up her call and texts now." I know he's trying to assure me, but it's pointless. I run my hands through my hair, trying to get a hold of myself.

A knock on my door jolts me out of my thoughts, and Phil eases carefully into my office.

"Sir. The feeds from the cameras should be on your drive now."

I pull up the different views, Raz hovering over my shoulder. We watch as Sam and Freddy leave the grounds, Samantha's hands flying through the air as she chatters away, Charity nowhere in sight. I feel Raz stiffen next to me. "Easy, friend, we'll find her." I wish I believed my own words.

I fast-forward through the different views until Raz points to one of the screens and shouts, "There!" We both watch silently as the shadowy image slips across the screen. The figure crouches in the dark, staying close to the greenery and wall, seeming to know how to hide in the shadows. One of the guards comes into view, and she stops short, waiting as he lights a cigarette before moving on, utterly oblivious to her presence. Seeing her threat of discovery gone, she continues until the cameras no longer track her shadow. If I weren't so inconceivably furious with her, I would almost be impressed with her cleverness.

"Who the fuck is that?" I demand, pointing at the guard. Phil stiffens.

"Jake, sir, he's new. Been with us around six months."

"Bring him to me. Now." I keep my voice steady, tamping down the fury. Phil gets on his earpiece and summons the guard.

"Cal—" Raz starts.

"Not one fucking word, Raz."

A knock at the door announces Jake's arrival. As soon as I see him, uncontrollable rage pulses through me. I jump out of my chair, round my desk, and launch myself at him. My fist connects with his face over and over until I feel bone splinter, his screams falling on deaf ears.

"I will not abide incompetence!" I roar at him. I pull back to hit him again when I feel Raz's hand grip my arm.

"Cal—enough! Killing him isn't going to help us find either of them!"

As if pulled from a trance, Jake's mangled face comes into view, my own ripped up knuckles dripping with blood. I turn away, wiping my hands on my handkerchief. "Get him the fuck out of here!"

Phil drags Jake's limp body up, and I give my next orders.

"Get Doc here to look at him. I want the names of every person on duty tonight, along with their positions on site. Start interrogating. If she had help sneaking out, I want that motherfucker's head on a goddamned pike."

Raz's phone pings. "It's Charity's phone logs. There's a call from Sam, followed by a text."

I watch as he pulls up the text and we both see the image of Sam on the screen, tied and bloodied. Raz roars like a wounded animal before I grab him, his eyes wild, accentuating the scars that I'd forgotten were there. It's almost as if his pain gave them new life.

"Raz!" I bark at him. "Here! With me, Brother!" I hold his gaze until I see the rage ease a beat.

He closes his eyes for a brief second, centering himself, his control washing back over him.

He goes back to work, pulling up the metadata, "It was sent from Sam's phone, but the location is all wrong." I see his fingers fly over his phone again. When he holds up his phone, I see a map, a marker indicating the origin of the call and text.

"He has her. Vardis has Sam." Raz's voice cracks slightly, revealing his vulnerability at the realization.

It all crashes together.

My words to her the day that she took my queen scream back at me: Sometimes you need to sacrifice your queen to save the game.

"Those stupid, stupid girls," I swear. "Vardis used Sam as bait, and she fell for it. The missed calls. I should have known something was wrong."

My desk phone rings, dragging us both back into the immediacy of the moment. I know who it is before I pick up the receiver.

I hit the speaker button and place it back on the cradle. "Vardis."

"Lose something, Mitchell? Or should I say…somethings?" The voice on the other end drips with satisfaction.

"You have my wife, Nikos." It's not a question.

"Beautiful photos you had delivered. Too bad that the entire affair was a sham. You see, Calahan. I know the truth. She is not your wife, not really. You married Charity Johnston, and we both know she doesn't exist. Sorry about Freddy, by the way. He was a good soldier, until he wasn't. Still, shame I had to put him down."

I clench my fist and see the tick in Raz's jaw.

"I will make Rhea mine soon enough. As for Samantha…I've already got two customers lined up. She'll need some training, of course—"

"Vardis, you motherfucker," Raz growls, cutting over me. I shoot him a glare, furious that he just gave Vardis what he was looking for.

"Ah, Raziel. Good to see Calahan still has his lap dog. I have to say, I admire your taste. Samantha is a pretty thing."

I pick up the receiver before Raz can reply.

"You do not want this war, Vardis. You will give us back our women, and maybe I will let you live." We both know that's a lie.

"Enough, Mitchell. I just wanted you to know it was me. Know that when you try to keep something of mine,

I will take it back double. While you two sit holding your cocks, I'll be fucking her with mine."

The phone goes dead with a click.

I slam the receiver down and unleash a guttural roar, sweeping my arm across the desk. Papers scatter, and I hear glass shatter—an image of Charity on our wedding day looking up at me from the floor. Her image fractured like some twisted foreshadowing I refuse to accept. I don't care who or what I need to destroy—I will bring my wife home.

FORTY-TWO
Charity

I squint my eyes, trying to see through the watery film covering my vision. The throbbing in my head keeps time with my racing heartbeat. I shake my head, ignoring the bolts of pain that shoot through my body with every movement. I need to break free of the cobwebs that blur everything.

The first thing that comes into view is yellowing teeth. I fight against the bile that surges to my throat when the stench of stale alcohol and rot permeates the space between us. I flex my fingers and pull against the restraints around my wrists, testing my strength, assuring myself that nothing is broken. My eyes start to focus, and I slowly arrange the pieces. Silver slicked back hair, a round, leathered face. Cruelty etched in the lines around his almost black eyes, mirroring the heartless fake smile taking up my field of vision.

"My apologies. You were not to be harmed. Unfortunately, my men can sometimes get a bit … exuberant when following orders."

He steps aside, and two men come into view holding a third between them. The man is gagged and struggles against their grip.

"The first order of business, recompense. You see, Rhea, men like this," he nods toward the man in the middle, "are like wild beasts. They must be controlled, and if they can't be controlled, you must put them down."

I watch in horror as he pulls a gun from inside his suit coat and fires a single shot into the struggling man's chest. His body jerks and then slumps, the bloom of wetness spreading across the dead man's black shirt.

Unable to stop myself, I let loose a scream and jerk against the ropes binding me. The rough fibers bite into my wrists and ankles, every nerve in my body screaming, RUN!

The crack comes before the pain. A sharp burst of heat explodes across my cheek, and my head snaps to one side.

"Enough!" he scolds. "Compose yourself."

The pain brings back my focus, and I swing my head back toward him with a glare. I keep my eyes clamped on him as the man who was just murdered in front of me is dragged away, a trail of red streaking across the floor.

A hand snatches out and grabs my chin in a vice-like grip as he studies me, disgust roiling in my chest.

"He touched what wasn't his to touch. This will serve as a valuable lesson to any other man in my employ. This is your world now. Accept it."

I don't react to his words. I won't give him the satisfaction.

"Where is Sam?" I grit out.

"Oh, Rhea," he lets out a dark chuckle. "So much like your mother. Tied, helpless, and still worried about everyone else. It was her undoing, and it will be yours. I truly thought Mitchell would make this harder. You were so easy to lure out."

He lets go of my face and nods at one of his men, who places a chair in front of me, and he sits.

Keeping my frustration under control, I size him up.

"My name is Charity Johns—Mitchell," I bite out. "I don't know who Rhea is, but I am not her. My parents are dead. You promised to let my friend go if I did what you wanted. I kept up my end. I demand you keep yours." I force the rest out, even though I'm not sure it's true. "I know you know who my husband is. He will pay you or give you whatever you want. He doesn't need to know it was you. You let us go, and we'll forget this ever happened."

I watch as his face contorts, and I can feel the rage coming off him. "Do not mention that man in this house. He is nothing but a thief. You will come to heel, or I will break you piece by piece until you are begging to join your bitch mother in her grave." He looks to two of his men. "Take her."

Before I can respond, the black hood is pushed back over my head. I feel the binds cut away, and hard hands force me to stand. I try struggling against them, but I'm no match for them. I'm blind to where they're taking me, and although I'm terrified, I try to pay attention as I'm dragged. The ground underneath me is rough, maybe stone, and the air is musty. The men talk between themselves in a language I don't recognize. We reach a set of steps, and I'm held firmly while I try not to trip as we descend. The air grows cooler, and the goosebumps rise to the surface of my skin.

We come to an abrupt stop, and I hear the grinding of metal on metal before the hood is ripped from my head again, and I see the cage. Before I can protest, I'm pushed in, and the heavy door is closed with a loud clang.

Finding my courage, I yell after them, "Assholes!" I frantically look around the cell I've been put in. A stained mattress is shoved into one corner, and a bucket, which I assume serves as a toilet, in the other. The back wall of the iron-barred cage butts up against a stone wall, with adjoining cages on each side. I gasp as I take in the small figure bundled in a threadbare blanket in the cell next to me.

"Sam?"

Her back is to me, but I can see her blond hair peeking from the top of the blanket.

"Sam!" I say louder. "Sam, it's me. It's Charity. I'm here! Wake up!"

I see her begin to move. It's slow, and when her head finally tilts toward me, I catch my breath. Her beautiful face is swollen and bruised. There's a visible cut near her left eye, and blood is drying near her mouth.

"Charity?" she croaks.

Tears are flooding my vision as I frantically try to reach her through the bars separating us.

"I'm here! Oh God, Sam, what did they do to you? I'm so sorry!"

I watch helplessly as she starts slowly crawling toward me. We both break into sobs as she reaches out and we clasp each other.

"You shouldn't have come, Charity," she sobs. "It's what he wanted. You shouldn't have come!" she insists again.

"Shhh," I try to soothe her. "I've got you. Of course, I came. It's okay. We're going to be okay."

"Vardis is a madman!" she continues. "He keeps calling you Rhea. Oh god, Charity. They killed Freddy. They shot him right in front of me. I tried to fight. I tried to run."

Before I can respond, a shadow moves in front of our cage.

"What a sweet sight."

I look up and get my first full view of Nikos Vardis. I realize now how little attention I paid him at the gala. He doesn't look like a monster. He looks like a sad old man. He's average height, with a barrel chest. His wrinkled hands are small with fat, sausage-like fingers. Other than the evil evident in his dark eyes, there's nothing remarkable about him.

I try to hide my fury as I look up at him.

"I hope you killed whoever did this to her. She needs a doctor." I nod toward Sam. "You want any sort of cooperation from me, you get her a doctor now!"

He sighs and then leans in closer, his eyes turning into black steel.

"You think I need your cooperation? You overplay your hand. I should come in there and begin your training now," he leers at me. "Fortunately for you, there's no time. We will be leaving soon. You have five minutes."

"Leaving? Where? Where are you taking us? You promised to let her go!"

He lets out a low chuckle, turns on his heels, and walks away without another word.

"Sam, listen to me," I whisper urgently to her. "Cal will come for us. I know he will. No matter what, don't fight. We need to stay alive until Cal and Raz can get to us."

Hearing Raz's name ignites a spark in Sam's eyes. She grips my hands tighter and nods.

I look her over and softly ask, "Did they…"

She shakes her head, "No, none of them touched me like that. Not yet anyhow."

Before I can ask any more questions, the sound of footsteps echoes as they get closer. Four men appear, and I clamp onto Sam tighter. "Remember, do not fight!" I whisper.

The door to my cage is yanked open, and two guards rip me away from Sam. Before I can protest, a third pushes the black hood back over my head before a sting pierces my arm. I hear Sam scream "NO!" before everything goes black again.

FORTY-THREE
Cal

Three days. It's been three days since Charity and Sam disappeared. Raz and our men breached Vardis's compound, but they were already gone. There was no trace of them.

Neither of us has slept. Food is tasteless. We're running on fumes, and we're getting desperate for any lead we can find. Desperation is a feeling neither of us is familiar with.

As I pore over files and information, searching Vardis's history and holdings for any clue about where he's gone, Raz's tactics grow more brutal. I've counted five of Vardis's men that he's taken for interrogation—there are probably more. Their silence cost them the mercy of a swift death. We've returned to the men we were when we purged my father's empire of its filth.

Raz walks into my office and drops into the chair in front of me. His eyes are bloodshot, his cheeks are hollow, showing the toll our search is taking.

"Anything?" I ask.

He shakes his head, rubbing his cut-up knuckles.

I rub my hands over my face, the frustration mounting again, and slam my fist on the desk.

"They couldn't have just disappeared!" I growl.

Without a word, Raz reaches over and picks up one of the files on Vardis.

"I've already gone through it, Raz. There's nothing."

"Cal, fuck off. It can't hurt to have another set of eyes."

I arch a brow at him, but I let it go. I know the stress is getting to both of us. We can't afford to let Vardis drive a wedge between us.

I watch as he pages through the documents. He's halfway through the file when he stills.

"Cal, Charity's mother. She was Greek, yes?"

My head snaps up. "Yes, why?"

"Did Malcolm or Cormack ever mention her maiden name?"

"What did you find, Raz?" I ask, my voice urgent.

He stands up and slaps the file open on my desk, pointing at a name.

Petros Karakis.

I grab Charity's file and flip to the front, searching for any information on her mother that might be hidden in its pages, and there it is.

Eleni Karakis.

I take a breath.

Raz locks eyes with me. "Vardis is in business with Charity's uncle. There's no way he's told Karakis that his niece is alive, Cal. I know his reputation. He would have burned everything and everyone in his path to find her."

I nod, but say nothing.

Petros Karakis is one of the most ruthless men left over from my father's world. I remember how close we came to a war when he believed, rightfully, that my father had something to do with his sister's death. Instead, he destroyed a mutual rival, believing my father's lies.

"This is the thread, Cal. If you don't pull it, I fucking will. It's not just Charity on the line. Sam is the most innocent one in this fucking mess—the mess you could've avoided. Pull the fucking thread, Cal."

The challenge in his eyes is unmistakable. I want to push back. To remind him who is in charge here, but he's right. I know when I do this, I risk never seeing my Charity again, but at least she'll be alive.

I nod, accepting his judgment.

"Have the team track him down. Get a location and a number. It's time Petros learns his niece is alive."

Raz lets out a breath.

"Thank you, Brother. I know what this means and what it could cost you." He heads for the door and then stops. "For what it's worth, I saw the way she was with you. However it started, her feelings for you were real. This doesn't mean it's the end."

Raz's footsteps fade down the hall, leaving me alone. I pick up the fractured photo still face down on my desk. I turn it over, glass biting into my fingers, and stare at her smile. It's a candid photo. I remember the exact moment it was taken. Both of us were distracted by the people around us, but then our eyes met—the smile she didn't mean to give me, lighting up my world.

For a second, the room feels too small, my chest too tight.

When I tell Petros Karakis what I know, it will cost me everything.

I set the photo upright, blood smearing the frame.

Hold on, Charity. I'm coming. And God help anyone between us when I do.

FORTY-FOUR
Charity

I feel the hum before I hear it—a slight vibration gently shaking me awake. I struggle to lift my head, expecting to see my room at Cal's house, but everything is wrong. The air smells of rotten leather instead of the lavender and mahogany I've gotten used to. I squint, adjusting my eyes to the dim cabin, the round covered windows only allowing in a small streak of light. My mind races to put the pieces together of where I am and how I got here. I move my arms and, feeling the now familiar burn of rope binding me, my body starts to shake with rage.

"Goddammit! Why do you people keep doing this to me?" My throat burns in protest as I scream and pull against the restraints tying me to the faded tan leather chair.

Cold water splashes against my face, and he comes into view.

"Quiet or I'll make you quiet!" Vardis growls at me. He lowers himself into the chair across from me, his eyes narrowed.

I stop moving, clamping my mouth shut. He looks like a predator ready to go in for the kill, and something tells me not to push him.

I give him a slight nod of acknowledgement.

Leaning over, he wipes my face with his handkerchief, his putrid smell making my stomach lurch.

"Good. Now we talk."

I take a deep breath, not taking my eyes off him, and ask, "Where's Sam?"

He leans back and waves his hand dismissively. "She's in the back." Tilting his head, he studies me, his eyes glazing over for just a fraction. "You look so much like her when you're angry."

"We had a deal, Vardis. I followed your instructions—you have me. Let her go, please."

I watch his face contort as he slams his fist down on the armrest of his chair. He leans forward, grabbing my face in his fingers, and squeezes. "Don't you fucking dare talk to me about deals! I had a deal with Eleni, and I had a deal with Malcolm Mitchell," he sneers. "Deals mean NOTHING!" He lets me go abruptly and sits back in his chair, smooths over his white dress shirt, and straightens his tie.

My heart races and my breath heaves as I see how utterly unhinged he really is.

"Your friend is of no consequence." He looks down and begins picking imaginary lint from his black dress pants. "She might live, she might die. I might sell her, I might keep her for my stables. Maybe I'll give her to my men to play with." He looks up and locks eyes with me, the madness swirling. "Her fate is up to you, Rhea."

Gathering my strength, I close my eyes, take a deep breath, and ask, "Where are you taking us?"

"We are going to my island. Somewhere we won't be bothered."

My stomach drops. I've seen enough true crime documentaries to know that if we make it to that island, we might not ever be seen again. Chess flickers through my mind. I hear Cal's voice in my head, "Don't just look at the pieces in front of you, look at the whole board," he reminds me. "Sometimes the Queen only needs to survive long enough for the board to change."

"For how long?" I ask calmly.

"As long as it takes for you to remember who the fuck you are, Eleni. Now shut the fuck up until we land, or I'll gladly make you." He stands abruptly, walking away.

What the fuck? Eleni?

The realization of how delusional Vardis truly is slams into my chest. I don't know who he thinks I am, but it's not me. How am I supposed to bargain with a madman?

FORTY-FIVE
Cal

Time stands still as I stare at my cell phone lying on my desk, willing it to ring. Raz sits across from me, the tension palpable.

"He should've called by now," Raz grumbles.

When I called the numbers that Raz tracked down through our network, I left messages for everyone. "I have information on his sister." That should've been enough to pique his interest, but it's been hours, and we've heard nothing.

Both of us jump when the phone finally sounds, "Unknown Number" flashing across the screen. I lock eyes with Raz and press the speaker button.

"Mitchell, why the fuck are you calling me, and what do you mean by daring to speak of my sister?" I can hear the fury in Petros Karakis's voice.

If the stories are true, he already knows my position, and there's a red dot ready to take both Raz and me out if he doesn't like my next words.

"My apologies, Petros. Please believe that reaching out to you at this time was a last resort." I see Raz cringe at my word choice.

Before I can stop myself, I continue. "You are going to have a lot of questions, and I swear to you, I will give you all the answers I have. Rhea is alive. I'm sending you a picture now. I think you'll find the resemblance to her mother uncanny."

I quickly send the last photo I have of my wife, our wedding photo.

I hear his phone ping and then a deep intake of breath.

"Eleni…" he exclaims softly, the pain seeping through.

"Karakis, I know you want to kill me, and you're probably within your rights, but that will have to wait. Nikos Vardis has my wife, your niece, and I need your help getting her back.

"What the fuck do you mean by your wife?" He booms at me.

I close my eyes, willing my patience under control when Raz jumps in.

"This is Raziel Verrick. As Cal said, all of your questions will be answered, but right now, Rhea is in danger. We know you are doing business with Vardis. We also know that at one time, Eleni was promised to Vardis, but she chose Cormack Brennan. He's been harboring that grudge, and now he's taken Rhea as payment, Karakis. We don't need to tell you what that means."

"Mitchell?" His tone is deadly.

"I'm here."

"Was it your piece of shit father who took my Eleni?"

I close my eyes and take a deep breath. "Yes."

"And the other rumors? Are they true, Mitchell? Are you the one who killed the great Malcolm Mitchell?" His voice drips with sarcasm.

I stare at the phone and reply dryly, "Yes."

I hold my breath during the silence.

"I will have my answers. Where is Rhea now?" Petros demands.

I explain that Vardis has gone dark and that our contacts haven't been able to find him or the girls.

"Give me an hour. Nikos Vardis is a cockroach. I make it a point to know where cockroaches hide. If I let you live when this is done, Mitchell, you owe me. There will be no questions when I decide what that debt is. Do we understand each other?"

I look to Raz, knowing that whatever he demands, it will cost both of us. He nods, accepting the terms.

"Understood. Just find that motherfucker!"

FORTY-SIX
Charity

I'm left alone in the plane's cabin, which looks more like a lounge area, and take in my surroundings. The pale tan and dark wood hint at its one-time opulence, but time and neglect have dulled its luster, and the musty smell permeates the space. The windows are covered with panels that are the same color as the leather and give me no clue as to what time it is or where we might be going. I see a guard dressed in all black at the front of the cabin and an identically dressed man at the back, where I'm assuming the bathroom is—and, if the old movies I've watched ring true, the stateroom.

"I have to pee!" I announce, looking between the two men left in the room with me. Both of them seem to ignore me, so I say it louder. "I have to pee, now!" This time, the guard closest to where I think the bathroom is shrugs. "Hold it," he replies gruffly.

"Listen, asshole, either let me go to the bathroom or I swear to Christ I will piss right here. Who do you think will end up cleaning up after me?"

He looks across me to his counterpart at the front, and thankfully, the guard nods. The guard nearest to me walks over, unties me, and grabs me by the arm, hauling me up. He pushes me toward the back of the plane, where I spot two doors. I know Sam is behind one of them.

"Sam, I'm here!" I yell out to her. "I'm here, Sam, can you hear me?"

"Quiet!" the guard scolds. He shoves me into the closet-sized bathroom and slams the door. I lean against the door and close my eyes, fighting against the tears threatening to take over. I can't afford to break. It's what Vardis wants, and I refuse to give it to him.

I want to believe with every fiber of my body that Cal will find us. The image of Cal on our wedding day feels like a million years ago. The look of adoration and lust in his eyes before I walked to him to take our vows replay in my head. It may not have been love, but it was something. I have to believe it was enough. I need to keep Sam and me alive long enough for Cal and Raz to get to us.

I quickly use the toilet, wash my hands, and take a deep breath before opening the door, only to see the wall of the man in black blocking my way. He steps back and nods toward the main cabin. When I exit the bathroom, I stop short, seeing Vardis sitting at a small table that has appeared between the lounge seat and two captain chairs. The guard nudges me, and Vardis's black eyes meet mine.

"Sit," he demands, looking at the seat in front of me.

I slowly walk to the chair opposite him and lower myself, preparing myself for what might be coming next.

"We land in thirty minutes," he states matter-of-factly.

I force my face to stay neutral. "Land where?"

He ignores my question and lays a thick folder on the table between us. He nods at the folder as if he's giving me permission to look inside. I don't move, something in my gut warning me not to open it.

"Open it," he commands me. I straighten my shoulders and shake my head no.

"Stubborn just like your mother," I hear him mutter. When he reaches out, I brace myself expecting a slap, but instead, he flips the cover of the folder open, the image revealed making me gasp.

A smiling couple looks at each other in the photo, the love unmistakable in their smiling faces. A tiny child held between them, maybe two years old, her innocent hazel eyes peering back at me. It's the woman in the photo who grabs my attention. Although her hair is darker, almost black, I recognize her face. It's my face, my eyes, my smile.

I look up at Vardis, confused, and his look of smug satisfaction makes my stomach turn.

"Beautiful, isn't she? I warned her that crossing me would be at her peril." He reaches out and flips the photo over, revealing the next image, and I gag at the image in front of me.

Two bodies covered in blood, faces battered, the woman's clothes torn half off her, exposing her breasts, empty eyes staring out, seeing nothing.

My mind blurs. A scent I can't name floods my senses, red flashes before my eyes. A sound, a distant, sharp crack. Oh God, so much blood. A feeling of terror overwhelms me, and my stomach lurches again.

I force the bile back down and look back up at Vardis, his expression unchanged.

"Eleni Mara Karakis survived by her only daughter, Rhea Cormack Brennan." There's a tone in his voice that betrays how much he's enjoying this reveal.

I shake my head, fighting back the truth that seems to be flooding every part of my body. "No," I whisper.

Vardis reaches out and flips the photo over, revealing the next image. The man I now know as Malcolm Mitchell, Cal's father, holds a young girl on his knee, both smiling for the camera. The realization hits me with a slap. I recognize the couch, the wallpaper, and I can almost smell the cigarette smoke permeating the air. It's my foster family's home. The pieces of a puzzle I didn't know existed start rushing into the blank spots of what I thought my life was.

I look up at Vardis. Satisfied with the realization on my face, he closes the folder and gets up.

I'm too stunned and confused to say anything. I can only watch as my captor turns to leave, but pauses. Looking back, he states plainly, "Mitchell knew. He knew everything." Without another word, he stalks to the front of the plane, disappearing behind another door.

The deafening hum of the plane is the only sound I hear as I sit frozen by what I just saw in the folder. Cal couldn't have known, could he?

The sound of a door opening draws my attention, and I look up to see Sam. She's still in a haze, her gait unsteady. I stand up to rush to her, but before I can move, a guard's hand clamps down on my shoulder, forcing me back into my seat.

"Move," the guard behind Sam demands, giving her a shove.

"Leave her alone, asshole!" I yell at him as I fight against the hand restraining me.

Sam raises her head at the sound of my voice, and I see fresh bruises near her jaw and a distinct handprint on her throat. My vision goes red, but Sam stares at me, shaking her head no. That's when I notice the scratch marks on the guard's face, fresh blood beading to the surface. I lock eyes with Sam as they continue toward me, and she gives me a ghost of a satisfied smile.

The guard forces her down into the seat next to me, her eyes never leaving mine.

"You sit. Stay. Move, and I shoot you."

Sam's fingers brush against mine, and I inch my hand closer, our pinkies hooking. I look into her eyes, and I see my message to her reflected back—*we're not done yet.*

I feel the plane begin to descend, and wonder what fresh hell is waiting for us when we land.

FORTY-SEVEN
Cal

The ring of my cell phone jolts Raz and me out of our blur. I see Petros Karakis's name flash on the screen. Without hesitating, I hit the speaker.

"Petros?"

"They're on Astypalaia. Your men will converge with my men in Athens. There is a private hangar. A plane will be waiting to take you to the island. I have already ordered my men into position. I am sending you the schematics of the island and its compound now. I've alerted my contacts with the Greek authorities. They will not interfere."

My heart hammers as I ask, "Will you be joining us?"

"Impossible until Vardis is disposed of. I do not need the war that entering his territory will cause over a girl that I'm not convinced exists. You are the son of a liar, and photos mean nothing—easily faked."

"Then why help at all, Karakis? What do you get out of this?"

I hear a dark chuckle. "You've lost your edge, Mitchell. If you kill Vardis, I absorb his territory, and you owe me. If the girl is Eleni's daughter, I get my niece back, and you owe me. If you die... well, these things happen. You have forty-eight hours to get your men to Greece and dispose of the cockroach."

With a click, the line goes dead.

I bristle at his words, but my only thought is getting to my wife. I will deal with Karakis when Charity is safe, back in my arms, where she belongs.

"Cal, the men are on the way to the plane. We're wheels up in thirty."

Without thinking, I scoop up my wife's wedding rings and the chess piece, an ache in my chest at the memory of how pleased she was to have taken my queen. I crack the already broken frame and cram her picture in my vest pocket.

"Let's go get our women. And Raz, if Karakis or any of his men turn on us and interfere—kill them."

Raz smiles ruthlessly, his soldier persona fully in place. "It will be my pleasure."

The matte-black interior of the plane screams our mission's intent. Its engines are louder than we've become accustomed to in the past years since deposing my father. Raz has secured six men, all former special forces contacts, all deadly and worth the price we paid for their loyalty. They are men who follow orders without hesitation or conscience. I watch and listen as Raz and the men pore over the schematics Karakis provided. He briefs the men and directs each man in their role. He's slipped so easily into the Raz who came up with me through my father's ranks—controlled, strategic, measured. I've watched him make the men review the plan again and again over the long flight. He's prepared them for any contingencies, including betrayal from Karakis's men.

I fight the restlessness threatening to take over as we near Athens. I feel Raz's eyes on me, and he gives me a confident nod. He's ready. Our men are ready.

I'm coming for you, Hurricane. Hold on a little longer.

FORTY-EIGHT
Charity

When the plane finally touches down, I'm surprised when we aren't bound and blindfolded. Each of us has two guards who herd us off the plane and then into a large black SUV with black windows. I scan around for Vardis, but he's nowhere to be found. I don't have time to question before the SUV speeds out of the airport hangar. Sam leans against me, partly because there's little room in the back seat for both of us and the two guards on either side, and partly because of the exhaustion I see on her face. Neither of us speaks, but we don't need to. I try to peer around the guard to get some idea of where we are or where we're going, but all I see is the black tint of the windows.

My instincts scream to fight, to do something, but Sam's weight against me reminds me why that would be an asinine move. I know Vardis will not hesitate to hurt or kill her if I make any attempt to escape. I listen to the hum of the wheels beneath us, and after what feels like only a few minutes, I feel us begin to climb and swerve as if we're driving up a mountain. The guard sways into me as we make a sharp turn, the smell of unwashed man hitting me, making me gag. The ping of gravel hitting the underside of the vehicle fills the space, and my ears give a small pop, confirming that we're climbing. Where the fuck are they taking us?

We slow again and then come to an abrupt stop. Sam looks at me, her eyes wide, and I give her hand a slight squeeze before the men beside us pull us from the car. The only lights visible are coming from the large house in front of us. I scan around us, trying to take in any detail as quickly as I can. The air is salty, I can hear waves crashing somewhere in the darkness, and the warm breeze tells me we must be somewhere coastal. I know Vardis is Greek, so maybe the Mediterranean?

The guards don't speak to either of us as they push us into the side entrance of a white stone building. The hallway we're herded into smells musty with age, and the temperature drop is jarring, making me shiver. As we're forced down a dim corridor, I notice there are no pictures on the wall, no feeling that this place has been lived in. The guards still say nothing short of barking orders. We make a turn down another bare hallway and are stopped short when we reach a door. The guard in front steps to a keycard reader, swipes the card, and I note where he stores it in his pockets. It's something, and I take that detail and lock it away just in case it might become useful. We're shoved through the doorway into a dark room before the door is slammed and locked behind us.

Sam immediately feels along the wall until she finds a switch, the click deafening in the silence. Yellow light flickers on, filling the room, and for the first time in days, I take a breath before grabbing Sam and hugging her, both of us silently breaking for a moment. When we pull apart, I put my finger to my lips, signaling her not to talk yet, as I look around the sparse room, my time with Cal reminding me we're probably being watched. There are two single beds but no other furniture. Off to the side, there's a small bathroom behind a half wall, leaving little privacy, but I think that's the point. I search along the ceiling for any signs of a camera, but there's nothing obvious.

"I think we should be okay if we whisper. They shouldn't be able to hear us, and I don't see any cameras," I tell Sam. Finally able to take her in, I reach out and touch her bruised face, flinching when she winces.

"God, I'm so sorry, Sam," I whisper to her.

"Charity, I need you to stop right now. I shouldn't have left Cal's. Raz told me to stay. If I'd listened…" her voice trails off.

I lean in, our foreheads touching.

"So what was so important that you just had to have it?" I ask, trying to add any lightness I can. If these are the only moments we get, I don't want to spend them on what-ifs.

She rolls her eyes. "When I tell you…"

"What?" I whisper. "Forget your vibrator?"

She huffs out something like a laugh. "No. I was getting lingerie. To—" She swallows. "To surprise Raz when he got home."

I blink. Then stare. Then the absurdity of it hits me square in the chest.

"Sam. When Raz finds out all of this happened because you went shopping for a nightie, he would've ripped off anyway—" I clamp a hand over my mouth, trying to choke down a hysterical laugh. "Oh my God." The laugh breaks through anyway, and Sam covers her own mouth to stifle hers. A loud bang jolts us out of the moment, and we both go stiff waiting, but not knowing what we're waiting for.

I grab Sam's hand, and we move further into the room and climb onto one of the beds, the springs whining underneath us.

The door swings open, and two guards enter the room, one carrying a tray of food. I see another guard standing right outside the door. It occurs to me at that moment how they all look the same. There's nothing that makes one stand apart from the other. The guard places the tray on the empty bed, looks us both over, and walks out of the room, with the second guard following behind him. The door closes, and we hear a click. It's only then that we both exhale at the same time.

We crane our necks trying to see what's on the tray, neither of us ready to move. It's sandwiches wrapped in plastic, chips, and bottles of water.

"Do you think they drugged it?" Sam asks.

I answer her with a shrug.

"I mean, it's wrapped, and they haven't been shy about using the needle. I say we take our chances."

I give her a nudge. "We're going to need our strength because we are not going down without a fight."

I get up and bring the tray back to the bed that's somehow become our safe space. We rip into our meal, eating in silence, the crunching of the chips almost deafening.

Sam finally breaks the silence.

"Why did you come after me, Charity? You had to know that he wasn't going to let me go."

"Sam, there is nowhere in this universe that I would ever not come after you. He took you because of me. I had to take the chance that Vardis would keep his word. Not going after you was never an option." I reach out and squeeze her hand.

We finish up and brush the crumbs off the bed. I lean back against the wall, and the weight of the past few days crashes over me. What the hell is my life right now? Three days ago, I was Charity Johnston, and today I'm Rhea Brennan. The photos of my birth parents holding me. The photo of their mangled bodies. Grief for people I don't remember and the life I could've had washes over me. Cal knew? Why? I lean into Sam, and she puts her head on my shoulder. I feel her breathing relax, and soon we're both drifting off. I try to fight it, I need to stay alert, but I'm so tired. I let myself slip into a fitful sleep.

FORTY-NINE
Charity

We're startled awake by the sound of the door crashing open. A guard steps into the room and throws a stack of items on the empty bed.

He turns to us, looks us over with a glare, and points at the open shower. "You. Clean," he grunts. Both of us watch wordlessly as he grabs the dinner tray and stalks out of the room.

"Christ," Sam huffs.

I walk over and rummage through the stack. There are a few light sundresses, towels, and a bar of soap. I take a breath and turn to face Sam, hoping that I'm showing all the bravery I don't feel.

"Okay, here's what we're going to do. We're taking a shower—we both need one. We're going to play the bastard's game," I whisper.

Sam is looking at me suspiciously. "Charity, why aren't we dead? Why does he think your name is Rhea? What aren't you telling me?"

I sit down next to her and relay what I know. I tell her about Vardis, my birth parents, and that Cal knew and kept it from me. By the time I'm done, I'm sweating and shaking.

"Wow," Sam replies softly, looking stunned. "That's, um, a lot."

I gape at her.

"That's it? Just, that's a lot?"

"Well, I'd say that's really fucked up, but I don't think you need me to tell you that. Didn't feel helpful," she shrugs and smirks at me. "Is that it?"

I give her a huff and manage a smile back at her.

"There's more, I'm sure, but I can't think about that now. Right now, we focus on staying alive, and hopefully, he doesn't move us again. We need to buy time for Cal and Raz to get to us."

Sam doesn't say anything, just nods in silent agreement.

"They will come Char…" she scrunches up her face. "Rhea? So do I call you Rhea now?"

The absurdity of this entire situation hits me, and I start to laugh. "I have no idea! Can I get back to you on that?"

"They will find us, Charity. Cal has already shown you how far he'll go to protect you. Besides, after the night Raz and I had, he'll want seconds." She flashes me a smile and a wink, then winces from the pain it causes her battered face. Everything in me is screaming to ask about the bruises, but I can't. There will be time to talk about all of this when it's over.

I roll my eyes at her and throw a towel and the soap at her. "Go clean yourself, heathen!"

She makes her way over to the small area serving as a bathroom, her battered body stiff and slow. I turn my head, trying to offer her what little privacy I can. As she strips out of the clothes she's been wearing for days, I stifle a gasp when I see the bruises out of the corner of my eye. The entire side of her torso is covered in angry blacks and purples, jagged scrapes and cuts mar her pale skin. Sam fought, and she fought hard. The guilt of her getting swept up in my mess engulfs me, and I choke back my tears.

Stop It! Tears won't help her. Don't put your bullshit on her. Keep it together and get her out—that's how you help her now.

After we've both showered, wearing our days-old underwear because of course the bastard didn't supply any, we almost relax.

"How much time do you think we have before they come back?" Sam asks quietly.

I answer her honestly. "I don't know. I don't think it will be long."

I barely get the words out before the door crashes open and four guards stomp into the room. They stalk toward us, two of them grab me, and the other two hold Sam down as she starts to struggle. As they start dragging me out of the room, I twist in their grip, trying to look back at Sam, but they block my view.

"Sam!" I scream. The only response I get is the door slamming behind us.

I pull back from them, trying to fight the hold they have on me.

"Slow the fuck down. You don't need to drag me, I'll walk you assholes!" I scream at them. "Do you think Nikos will appreciate you manhandling me? Ask your buddy Van how that worked out!" I don't know if it will work, but it's the only card I have to play.

They come to a stop, and I hear one of them growl at me.

"You walk then," the guard on my left grunts.

I straighten myself, lift my chin, and walk, their vice-like grips steering me where they expect me to go.

I try to count the turns and get some idea of where they're taking me, but the hallways look all the same. We come to a door, and when it opens, the first thing that hits me is the light. I squint, trying to focus against the blinding glare. When we step into the large space, the overwhelming musty smell of age hits me, and I scrunch my nose. I look around and am barely able to take in the dusty furniture and cracked paintings before they steer me down more hallways. The carpets are dirty and worn. I notice closed doors intermittently spaced along the corridors and can't help but wonder what horrors hide behind them.

We turn another corner, and the guards turn me to face the doors before giving it a knock.

"Enter," Vardis's voice bellows, making my stomach roil.

The guards push open the door and nudge me to move forward.

I step into the room. I shake my head and steady my hands. I try to own the space I'm standing in, hoping my bravado hides how truly frightened I am of this monster.

"Ah, Rhea. Welcome!" His smarmy smile causes my skin to crawl, but I refuse to let myself react. I won't give him that satisfaction.

He waves a hand toward a worn leather couch, "Come in, sit."

At Vardis's nod, both of the guards release me, and I carefully make my way over, inching by him to avoid any physical contact.

"I apologize for the poor accommodations. Our departure required haste, and I was unable to make the necessary arrangements. Soon enough."

He walks over to his desk, where a decanter of brown liquid sits half full. He fills two tumblers, walks over, and holds one of the glasses out to me. "Go on, take it. Metaxa… It's what you Americans call brandy, but better."

I watch him, taking in his overly friendly demeanor, then hesitantly take the glass from his hand, sniffing at the liquor. The smell of dried fruit, and almost too sweet, spiced honey hit me. The warmth of the drink adds to the suffocating weight of the room.

He lowers himself into a chair across from me and takes a long swallow of the drink.

"Go on," he nods at the glass, "It's good. It tastes like home."

I take a deep breath, reminding myself that I need to play along, and take a small sip, wincing at the syrupy sweetness.

Vardis watches me and chuckles. "You will get used to it, Kóri mou. I will teach you many things."

I feel a cold shiver run down my spine at his words, and I grip my glass.

"What does that mean? Kóri mou?" I ask, afraid of the answer.

"Yes, we will need to work on your Greek. It means 'my girl,' which you are now," he says matter-of-factly.

My spine stiffens at his possessive declaration, but I don't say anything. If I can keep him talking, maybe I can learn where we are.

He tilts his head and studies me, and I feel my face grow hot under his scrutiny.

"It is so incredible how much you look like her. Hardly any trace of that Irish bastard," his voice is almost wistful, making alarm bells set off in my head. If I don't do something, he'll slip into that place where he sees Eleni, not me. I need him to see me right now.

"My mother," I start, carefully measuring my tone. "What can you tell me? You seem to have known her well, and I've been told nothing."

I watch as his face brightens, and it's almost as terrifying as his anger.

"Eleni was beautiful, and she was also brilliant. Not cunning like you, but I do see her fire in you. Fierce, and strong but tender."

"How…" I stutter, feeling conflicted at how much I need the answers. "How did you meet her?"

He looks down at his drink, and for a moment, I see the brokenness. "Our families were long-time friends. Your mother and I were promised to each other. She was much younger than me, but no matter." He waves a hand dismissively before continuing. "We were to make an unbreakable alliance. You do not know the power you should have been born in, Rhea." He clears his throat, straightens, and I see the monster return.

"Instead, she ran away. Ran away to fucking Cormack Brennan. I'd have killed them both myself if Mitchell hadn't."

My eyes widen, and I feel the blood rush from my body.

I watch as he registers my shock and delight dances in his eyes.

"Oh, did your dear husband not tell you?" he chuckles darkly.

"But—" I protest, but Vardis stops me with a look.

"Enough. No more talking about the past. It no longer matters. You are here now. Things have been made right." He finishes his drink and looks down at his watch. "They should be finished now. I will have a dress brought to you, and you will join me for dinner." He walks briskly to the door and gives it a knock before turning back to me. The two guards enter the room.

"Take her back but blindfold her. My little fox is too smart for her own good. No need to fill her head with fantasies of escaping me."

One of the guards steps behind me, and a black cloth is secured over my eyes.

"You don't need to do this, Nikos. I'm not trying to fight you." I try to convince him. I need him to believe that I'll be compliant if I'm to gain any freedom.

I feel his breath against my neck and hear him inhale, taking in my scent, and I jolt.

"Please remember, Rhea, the more you fight me, the more Sam will be punished for your actions. Be good, Kóri Mou, and all will be well."

Before I can say anything more, the guards grab me by the arms and lead me back to my room.

FIFTY
Charity

When we get to the door of the room Sam and I are being held in, I hear the beep of the keypad before the blindfold is ripped off, and I'm shoved into the room. Before I can look back, the door slams behind me.

My eyes go to Sam, curled up in the corner of the bed we've been sharing. When I hear her whimper, my mouth goes dry, and I rush over to her. She's not in the dress she had on when I left. Instead, she's in a black low-cut tank top.

"Sam?" I whisper as I gently reach for her.

"Don't touch me!" she screams and pulls away from me. Her head snaps up, but she looks at me like I'm a stranger.

"Sam, it's me. What happened?"

She snaps out of her fog. When she turns toward me and sees me, I watch wordlessly as she starts to crumble. Her shoulders shake, her body trying to catch its breath.

I scan her body, looking for any sign of what happened when I was taken from the room. Then I see it.

Just inside the hollow of her neck, the skin is raised and angry red. I try to make sense of what I'm seeing: the letters N and V inside a tight circle. I search my mind for where I've seen the mark before. Vardis's ring. I have to fight back the bile rushing to my throat at the sight. Oh God, he fucking branded her.

She finally lets me pull her in. I don't say anything. I just hold her, my own tears wetting my face.

I'm not sure how long we sit wrapped in each other, before I finally softly ask, "Do you want to tell me what happened?"

She stiffens and pulls away from me, and I let her go.

"After you left, the two guards that held me…" I watch as her eyes glaze over, like she's reliving it, and my heart screams for her.

"Two other guards came in. They were saying things, but I couldn't understand them. The more I tried to ask what they wanted, the angrier they seemed to get. Before I knew what was happening, they tore my dress off and pinned me to the bed." My breath hitches, but I don't say anything.

"God Charity, their hands. They kept grabbing, pinching, and laughing. They were fucking laughing." I watch as she angrily wipes a stray tear from her face. "I don't even know where it came from. I just saw this thing come at me. Do you know what it's like to smell your own skin burn, because I do."

"I hurt so fucking much! There isn't a part of my body that doesn't hurt."

"It's okay, Sam." I know my words are a mistake as soon as I say them.

Her face contorts, and I can see her rage coming to the surface.

"Fuck, Sam, that's not…" I start before she cuts me off.

"Okay?" She scowls. "Seriously? Do I fucking look okay to you, Charity? Where are your marks? Have they touched you? Have they beaten YOU? Why haven't Cal and Raz found us? Where are they, Charity? They should have found us by now!" She shoves at me and I don't fight her.

"I've got Nikos Vardis's goddamned initials burnt into my skin," she screams at me, "don't fucking tell me it's okay!"

I lower my head and stare at my hands.

She's right. None of this is fucking okay. I don't know how to save her, or save us. Sam turns away from me. The fight is leaving both of us, and I don't know how to stop it.

When the door bangs open again, neither of us reacts.

The scene repeats itself. Two guards enter, one throws something on the bed, grunts, and they leave. I'm numb.

When I finally walk over to see what the guard left this time, I gag. I lift the thin red garment. It's red with thin straps, and other than its length and color, it could be a replica of my wedding dress. The memory of my wedding day makes me ache. Cal. His smile. His touch. It's breaking me all over again in real time. I collapse to my knees and sob.

I feel Sam move behind me. She takes the dress from my hands.

"Sick fucking asshole," she huffs before throwing it back on the bed with disgust.

"Get up!" she demands.

I don't move—my limbs won't work.

"Goddammit, Charity, get the fuck up!"

I look up at her from the floor and see her determination back.

She grabs me by the arms and pulls me up, wincing through her own pain.

"He doesn't get to win. Do you hear me? Don't you dare let them win. Not Vardis, not Cal."

I wipe my eyes and look into hers. "Sam, I'm—" she cuts me off.

"Jesus, we have to stop. This isn't our fault. Neither of us did anything, other than get caught up in something we had no part in. We need to keep our shit together. Now, what happened when they took you to Vardis? What's with the dress?"

I shake my head. "We talked. He told me about my mother, how he knew her, how Cal's father killed both my parents." I take a deep breath, not wanting to finish, knowing that when I say the next part out loud, there will be no coming back, even if they reach us in time. "He said that Cal knew. He didn't just know who my real parents were. He knew that Malcolm killed them both." I close my eyes, my heart quietly breaking at the betrayal.

Sam's eyes go wide with shock.

"That bastard! He kept all of that from you and then married you? I'm going to fucking kill Raz!"

Seeing Sam turn her rage at our situation on Raz tells me she's still with me.

We're still okay.

"This doesn't have anything to do with Raz. This is all Cal's doing. We don't even know if Raz knows any of this."

She scoffs at me. "Don't you dare defend him. We both know he knew. Neither of them does anything without the other being involved. It's actually kind of weird now that I think about it. What else did he say? Did he give any idea of what he's planning?"

I think back on the conversation, reaching for anything that might help.

"I don't think he plans on moving us. He believes he's safe here. He thinks that now he's got me here…he thinks I'm 'his.' He said something about renovations happening soon."

I can see Sam's mind working. "That makes sense, actually. I'm no expert, and maybe I'm wrong, but I don't think he plans on selling me. I can't see anyone else accepting me with his initials on my skin."

I wince at the reminder of the mark, and my eyes immediately go to it. I feel Sam's eyes on me.

"Hey, Charity?"

I raise my eyes to hers.

"What did you see? Were you able to see outside? I think we're near an ocean or the sea. I could smell salt on the guard's clothes. It reminded me of visiting the beach when I was a kid."

I tell her about the hallways and the room with the enormous windows, the dinginess. "This place hasn't been lived in a while—that was obvious."

"How many guards did you see?"

It dawns on me how empty the hallways were. "None."

Feeling our first concrete glimmer of hope, we smile at the same time.

"We're a good team. If those two lying bastards can't save us, we save ourselves. I'm starting to believe what you said before. We just need to stay alive long enough for the board to change."

She picks the dress back up and tosses it to me.

"Get ready. You have a dinner to go to. Try to get as much out of him as you can, but be careful."

I nod and start changing.

Once I'm dressed, Sam and I sit on the bed and wait, the air thick with our nerves.

As if on cue, the door swings open, and I stand before they get through the doorway.

One stands by the door while two stalk toward me. I'm past scared, now I'm annoyed.

Fuck this.

"Only three this time?" I taunt.

I walk toward them, determined to escort myself. I almost make it by them before an arm swings out and a sharp tug of my hair jolts me back.

"Get off her, asshole." I hear Sam scream before she lunges at the guard. Before she can get to him, the other guard steps in front, shoving her back with too much force. I see Sam hit the stone wall, her head making a cracking sound before crumpling to the floor.

"Sam!" I scream before being pulled from the room.

FIFTY-ONE
Charity

I struggle against the men who are holding me. I feel one of the straps of the dress slipping, but I don't care. I don't care about my dignity. I only care about Sam.

"Get her a doctor, you assholes," I scream at them.

They ignore me as they drag me further away from her.

By the time we reach our destination, I'm nearly hysterical. The guard behind me pushes me into a room, and I stop short.

Vardis stalks toward me, rage in his eyes. Without a word, his hand flies out and lands on my right cheek with a sharp slap, my head swinging from the impact.

"Compose yourself, Eleni!" he thunders. "I will not have my wife acting like an untamed animal!" He turns to the guard and growls, "Leave us!"

Eleni. Oh fuck. He thinks I'm her again.

I straighten myself, realizing what I need to do. Maybe being my mother's ghost will get us out of here.

"I'm sorry, Nikos, but my friend—she's hurt. She needs a doctor. I'm worried about her."

He studies me for a moment, and I see the confusion flash over his eyes before he can mask it.

"My men will take care of it. Now, be a good pet and come sit." He places his hand on my lower back and nudges me toward the table.

There are two places set, and I carefully lower myself into the chair next to the head of the table. Two dark glossy green rolls, veins visible on the skin, sit on the plate before me. A faint lemon-and-herb scent wafts from the strange-looking food. My stomach growls but nothing about what's in front of me looks appetizing.

Vardis sits and tucks his napkin into the neck of his shirt. His paunchy stomach stops him from getting too close to his plate. I would laugh at how cliché this all is if I weren't so terrified.

I watch as he picks up one of the oily rolls, stuffs it into his mouth, and licks his fingers. My stomach lurches.

He nods at my plate. "Go on, eat. I remember how much you used to love Dolmades. I had my chef make them just for you, my love. They are not as good as my mother's, but it's close."

Feeling his eyes on me, I pick up my knife and fork. I want nothing more than to drive the knife into his neck, but if I do, Sam and I are as good as dead, whether he dies or not.

I cut a small piece and slowly raise it to my mouth, chewing carefully. The tangy, earthy flavor overwhelms my senses. Another time, under different circumstances, I might enjoy them. But now, now I'm only focused on getting through this ridiculous charade so I can get back to Sam.

I begin to cut another piece when Vardis wipes his hands on his napkin and pours me a glass of wine from the decanter.

"So tell me, Wife, how was your day?"

His use of the word "wife" feels like an assault, and I drop the silverware. I can't do this.

"Eleni, look at me when I speak to you!" he demands.

I lift my gaze and lock eyes with him.

"I am not my mother, and I am not your fucking wife! My name is Charity Mitchell. My husband is Calahan Mitchell. And you are fucking delusional if you think my mother ever loved you!"

As if my words reach in and grab whatever sanity he has left, I see the realization wash over him.

"You disrespectful whore!" He booms, slamming his fist down on the table.

I push back, ready to make a run for it, but he grabs me before I get far. He picks me up, slamming my back on the table. I thrash against his hold, but he's too heavy. Forcing my hands over my head, he leans over me and licks the side of my face. I cringe, trying to pull away from his stench.

"It's time to come to heel, Rhea. I will teach you not to defy me." His tone is deadly cold.

He adjusts his grip until one hand is wrapped around both wrists. His contorted face looms over me while he rattles off words in a language I don't understand. I don't need to—his intent is crystal clear. He reaches down and I feel him fumbling with his pants. He pushes my dress up, rips away my underwear, and grinds into me. I squeeze my eyes shut, trying to brace myself for what's coming— but there's nothing. I look up at him. He's breathing heavy, his face red with rage, and I realize as much as he wants to—he can't do it. The absurdity must register on my face before I can stop it. He snarls, rears his fist back— but I hear nothing but a roar.

"Get your fucking hands off my wife!"

FIFTY-TWO
Cal

We land in Athens ahead of schedule and taxi directly to Karakis's private hangar. We're on the outskirts of the city, out of sight of the usual authorities. There's a smaller plane ready for us. Along with the six men we have, Karakis has four men waiting for us—two have already gone ahead to the island as scouts. According to Karakis's men, this should be an easy, clean operation. They've counted approximately twenty men around Vardis's compound. His men are known to be well-trained, but still no match for the hell we're bringing to his doorstep.

As soon as we hit the air for the forty-five-minute flight, Raz reruns the briefing. The men will provide cover so he and I can get in clean. They are equipped with assault rifles with suppressors. Raz and I are equipped with the bare minimum needed for close-quarter combat, a semi-automatic handgun, and Bowie knives. As we get closer to the abandoned airstrip where the SUVs will be waiting, courtesy of Karakis, I stand.

"One more detail. Listen to me and listen well. If you find our women, you neutralize any threat, and you radio immediately. Under no fucking circumstances do any of you touch them. Am I understood?" I look around the hold and wait until every man nods their acknowledgment before locking eyes with Raz. A silent message crosses between us. There is no room for failure.

The plane lands, and we deboard, piling into the vehicles. We split off in one direction while the other speeds off in another. My adrenaline is spiked, and my heart feels like it will pound its way out of my chest. I look at my right-hand man. Unlike me, he's locked in. His face is stone as he checks his weapon one last time, showing nothing but calculated efficiency.

Although the air is still uncomfortably warm on the island, the fog coming in off the water and the waning moon help hide our approach. As we get closer, the driver cuts the headlights, driving in almost complete darkness. The drop-off spot is rocky and uneven, and as we silently make our way to Vardis's property, I have one thought— get my wife out alive. I don't care if I make it, but she has to. There is no world without Charity in it.

Raz and I each have a man on our flank, and it isn't long before I see the compound come into view and hear the first pops of gunfire. We speed up our approach, the other team already having breached the perimeter. The iron gates are flung open as if we're being invited into the devil's lair. The gunfire increases, and I see a few of

Vardis's men fall. I don't take the time to confirm that they're dead. My only mission is to get into the house. As we come to our breakaway point, Raz gives me a nod, then splits off to the side of the house following the plan to the letter.

Gun in hand, I approach the front door. Before I can enter, someone steps out from the shadows. I raise my weapon, but the man drops before I get a shot off. I scan the house's interior. Old, worn, it reeks of Vardis. I hear more gunfire, but I keep my eyes trained on my surroundings. I race through the house, opening doors, searching for any sign that Charity is here. I see movement down one of the hallways and, without hesitation, fire my gun, dropping the man before he sees me. I'm getting closer—I can feel her.

I take two more of Vardis's men out and swing open the last door. I see him. It all flashes too quickly. Vardis. Charity pinned beneath him, her clothing shoved above her legs, his fist raised—about to strike. I can't get a clean shot. I can't risk shooting her. With a roar, I fly across the room. I tackle him, sweeping him off her. We land on the floor and I strike him with my gun again and again. His arm flies up, grabbing at me. He wrestles me for the gun. I hear the bang, and it flies out of my hand.

The last thing I hear before the darkness overtakes me is my wife's scream.

FIFTY-THREE
Charity

I hear the roar, but everything is a blur. Vardis's weight is thrown off me, and I see him—Cal. Oh God—Cal! My heart leaps inside my chest, but there's no time for celebrations yet.

I watch, horrified, as he smashes his gun into Vardis's face over and over. They struggle, and a deafening crack fills the air as the gun goes off. A scream rips from my throat as I watch Cal's body jolt and then slump on top of our enemy.

Vardis rolls Cal's body off him, and I can see the blood seeping across the floor. Both Vardis and I lock eyes on the gun at the same time, and I watch as he begins dragging his injured body toward the gun.

"No!" I scream. My hand searches for the knife I know was on the table, and when I have it in my grasp, I launch myself on him.

I stab the table knife into his neck, pull it out, and stab again, and again, and again. Fury takes over. Even though

I'm covered in his blood, I don't stop until he's limp underneath me.

I crawl to Cal through the blood-slicked white stone floor.

"Cal!" I instinctively kiss his face, my hands searching his body to find where the blood is coming from.

"No, no, no! You do not get to do this to me, Cal Mitchell! Don't you fucking come all this way to just die on me! Don't you dare make me a widow, you bastard!" I scream at him.

I tear open the tactical vest he's wearing, and I see the blood soaking his black t-shirt, and I press my hands, putting as much pressure as I can on the wound.

I don't hear the door open. I don't see the man who storms into the room. I focus all my energy and will into keeping my husband alive.

"Charity, MOVE!" Something shoves me, and before I turn my rage toward it, Raz comes into focus.

"Raz?" I croak. "Blood. There's too much blood." I look down at my hands, Cal's blood mixing with Vardis's blood.

"Charity, you need to help me now," he commands. "There's no time for panic. You've brought him this far— help me save him now."

I watch as he rips Cal's t-shirt. I can see Cal's skin going paler by the second. I start to panic at the realization that I'm watching him die.

Raz rolls him and searches for something before nodding to himself.

"It's a through-and-through wound. Good. Grab whatever you can to stop the bleeding."

I get up, run to the table, grab my unused napkin and the cloth placemats, and rush back to Cal, handing them to Raz.

"Good!" He rolls the napkin up and places it over the exit wound under his right shoulder.

"Hold this, right here. Pressure, Charity, as much as you can muster."

He grabs the placemat and does the same, clamping it over the entrance wound, the pressure pushing a groan out of Cal's incoherent body.

"Cal, it's Raz. We've got you, brother. I need you to hold on, man. We're going to get you to the hospital, but they won't treat a dead man, so let's not waste the trip, yeah?"

Raz touches his earpiece and barks something into the air. I don't comprehend what he's saying—my only focus is pushing all my will to Cal to survive. To live.

Seconds later, four men pound into the room, and Raz begins barking orders I don't hear. I feel hands tugging at my arms.

"Charity, you have to let go now. We need to get him to the hospital now. Let him go, Charity. We've got this now." Raz's voice sounds like a faraway echo.

He peels me away, holding me back, and the men roll Cal onto the tablecloth, making a makeshift gurney, and start leaving with him.

"NO!" I scream. "I need to go with him!" I fight against his hold and scream again, "Raz, I need to go with him. He needs me!"

Raz turns me and gives me a hard shake. "Charity, look at me!" His gruff tone snaps me out of my fog, and I look up at him.

"You did good. You did so, so good, but there's no room in the helicopter for us. We're going to go now. We'll meet them at the hospital, but I need to know if you're okay. Are you hurt?"

"I'm fine. Please let's go!"

It hits me in that moment.

"Oh God, Raz—Sam! She's hurt, we have to go get Sam!" I feel myself spiraling. Sobs break from my body, and I can't seem to stop them. Firm arms wrap me in an embrace.

"We got her, Charity. She's already at the hospital. Take a breath. Breathe."

I squeeze my eyes shut and breathe, getting myself somewhat under control even though I want to rip my skin open to get away from all that I'm feeling.

"Good," he rumbles. "Now, let's go. They both need to see us when they wake up."

He catches my face in his hands. "You did so well, Charity. Thank you for saving them."

He takes me by the hand and leads me away from the blood-covered room.

FIFTY-FOUR
Charity

I barely hear the beeping of the machines anymore. It's been twenty-four hours since Cal and Sam were airlifted to Athens. Raz has been handling most of the arrangements since I have no documentation of who I am or what I am to either of them; he's Cal's next of kin. Cal needed surgery and is still getting blood transfusions, but the doctors are optimistic that he'll make a full recovery. They stressed that the first forty-eight hours are the most critical. I log the hours in my head and watch him for any signs, better or worse.

Sam's treatment was a bit trickier. We agreed that keeping Sam's family in the dark was best for now. It's up to her if she wants them to know about all that's happened. I'm not sure how Raz got the hospital to go along with it, but it won't surprise me if Athens has a new Mitchell trauma center by next year. We haven't spoken much, other than brief moments when he checks on them. He's mostly pacing up and down the halls outside their

301

room, doing damage control or whatever it is that Raz does.

I get up, stretch, and rub my eyes. Out of the corner of my eye, I see an older gentleman in a gray suit enter the room, and I feel my skin prickling. Before he can get further into the room, Raz busts in and stops him by stepping in front of him.

"Karakis, no disrespect, but now is not the time," he tells him quietly. My ears perk with recognition.

"Raziel, I will see the girl with my own eyes."

"Raz," I interrupt. "It's okay, let him in." I look around Raz at the stranger, and the first thing I recognize is his eyes. Raz gives me a nod and steps back.

"Karakis? Are you related to my mother?" I ask hesitantly. "I'm told that was her maiden name."

I watch him as he looks me up and down until he reaches my face and takes a sharp intake of breath.

"You look just like her."

When I see the tears well in his eyes, I instinctively step forward.

"Rhea, we were told you were dead." I can see the disbelief on his face before he collects himself. "Please forgive the intrusion. I had to see for myself."

He holds out his hand to me, "I'm your uncle. Your mother was my younger sister," he explains. "Please call me Petros."

I take his hand, and he squeezes mine. "As I understand it, your marriage to Mitchell was a bit... unconventional?"

"Karakis," Raz warns.

"Easy, Raziel. I'm not here to fight. I'm here to ensure my niece is safe and where she wants to be now that things have been... neutralized." He turns back to me and raises an eyebrow. "Are you where you want to be?"

I'm taken aback by this complete stranger and the genuine affection I see in his eyes for me. "I am," I assure him. "I'm okay."

He nods. "We will have time, Rhea. I have much to tell you. You have family that will be over the moon to hear that you are alive and safe. In the meantime," he reaches into his pocket and holds a card out to me. "When you are ready." He gives my hand another squeeze and then turns around and walks out the door.

I let out a breath. "Well, that was interesting," I say out loud to myself.

One of Sam's machines beeps, and we hurry over to her side of the room, hoping it's her waking up. We watch as she mutters something incoherent and then settles back in. Raz reaches out and gently moves a strand of her hair out of her face. I can see how much he cares for her, and in this moment, I'm so glad for that.

"Raz, you should have seen it. She was so fucking fierce."

Raz gives me a long look, "She wasn't the only one. You saved him when you didn't have to. You could've been rid of Cal along with Vardis, and you chose not to. It would have left you a wealthy woman. Why?"

I look over at Cal, still asleep in the hospital bed. The white of the sheets so stark against his black hair, that serious look on his face, even in sleep.

I walk over to him, smooth a lock of his tousled hair away from his forehead, unable to take my eyes off him. If I stay close—if he can feel me next to him—maybe it will be the thing that keeps him alive.

"I need answers, and he's the only one who can give them to me." I wipe away a stray tear. "Besides, what the hell am I going to do with a bunch of old stuff and BDSM clubs?"

I feel Raz watching me, and when I look into his tired, bloodshot eyes, I see a shadow of a smile.

"Just after the answers, huh?"

I shrug and look back at my husband. "Fuck off, Raz." And in that moment, things almost feel normal.

The quiet between us hangs in the room, offset by the beeping of machines.

"So, Rhea, huh?" he asks cautiously.

"Don't act like you didn't know." I side-eye him.

"Listen, Charity—I," he starts.

"Stop right there, Raz. I don't want any excuses or reasons. I already know yours. Your loyalty is to Cal. Hell, even Sam thinks you two are a little too weirdly connected.

As far as Rhea," I sigh. "I don't know who she is. Hell, I was barely getting to know who Charity Johnston was before I became Charity Mitchell. Now I'm Rhea Cormack Brennan. Who the fuck is she?"

Raz puts his arm around me and squeezes me.

"You'll figure it out. You're still a brat, so we're good."

It takes another few hours before Sam finally wakes up. At first, I was a little upset that it wasn't me by her side, but when I saw the happiness in her eyes when she saw Raz, I didn't care anymore. She's awake, and she's safe—that's enough.

"Hey!" I squeeze her hand.

"Hey, back. You're okay," she manages a small smile.

I nod. "Better now that you're awake."

"Is there anything to eat? I'm starving!"

I stifle a laugh and look to Raz. "You heard her, get the woman some broth!" Raz grumbles and goes off in search of Sam's dinner.

By the next morning, Sam seems stronger. We've talked a little bit, but neither one of us is ready to dissect the past five days. We've got time for that. The doctor assured us it would be safe for her to travel as early as tomorrow, and she's antsy to leave the hospital and return to the States. There's just the logistics of where we're going when we get there. I think I have an idea.

"Hey, Raz," I start. "What's my situation?"

He narrows his eyes at me suspiciously, which I suppose is fair considering what's coming next.

"What do you mean by 'situation,' Charity? What are you getting at?"

"Raz," I say gently, "you know I can't go back to Cal's house, not after everything he kept from me."

"Right," he clips. "I thought that might be the case. We've got two houses that I can get you and Sam into immediately. Both are in proximity to the main house." I start to protest, but he stops me.

"Let me finish."

I narrow my eyes at him, but tilt my head in agreement.

"We don't know what the fallout of all of this is going to be. You will be somewhere that is protected, regardless of your status with Cal. I've already set up a bank account for you, and one for you, Sam." She gapes at him.

"Whaaaat?" she stammers.

Raz holds his hand up to stop us both from arguing.

"As I was saying, accounts have been set up. I added enough to get you on your feet and to cover any expenses from this, and there will be expenses. When do you want to leave?"

I look over at Sam, and she nods.

"Tomorrow. As soon as Sam is given the all clear."

Raz takes a deep breath. "Okay. I don't like it." He nods at Cal, "And he's really not going to like it, but it's time you decide for yourselves. I owe you that. I'll go make the arrangements." He stands and, without another word, walks out the door.

Sam grimaces. "Oh, he's not happy."

"No, he is not," I chuckle. "But you know as well as I do, he'll find a way to stay in our business. He'll be fine."

Cal finally starts waking up the next morning. If I didn't know better, I'd think he sensed our plans and is waking up in protest. Always the control freak.

I watch him struggle, as if he's fighting something holding him down. I stand and walk to his bedside.

"Hurricane..." he rasps, squinting up at me.

"Hi," I reply, trying to hide the worry etched on my face.

"Where..." his eyes dart around the unfamiliar surroundings.

"Shh, Cal. You're in the hospital. In Greece." I place my hand on his bicep, trying to soothe away his instinct to sit up. "You've been shot. It was touch and go for a minute, but thankfully, Raz was able to stop you from bleeding out until we got you to the hospital."

I watch as he scans over what he can see of my body, and I see the confusion on his face. "Are you okay? Samantha?"

"Sam is banged up, but she's okay. She's in the bed next to you, actually. Raz and I used some of that Mitchell clout and money to get you in a room together so we could stay close to both of you."

He sighs in relief, the breath causing a spasm of pain. Closing his eyes, I see him fighting through it. "Vardis? How did you get away?"

"Dead," I tell him, keeping the emotion out of my voice. "I killed him. The rest of it doesn't matter."

I can see him searching my face, but I don't know what he expects to find. I was so scared that he would die, but now that he's awake, that worry is getting shoved aside by anger.

He tries reaching for my hand, but I pull away.

"I'm so fucking sorry, Charity." My eyes flash when he says my name, and it jolts me back to what he's taken from me.

"Don't you mean, Rhea?" It comes out sharper than I mean it to.

"Rhea..." he rasps. "I was going to tell you, I swear I wanted to."

I straighten myself and clear my throat. "We're not going to discuss that right now. When I get the truth from you, I don't want it to be while you're under the influence of drugs. As you'll remember, I know how they blur everything. I want you crystal clear so you have no excuses. Nothing to hide behind." I turn my face away from him and furiously wipe a tear from my eye.

He tries to reach for me again, but I shake my head no. He doesn't have the right to touch me right now.

"So, I don't know how this works. I'm going to stay until Sam gets the okay to travel. Raz has already taken care of the arrangements. Oh, I met my uncle. I got the feeling he's not a fan of yours." I can't help the slight snark sneaking into my voice.

"By the way, are we married, for real? Do we need to get a divorce? Jesus, Cal, I don't even know what my legal name is." I know I'm rambling, but I don't care.

"Hurricane, take a breath," he soothes. My eyes snap to his with a glare.

"Do not tell me to do a fucking thing, Calahan Mitchell."

I see the glimmer of a smile. Bastard.

He nods and locks eyes with me. "Understood. I'll tell you what I know. I know that you are legally Charity Johnston Mitchell. I know that we are legally married." He begins to cough, and I can see the spasms of pain start overtaking him.

"Oh, for fuck's sake, Cal, enough. Just stop." Any patience I had for him, for this situation, evaporates.

My eyes lock on his pain pump. I can't help the smile that creeps over my face when I reach over and press the button.

"Whaaat...?" That's all he gets out before I watch his eyes go glassy.

I lean forward and whisper in his ear, "Shhhh. It's just pain meds. It's my turn to drug you, husband." I reach over and kiss his temple. "Goodbye, Cal," I whisper.

"Raz," I call to him, "Can you get the doctor in here to sign Sam out?" I look at Sam, knowing that there's no way she didn't hear all of that.

"Let's go home," she says quietly. I settle into the chair next to her and wait.

FIFTY-FIVE
Cal

The treadmill beeps and comes to a slow stop. I'm sweaty and a little sore, but I lasted longer today. I'll take the progress. It's not the run I need, but it will have to do for now. Wiping my neck with my towel, I pull the picture from my pocket, its edges tinged with blood. I'm not sure whose blood it is, mine or Vardis's, and it doesn't matter.

What matters is the woman's smile in the picture.

It's been a month since my hurricane knocked me out and stole away like a thief, but I understand why. Once I was coherent enough to grasp it, Raz recounted everything. The irony that I was there to save her, and she saved us both, isn't lost on me. I've stayed away—given her her space, as Raz calls it. I call it bullshit. At first, it made sense. I didn't want to go to her until I felt whole. I need to be strong enough to withstand the wrath I'm sure she'll unleash on me. Again, warranted. Now, all I know is that this house is too quiet. Too empty. I need her back here, with me. I stuff the picture back in my pocket and start heading for the shower when Raz comes in.

"Morning," he grunts as he walks over to the treadmill I just vacated.

"G'morning," I reply, then stop. I turn back to him. Maybe he'll give me answers this time.

"Raz," I start, which earns me a dramatic sigh.

"Cal, don't. If you want to know anything about her beyond logistics, you're going to have to go talk to her yourself. It's too early for this. If you don't mind—" He turns back to the machine.

"She's my fucking wife!" I shout at him.

"Then start fucking acting like it," he throws back. "Go talk to her or let her go, but keep me out of it!" he shouts back stubbornly.

He steps off the treadmill and sighs.

"Here's the one thing I'll tell you, then for fuck's sake, Cal, drop it." His face softens.

"She's as miserable as you are—she's just not being a prick about it. I don't know if she misses you or is miserable because she's still tied to you, even if it is just on paper. All I know is she's not happy. So, since you like proclaiming the title of husband, start acting like it. Make her happy—no matter what it costs you."

I nod in recognition and leave him to his workout. I know what I need to do. It's going to gut me, but it's what she deserves.

FIFTY-SIX
Charity

I walk through the door and hang my keys up, exhausted from my last therapy session. Raz referred Sam and me to a therapist from the Phoenix Group who works with women with trauma. I scoff at the word. I know the ordeal with Vardis left a mark. I don't feel guilty about what I had to do to save Cal and me. I don't feel anything at all, and maybe that's why I need the sessions.

It's been over a month since I left Cal in Athens. Raz has kept me updated on his recovery, but other than that, he refuses to give me any information. He just growls about the two of us being the most pig-headed idiots he's ever come across.

The door opens, and Sam walks in, sweaty from her run. The guards that Raz assigns to us hate pulling Sam as their assignment. Since she's healed enough to start working out, running has become her passion, which means whoever is guarding her had better keep up. Raz has already lectured her twice about trying to outrun her man. We're each managing as best we can.

"Hey," she says brightly. "I'm glad you're home. I'm going to grab a shower, and then I thought we'd order in. Pizza and a rom-com?"

"Sure," I answer. "Sounds great. How was your run?"

"Awesome!" she beams, "But I think I broke the new guy. He's out there huffing and puffing. You would think Raz would have standards for physical fitness."

I see the mischief in her eyes, and it can only mean we can expect another visit from Raz soon.

She turns to head to her room and stops. "Oh, hey, one of your husband's guys dropped that off," she nods to the coffee table.

"Husband?" I roll my eyes at her.

She puts her hands up and smirks. "Hey, don't kill the messenger. He is, in fact, still your husband. It's not my fault you were foolish enough to fall in love with him."

"Just go," I tell her. I'm not having that conversation with her again. I hear her laugh as she heads down the hall.

I walk over to the coffee table, expecting to see the usual manila envelope with more forms to sign, or not sign, as is the usual case. I haven't heard from Cal, other than through legal documents stating that investments are supposedly now in my name. I usually write "fuck off" on the envelope and hand it to Raz when he comes to check up on us. I don't know what I expect from Cal, but paperwork definitely isn't it.

Instead, there's a long, plain white box. No label. I pick it up and shake it, but nothing shifts inside. Something feels off about this. I carefully run my fingernail along the tape securing its edges and lift the lid. The first thing I see is the chess piece. The one I left behind when I went after Sam. I take a deep breath and pick it up, remembering the day I took this from him and won my freedom from that room. I slip it into my pocket, recalling my old habit, and look back at the box. A folded note with "Charity" scrawled in Cal's measured hand. The room suddenly feels heavy, and my hands begin to shake when I lift the note and open it.

Hurricane,

Everything I know about you is in this file. The details will tell you who you were, but they don't come close to showing who you are. I told you the night before our wedding that I didn't know if I was the type of man who could love.

I was wrong.

—C

I open the file and start paging through my life. It's all here. Facts about my parents, their lives, and their deaths. Facts about my foster home. How Malcolm set it up and what his plans were for me, and even notes on when he changed his mind and decided not to turn me over to Vardis. I see photos from different ages. School transcripts. A running list of jobs I lost, and apartments I got kicked out of. There's even an entry about my job at the gala—the last entry. But that's all they are—facts. I lift the file out of the box, set it on the table with the note, and see one more document. My face goes hot. "Petition for Dissolution of Marriage."

What the actual fuck?

I pick it up expecting to see another note or something, but instead, there are just tabs marked 'Sign Here.'

"How fucking dare he!" I yell.

Sam comes running into the room, finding me stuffing the contents back into the box.

"Charity, what's wrong? What was in the box?" Sam asks, concern lacing her voice. "Do I need to call Raz?"

"Do not call Raz!" I bark at her. "He'll just warn him I'm coming!"

"Charity," Sam's concern now sounding more like alarm, "What are you going to do?"

"I'm going to go have a long overdue conversation about making decisions about my fucking life!" I slam the lid of the box down, pick it up, and stalk to the door.

Swinging it open, I point to one of the guards. "You." His eyes go wide. "You're taking me to Cal Mitchell's house right fucking now!"

"Yes, ma'am," he nods nervously, and we head for the car.

By the time we reach Cal's house, I'm shaking. We go through the gate, and I practically jump out before the car's even stopped. I stomp up the front step and bark at the guard, "Open it, and if you radio to anyone that I'm here, I'll cut off your balls!"

I storm down the hall to his office. I know exactly where my dear husband is. He wants the hurricane, well, here I am!

When I reach his office door, I fling it open, not bothering to knock.

As usual, Raz, the ever-loyal watchdog, stands by his desk while Cal lords over his kingdom. Both of their eyes snap up, and I clock Cal's surprise before the calm drops back into place. The intensity of those icy blue eyes threatens my resolve for just a heartbeat before I lean into my anger.

"You!" I point at Raz. "Out!"

I lock eyes with Cal, still speaking to Raz, and sneer, "My husband and I need to have a little chat." I throw the box on his desk.

I hear Raz chuckle as he exits with a quick, "About damned time."

Cal calmly places the cap on his pen and lays it on his desk.

"Charity."

"Don't you 'Charity' me, Cal Mitchell! Who the fuck do you think you are? You send that," I point to the box, "and fucking divorce papers?"

He stands and walks around the desk, leaning back against the front edge, his eyes not moving from mine.

"I promised you answers," he begins, his voice too steady. "I promised I would set you free when the Vardis situation was resolved. It's been resolved, by you, I might add. Per the conditions of the contract, you are free."

Without thinking, I stalk up to him and swing my palm toward his face, his hand catching me before I make contact.

We are so close, I can feel his breath on my face, our pulses mingling in his firm grip.

"Charity," he says calmly. "What do you want?" I see the challenge in his eyes. I'm not backing down, not this time.

"I want you to stop being a fucking coward and give me answers. Not a file of facts, Cal—answers! The divorce papers, along with the note basically telling me for the first time that you love me, were a nice touch, though. 'Sign here?' Go fuck yourself!"

He drops my hand and braces himself on the desk.

"I was there when your parents were killed. He made me watch. I thought he had killed you, too." He closes his eyes for a moment, then continues. "That night, I decided that someday, somehow, I would end him, and I did. You were eighteen when I learned you were alive. You were the last of my father's sordid secrets. My inheritance," he tells me, his voice cold.

"If you're asking why I didn't tell you, recent events should have made that clear. You were supposed to stay away from all of this. I wanted to protect you, and before you say it, I assure you it wasn't out of guilt. You were owed a debt. I tried to pay that debt as well as I could without you being dragged back into this."

His eyes soften. "If you want to know when I started loving you... it was the night of the gala. Do you want the exact moment? It was when you had the nerve to spit in my drink, though I didn't realize that love was what I was feeling." A smile tugs at the side of his lips. "My God, you were—*are* spectacular!" He sobers again, and stoic Cal is back.

"What answers do you need, Charity? What will make any of this okay? You deserve to start whatever life you choose without the tether of a marriage you never wanted."

"Oh, don't you dare turn this around on me." I push back. "You don't get to define what kind of life I live. You don't get to decide. I decide!"

I see the control drop from his face and finally see my Cal return. He drops his eyes, takes a breath, and snaps them back up to me.

"Then decide, dammit. Living in limbo with you two miles away is something I can't live with, and I don't think you can either."

I search his eyes and see familiar pain. The same pain I've been carrying since I left him in that hospital bed.

I lean in and grab him, kissing him fiercely, and feel him stiffen for a heartbeat before returning the kiss

FIFTY-SEVEN
Charity

Cal's hand grips my hair, tightening as he kisses me deeper. He isn't gentle, and I don't need him to be. I let my hands roam over his chest, careful to avoid his wound. He moans into my mouth as I fumble with his buttons, and he pulls back, searching my face.

"Cal," I smirk, "in case you're wondering—this is me giving consent. Now fuck me." I see his eyes darken.

"That sassy mouth," he growls. His hand connects with a sharp crack, knocking a laugh out of me—and then I see it. He tries to hide it, and it's the tiniest flinch, but I see it.

I lock eyes with him and finish unbuttoning his shirt. I carefully sweep it from his shoulders, kissing my way over his chest. When I see the bullet wound, I stop. I lean in and let my lips linger on the angry red scar. When I reach his neck, I whisper, "Do you trust me?"

He reaches up and cups my face, staring into my eyes. "With my life."

I grab his arms, pulling him forward, then guide him back until his knees touch the chair in front of his desk. He cocks an eyebrow at me.

"Sit," I tell him, not breaking contact.

"Enjoy yourself, Hurricane. You're writing checks that I'll be cashing later."

"Noted," I reply, a smile quirks at my mouth.

I lower myself in front of him, and I see his attention sharpen.

"Charity," he warns quietly.

Watching every reaction to my touch, I stroke the inside of his thighs, my hands skimming higher over the bulge his black dress pants can't hide. I linger there until I see the challenge in his eyes, like he's daring me to go further.

I reach for his belt buckle, open it, and unzip him, easing him free. I lick my lips, making his cock twitch.

His hands grip the armrests, knuckles going white.

He hates this. Not what I'm doing but what he can't do. All he can do is sit there and let me have him.

And God, that knowledge is doing something to me.

I wrap my fingers around him, stroke once, and watch his jaw clench.

"You're enjoying this," he says. It's not a question.

"Little bit," I smirk at him.

Holding his stare, I lower my mouth and drag my tongue along the underside of him, base to tip, licking the bead of precum gathered there. I work slow and deliberate. His hips jerk, just barely, and I feel the effort it costs him to stay still.

"Charity." His voice, rougher.

He makes a sound that goes straight through me. Low and raw. His hand comes to the back of my head, fingers threading through my hair, and holds on like he needs something to anchor him.

I take my time, hollowing my cheeks on the way up, tongue swirling over the head before sinking back down. I want him to feel every second of this.

I can feel the tension coiling tighter in him with every pass of my mouth, hear it in the way his breathing has gone ragged and uneven.

He grips my hair, lifting my head. "You look so beautiful sucking my cock," he breathes, before lowering me back down, guiding himself deeper until he hits the back of my throat.

"Fuck—" His fingers flex in my hair. "Just like that."

His head falls back against the chair. The column of his throat is exposed, muscles straining, as he fights for control.

He's completely at my mercy, and we both know it.

I speed up, adding my hand to what my mouth can't reach. His hips start moving in short thrusts, and I can tell he's close. I can feel him swelling against my tongue, the grip going tighter in my hair.

"Charity." His voice is strained. "Stop."

He drops my hair, reaching for me, hands gripping my hips and hauling me up.

"I need to taste you," he commands.

He guides me up onto the chair, helping me to kneel on the armrests so I'm bracketing his shoulders. I grab the back of the chair for balance.

"Cal, are you sure?"

He slaps my ass harder this time.

"What did I tell you about interrupting me?" His breath is hot against my inner thigh. "Now hold still and let me taste my wife."

He pushes my skirt up around my waist, yanks my underwear to the side, and then his mouth is on me.

I gasp, hands flying to his shoulders. There's no buildup, no teasing. He latches on to my clit, licking and swirling his tongue. His lips close around the bundle of nerves, and he sucks.

"Oh God. Fuck, Cal!" I scream, throwing my head back.

His fingers dig into my hips, holding me while he devours me.

"Grind against me, Hurricane," he murmurs into my pussy, vibrations intensifying the feeling. "Take what you need."

I push closer to him, offering myself. "Cal, I can't—"

He hums against me, and my vision goes white.

I grab onto the back of the chair, the orgasm tearing through me as I scream his name.

I'm still trembling when he starts lowering me down. His hands are gentle now, careful, easing me into his lap until I can feel him pressing into me.

"Slow," I tell him. "I want slow."

He guides himself to my entrance and pulls me down onto him, inch by inch.

My body opens for him, hungry for what it knows he'll give. Once he's all the way in, we both go still.

His hands come up to cup my face. Thumbs brushing my cheekbones. Ice-blue eyes searching mine.

In this moment, it's just this—just us. Him inside me, his hands on my face, his eyes holding mine like I'm the most precious thing in his world.

I begin moving my hips, and when I feel him start to shift, trying to meet my movements, I give him a slight shake of my head.

"No, let me." And he stills.

It's slow. A rolling of hips, a gentle rocking, nothing like the frantic need from before. His hands slide down my back, over my hips, back up to my face again. It's like he can't stop touching me. Like he needs to feel all of me at once.

The pleasure builds differently this way. Not a sharp climb but a gradual, rising swell, until I can feel him in every nerve ending, every heartbeat.

My eyes start to drift close, and Cal gives me a little shake.

"Oh no, Hurricane." His voice is rough. "When we come, eyes open. I need to see all of you."

My eyes rise to his.

He holds my gaze. Thrusts up into me, once, twice—and everything crests. I feel myself clench around him, feel him pulse inside me, hear the groan rip from his chest as we fall over the edge together.

For a few seconds, there's nothing but the feeling of him buried deep and the aftershocks rolling through us both.

When I come back to myself, I'm slumped against his chest. His heart is pounding under my ear.

He presses his lips into my hair, and his arms tighten, pulling me closer.

"So fucking perfect," he whispers. "And I'm fucking yours."

I pull back and look into his eyes, seeing all the unspoken words, all of the feelings that Calahan Mitchell has never allowed himself to feel.

"Mine," I whisper back. "And I'm yours."

FIFTY-EIGHT
Cal

Charity dozes in my lap, my arms wrapped around her. My body aches from our lovemaking, but I'll stay here. I'll hold her as long as she'll let me.

Closing my eyes, I lean into her, taking in her scent. My hurricane.

I thought I'd lost her, so I let her go. Instead, she stormed back into my life, upending everything in her wake like the force of nature that she is. I don't deserve her. I'll spend the rest of my life proving I know that—if she'll let me.

Her eyes flutter open, a small smile spreading across her face.

"Hi," she whispers shyly.

"Hi," I whisper back.

She snuggles closer into me, the movement causing me to wince.

Realization, then worry, flash across her face, before she tries to move. "Oh God, Cal, your shoulder—"

"Don't you even think about moving," I growl, pulling her closer. "If I have my way, we're never moving from this spot."

She settles in again, and we sit in silence for a moment.

"I'll arrange for your things to be brought home today. Of course, we have plenty of room for Samantha, unless she'd rather stay at the house. Marie and Cora will be relieved. Maybe Cora will stop over-salting my dinner. She was less than pleased with me when I came home without you. And Marie," I grumble, "it seems her loyalties also shifted." I raise a teasing eyebrow and look down at her.

"Cal, I'm not coming home," she says carefully.

Something in my chest drops. "Excuse me?" I ask, rougher than I mean to. "But I thought—"

She places a hand on my chest to stop me.

"I'm not coming home... yet." Her eyes meet mine, and I see the playfulness dancing.

My God, she is beautiful.

"So tell me, wife. What schemes do I need to plan for next?"

She takes a deep breath. "I want to get married."

I pull back, confusion and worry tightening in my chest. "Charity, we are married. Our marriage was never a lie."

"No, I mean..."

I watch her search for the words to ask for what she needs.

"I want to do it right this time, Cal. No secrets. No contracts. Just you and me, no conditions." She looks like she's afraid she's asking too much. I know it's not nearly enough.

"Is that all?" I look down at her, amused. "Done. I'll have everything arranged. We'll remarry this weekend."

She rolls her eyes at me. "No, you will not 'arrange' anything. I will arrange it. I will pick the place, the time, and what I wear." She narrows her eyes. "You, husband, will keep your hands off and nose out of it. You just show up when I tell you to."

I give her a playful swat. "Careful with that tone, Hurricane."

"I think I need maybe three months. I'll move back home after."

"Three months?" I ask, sharper than I intend. "Absolutely not. I'll give you one month. And you're in my bed tonight."

"Two months, Cal, and that's my final offer. And I will not be living here until then—unless you plan on kidnapping me again?" She smirks.

"Do not tempt me, Charity."

She huffs.

"Fine," I concede begrudgingly. "You have exactly two months from right now." I look at my watch. "Not a minute longer."

She settles back into me, leaving me to count the minutes until she's in my arms for good.

EPILOGUE
Rhea

I take one last look in the mirror before standing, ready for my future with Cal to begin.

True to our agreement, Cal has left this day in my hands... well, almost. He did send a wedding planner to help. At first, I was a little pissed off, but after I realized how much there was to do, I conceded. Nelle has been a godsend, though I'll never admit it to Cal. I had to recruit Raz on a few things, like securing the venue and rushing some of the paperwork I needed. I may have the Mitchell last name, but I'm not ready to use it to get my way—Raz has no problems clearing those roadblocks for me.

We hear a short knock on the door, and Sam looks at me.

"Expecting someone?" she asks.

"No, and if it's Cal, shoo him away," I laugh.

Sam opens the door a hair, and I hear my uncle's voice.

"I'm sorry for the interruption, but may I have a moment with the bride?"

Petros has made a point of becoming part of my life despite the distance. Getting used to the idea that I have family who hasn't seen me since I was a little girl has been challenging. Petros and his sons, my cousins, have been respectful but a little pushy. He's still not a fan of Cal but has been careful not to overstep.

Sam checks with me, and when I nod, she steps aside to let him in.

I reach out, offering him a small hug, and he kisses me on the cheek before holding me away from him, looking at me with adoration.

"You look beautiful, Kardia mou," he says, beaming with pride. The Greek endearment for "my heart."

"I'm so happy you could make it, Uncle Petros. Thank you for making the trip." I tell him, and I truly mean it. Having him here feels like having a piece of my parents. I may not have known them, but now that I've learned about them through my extended Greek family, I feel their absence.

"You think I would miss this?" he asks teasingly. "Psht, impossible," he waves the thought away. "Your cousins are in the main area, throwing your husband daggers, but your grandmother wasn't able to come. Travel is hard for her these days."

I nod in understanding.

"I appreciate your decision to walk yourself on your wedding day, but I was hoping that you would allow an old man an indulgence for his only niece?" He reaches into his pocket and pulls out a small bundle.

He hands me a small mesh bag with five oval candies.

"First, Koufeta," he starts. "Your grandmother made these herself. Usually, they are given to guests as a trifle, but the meaning is the same. May the sweetness of marriage endure the bitterness of the almond. May your marriage be filled with health, wealth, happiness, longevity, and fertility." He gives me a wink, and I feel myself blush.

Next, he hands me a small sprig of greenery. "Laurel, for your bouquet," he tells me. "A symbol of endurance and survival." I take it from him, and we exchange a knowing look.

"And finally," he takes a breath and hands me a photo I haven't seen before. It's a picture of my parents on their wedding day. Tears spring to my eyes, and he squeezes my hands. "I thought maybe you would like them near today."

He gives me a final squeeze. "Now, if you'll excuse me, I need to get back and make sure that my sons haven't already made you a widow." He kisses me lightly on the cheek, tips his head at Sam, and leaves.

Sam puts her arm around me and looks at the picture in my hand. "She's so beautiful. And her dress... Charity, your dress is so close, it could be hers."

I turn to the mirror, taking in my reflection. The ivory dress is simple and flowy. The fabric is gathered at one shoulder and held by a simple mother-of-pearl brooch.

We both take a minute before she gives me a little shake and dabs my eyes with a tissue. "Okay, enough of that. You'll wreck your makeup." We exchange a smile. Everything we are and all that we've gone through together passes between us.

Another knock sounds on the door, and Nelle pops her head in, the sound of the music from the small quartet drifting into the room.

"Ladies, it's time."

I take a deep breath, and Sam hands me the small bouquet. The scent of olive branches and heather fills the air, and I adjust the shamrocks peppered in, slipping the sprig of laurel and small photo in between the greenery. I give her a smile. "Let's go get me hitched."

As we reach the entryway into the temple's exhibit room, the haunting sounds of a single cello fill the air. Sam gives me another squeeze. "I love you, Charity!" she whispers. Then she turns and walks down the pathway toward the two men standing at the temple.

It feels fitting that we start over where we began. I see Cal standing in the exact spot I saw him that first night. My breath catches when his eyes meet mine, and I begin the walk toward our new beginning. The space is filled with family, friends, and Cal's business contacts, but they all fall away. All I see is him.

When I finally reach them, I look at Raz, and he gives me a nod, assuring me that everything is in place.

The music halts, and I hand my bouquet to Sam. Cal takes my hands in his, his eyes gleaming. I've never seen him so unguarded, and that's what I need him to be for what's coming next. The officiant goes through the usuals, and when she gets to the part for any objections, I hear a throat clear. Throwing a look over my shoulder, I see Petros, and he gives me a wink. A quiet chuckle goes through the crowd of onlookers, and with a smile, we continue.

"Do you, Cal, take this woman to be your wife? Do you promise to love her, honor her, and consult with her on all things?" Cal raises an eyebrow at me, and I tilt my head at him, challenging him to concede. He clears his throat. "I do."

I smile at him, knowing what he just gave me.

"Then repeat after me."

"I, Calahan Malcolm Mitchell, take this woman..." I listen as he repeats the words.

"Rhea Brennan Mitchell," the officiant continues. At that moment, I see Cal's face soften with recognition. "Rhea Brennan Mitchell," he repeats almost in a whisper, his eyes glistening.

He continues without prompting, "to be my wife. I promise to love you, honor you, and worship you. I promise to consult with you and cherish you for as long as I have breath in my body." Emotion blurs my vision, and Cal reaches up, brushing a tear from my cheek with his thumb.

"And you, Rhea, do you take this man—" I interrupt her and continue my vows unprompted. "I, Rhea Brennan Mitchell, take you, Calahan Malcolm Mitchell, to continue being my husband. I promise to love you, honor you, and sometimes obey you." I smile through my tears when I see his mouth curve just slightly. "As long as there is breath in my body, I am yours," I finish.

Unprompted, Cal reaches into his pocket and slips my rings back on my finger. He's never taken his off.

I look down at them, remembering the words he said to me the first time he put his mother's ring on my finger, and I understand now.

Leaning in, he says quietly, "Let these be a symbol of my vow."

"Ladies and gentlemen, I present to you, Cal and Rhea Mitchell."

Cal scoops me into his arms and kisses me fiercely before looking into my eyes and whispering, "Let's go home, wife."

The End

PLAYLIST

"Everybody Wants to Rule the World" — Lorde
(from *The Hunger Games: Catching Fire* soundtrack)
"Gasoline" — Halsey
"Red Right Hand - 2011 Remaster" — Nick Cave & The
Bad Seeds
"I Did Something Bad" — Taylor Swift
"Mr. Sandman" — SYML
"Arsonist's Lullabye" — Hozier
"Bloodline" — Alex Warren & Jelly Roll
"Black Wave" — K.Flay
"Butterflies" — Zendaya
"Boss Bitch" — Doja Cat
"Wicked Games" — Chris Isaak
"Blood // Water" — grandson
"Familiar Taste of Poison" — Halestorm
"Ain't No Crying" — Derivakat
"The Death Of Peace Of Mind" — Bad Omens
"Million Reasons" — Lady Gaga
"I Found" — Amber Run
"Desire" — Ryan Adams
"If You Love Her" — Forest Blakk

ACKNOWLEDGEMENTS

Thank you for reading *Inheritance: Blood Legacy*. If you made it to the end, I'm grateful that you trusted me with Rhea and Cal's story. I hope you enjoyed the tension, the emotional warfare, and the consequences as much as I enjoyed writing them.

First and foremost, to my guy. No matter what I dream up, you're always ready to go on the adventure with me. Thank you for supporting me, picking up the slack when I've had to check out to meet a self-imposed deadline, and always asking, "And then what happens?"

To my tribe, when I say this book wouldn't exist without you, it's not hyperbole. I've told you a million times, and I'll say it a million more–I'm so damned lucky to have you in my life! Danielle, without your gentle but firm push, this would still be in my drafts waiting to get scrapped. You said, "We're doing this," and **we** did it! Thank you for your knowledge and guidance, your patience while I spiraled (so many times), and all the invisible work you did to help make this a reality. Meghan, your feedback and encouragement kept me going. There were more than a few times that I was ready to scrap this——seeing your excitement renewed mine. Marla, you are so amazingly talented. My next dream is that someday soon, I'll get the privilege of saying, "She's the engineer on my audio book(s)!"

One more thing..."**Shots Fired!!**"

ABOUT THE AUTHOR

Tess Hollis writes dark, emotionally intense romance that explores power, obsession, and the psychology of desire. Her stories center on morally gray characters and relationships shaped by control, consequence, and choice. You can expect sharp dialogue, grounded tension, and an unflinching look at love in its most dangerous forms.

When she's not writing, Tess is dreaming up new stories while she juggles her day job, manages her golden retriever husband, and the menagerie of furry creatures that share her world.

Come stalk me:

BOOKS BY THIS AUTHOR

Coming Soon
Inheritance Book 2: Fall 2026
Inheritance Prequel: TBD